World of Myth XIII

<u>Tranquility Lost</u>

Travis Bughi

DEDICATION

To Steven,
For a friendship worth aspiring to

ACKNOWLEDGEMENTS

Patricia Hamill for the editing

ISBN: 9798762381215

World of Myth Series

Emily's Saga

Beyond the Plains
The Forest of Angor
The Fall of Lucifan
Journey to Savara
Juatwa
A Legend Ascends

Takeo's Chronicles

Fated for War
An Enchanted Sword
Fortress of Ruin
A Dagger in the Light
Battle for Redemption
A Legend Falls

Cyrus' Legend

Tranquility Lost

Prologue

Lord Takeo Karaoshi considered Lucifan to be the greatest city ever created and an objective failure.

On one hand, this city had been created by angels. It was made of buildings so thick and tall that no man-made structure could match their height outside the lost wonders in Savara. It was the densest populated place by far, owing to its deserving status as the world's trading hub and as an exceptionally tolerant city for all manner of creatures. Even a kobold could find protection under the law here, owing to the angels' legacy, upheld by the Knights' Order and a majority of peaceable citizens just looking to get on with their lives. Although hunger came and went with the seasons, starvation was rare, for this city imported enough food and goods that what was thrown away was enough to provide for the crippled and destitute. It should have been heaven, but to Takeo, it was a warning.

For on the other hand, Lucifan squandered its potential.

Those large buildings that could house so many became cesspools for criminals and thieves. Those very same laws that protected the innocent were more often used to protect the guilty. In a world of plenty, civilization had elected not to share its bountiful gains, but instead to covet the wealth and power into the concentrated few. When Takeo looked upon Lucifan, he saw a mistake. He saw how even a literal utopia could be desecrated by selfishness and cruelty if left unchecked. In the world he would create, a mistake like Lucifan would not be allowed to exist. In fact, in the world he was about to create, Lucifan would be destroyed.

It was only fitting really. After all, no creation that kills its creator should be allowed to live. Not when those creators were angels.

These were the thoughts that filled Takeo's mind as his ships pulled into Lucifan's harbor. The grand city of grey and black stone was like a beacon of darkness against the golden background of the Great Plains, which surrounded it. At least, that's how Takeo imagined it, because under the cover of night, the entire coastline seemed a fortress of solitude. Foremost in the waters, greeting every ship that came and went, stood the lone colossus that had survived from a time so long ago. Motionless, yet intimidating, that great statue of a male warrior hadn't moved since its last puppeteer died.

Her name was Emily Stout, and Takeo had loved her with all his heart as she'd died in his arms.

"My lord, if you insist on landing at night, then I shall insist we send one of the other ships to clear the way for you," Aiguo said, interrupting Takeo's thoughts.

Normally Takeo found his underling's voice irksome on the best of days, and admittedly the trip across the seas had been an exercise in patience. More than once, the urge to kill this man had passed through Takeo's mind only to be wrestled down by the strong, yet steady hatred for someone far more dangerous. That is to say, Aiguo was only alive because he was useful.

"No," Takeo said as he gazed upon the colossus. "It's been too long since I've touched solid ground. Dock us at once."

"Of course, my lord. I'll have your orders obeyed at once. Yet, if I may explain my first suggestion, I only asked if you wished another ship to go first so that they could test the waters, so to speak. You have not been to Lucifan in some time. We cannot know how a lord of your stature will be received, or if you'll be received properly."

"There's no need to be cautious," Takeo said. "Doing so will give O'Conner time to think."

They sailed beneath the colossus's legs. Now that they were close enough to see the thing in the cover of night, each person on the ship gazed up at the magnificent mountain of stone that had once upon a time laid waste to an invading army. Takeo was almost certain the colossus had stood dead since then, and that it would never move to protect the city once more. However, 'almost certain' wasn't good enough. He needed to be completely certain, and for that, he needed to find the last angel in existence.

As for Aiguo, Takeo had another task for him.

Takeo's fleet reached the Lucifan docks without trouble. There was room enough for half his fleet, while the other half had to anchor in the bay. His honor guard poured out first hastily and with vigor because Takeo would not be delayed. He came down off the wooden docks just in time for word to finally reach the inner city, and a small legion of winged beasts came pouring down from the skies.

Pegasus, that was the creature's name, and they were the prized possession of the Knights' Order. With them, Lucifan's enforcers could traverse the grand city in a moment's time, covering large swaths of ground with a fraction of the men it would require to do so on foot. A pegasus was impressive to behold, honestly, and Takeo could understand why the creatures were not allowed to be used by anyone else. In Juatwa, too, precious weapons were reserved for the elite.

Two dozen knights, which rivaled Takeo's honor guard, landed on the shores, but the lord could only assume more were on the way. They'd have to be, to pose a threat, for Takeo's other ships were unloading additional soldiers. The knights were encased in heavy metal armor and carried wide shields. They formed a defensive line along the docks with practiced efficiency.

They did not draw their swords, though, and so Takeo took his hand off his.

From the center of the group, Sir Mark O'Conner marched out. Even under the darkness of night, even after decades apart, Mark O'Conner was an easy man for Takeo to distinguish. The old man had many features that stuck in one's memory, like his aged face, bald head, stiff mannerisms, and, of course, piercing blue eyes of a vampire.

Mark's presence brought a literal chill upon the scene. The temperature plunged wherever a vampire went, and Takeo's and Aiguo's breath materialized as white steam in the supernatural change. Yet the coldest thing about Mark was neither his eyes nor his presence, but his scowl.

The vampire stopped just two paces from his knights, leaving a wide gap between him and Takeo. That was telling, Takeo thought, because as a vampire, Mark possessed strength and speed far beyond any normal human. That and, well, he was immortal—for the most part. Although Mark would never age or die of hunger, he could still be killed by more difficult means, such as sunlight, basilisk poison, or having his head completely detached from his shoulders.

And perhaps that was why he stayed away.

"Karaoshi," Mark called out in a tired voice. "I can see you back there, behind your guards."

"That's Lord Takeo Karaoshi!" Aiguo shouted in reply. "You will show our lord the respect he deserves."

"Do not speak for me again," Takeo whispered.

Aiguo's lips snapped shut.

"Step aside," Takeo commanded to his guard.

His guards parted like a wave, and Takeo strode through.

"Sir Mark," he said. "It's been a while. You haven't changed much."

"I wish I could say the same," Mark replied. "When you left this city, you were a poor, broken man accompanied by three friends. I never thought I'd hear from you again, to be honest. Unfortunately, I did, and Takeo, what I've heard are some disconcerting rumors. They say you rule all of Juatwa, now."

He paused. Takeo gave a slight nod.

"They say you carry an enchanted sword that belches fire and turns you into a fiend," Mark broached.

Takeo paused this time. He decided there was no harm in admitting this one. He nodded again.

"They saw you lead an army of demons, and men who fight like demons," Mark pressed. "They say you've launched warships bound for Savara and The North, intending to start a war."

"From my perspective," Takeo said, "it seems like you're the one preparing for war."

"That's what I'm trying to say. There is no war here unless you've brought it with you."

Takeo sighed. He had wondered how thoroughly his reputation had preceded him across the world. It seemed he didn't have the element of surprise like he had originally thought. If Lucifan knew this much about him, then all the world knew about him and had invented a fair bit more. Trading hubs traded information just as much as goods.

"If I came to invade Lucifan, don't you think I'd have brought more ships?" Takeo asked.

"Come off it, Takeo. I haven't even said the worst of the rumors. I heard you killed Gavin. And your wife. On your wedding night. While, they say, she was pregnant with your child. Is any of that true? Even half true? How could you? What happened to you?"

Takeo dropped the lingering smile from his face. He shouldn't have been surprised, really. Nothing spread faster than rumors and tragedy. Of course, these ones were true, but how could Takeo possibly explain in short time that all his actions were well justified under the circumstances? Not that he would, of course. Lord Takeo Karaoshi, The Dark Lord, didn't need to explain himself to anyone. He didn't need approval, or even crave it, and especially not from an old coward who had let the world's greatest city descend into a sickening pool of decadence.

Takeo smiled, knowing how much pleasure he would take in when he burnt this city to the ground.

"Firstly, what you've heard is true," Takeo said. "I am a lord now, actually an emperor, and I will be addressed as such. Secondly, I am not here for you or your city, and I would strongly encourage you to think about your actions lest I change my mind. I am merely passing through, looking for one old friend and one dangerous fugitive. After I have both, I'll be on my way."

Takeo's confident reply put Mark off balance, which Takeo knew would happen. Mark had been turned into a vampire in his old age, but he'd been cursed long before that with a severe case of cautiousness. He contemplated and worried so much that he often missed the forest for the trees or delayed to the point where decisions were made for him. That's how he'd gotten wrapped up in the plot to destroy the angels that had eventually led to him becoming a vampire. Mark never was able to understand that power came from control over a situation.

Mark's biggest problem, however, was that he wasn't willing to risk the city. He felt morally bound to it, as if serving the city could pardon his past sins. Like a fool, he sought redemption, and Takeo knew it.

Men like Mark would rather appease a tyrant than stand up to one.

"A fugitive?" Mark said, easing up for the first time. "What sort of fugitive?"

"I came at night for a reason," Takeo said. "I wanted to talk to you, to come in peace, and perhaps get your help. Gavin is dead, but his blood is on the hands of another, and it's her I'm after. My man, here, Lord Aiguo Mein, is tasked with finding and bringing her to me, dead if need be. From my understanding, she passed through here or perhaps lingers here still."

"And after you have her, you'll be on your way?"

"Well, regardless, I'll be on my way shortly. As I said, I'm merely passing through, and I have no reason to stay in Lucifan so long as I'm not given one. Honestly, I thought you were a man of the law, Sir Mark, and I fail to see what law I've broken on Lucifan soil. I've only just arrived."

The lines in Mark's forehead deepened in thought, as he tried to weigh the far-reaching consequences of every action. Takeo knew where such thoughts would lead, only into uncertainty and doubt. Takeo's smile grew. This was too easy.

"I, uh," the vampire said. "I suppose it's not Lucifan's business what occurs between Juatwa, vikings, and Savara. Besides, it's not like you'd assault Lucifan anyway. Not after seeing what happened to the last army that tried that."

Mark forced a cordial grin and flicked his gaze up at the colossus.

"And what friend are you going to see?" he asked.

"That's my business, and he's not in Lucifan."

"But this fugitive is? Need I remind you that your man here can't go about exerting authority. He needs to obey our laws and respect our customs."

"I highly doubt she's still here, but if she is, he'll be sure to alert you immediately as to his intentions."

Mark shuffled in place, searching for more questions. Takeo's short and cooperative responses were not giving the opening to the conversation he wanted. In the end, he decided to force the question anyway.

"Emily's brother passed through here some time ago, my men report," Mark said. "Rumors say you two parted ways."

Takeo stood as motionless as the colossus. Mark sighed.

"Listen," the vampire said. "I don't know what happened to you over there, but I hope you remember that Emily loved this city, fought for this city, and died for this city. The angels died for this city. Maybe this won't mean anything to you, but I was turned a monster for this city. Remember that, and don't become a shadow of your old master."

"Are we done here?" Takeo asked.

Mark sighed and dropped his head.

"Yes, I suppose so. I'll need to know where you're staying tonight. You have a large number of warriors with you. That's something the knights will need to keep an ear open for."

"I'll stay on my ship, thank you," Takeo replied. "As will my samurai."

Mark nodded and shook his head. Unable to conjure any more questions, he signaled to his men. Most mounted up, ready to take to the skies, while a handful took up watch on the shores. This wasn't an insult to Takeo, however. He knew it was Lucifan's policy ever since an attack on a Juatwa royal ship had occurred so many years ago. Takeo knew about it, too, as his brother had died in that attack.

However, before Mark could mount up and fly away, Takeo couldn't resist getting in the last word.

"Just so we're clear," he said, making them all pause. "The angels didn't die for this city. Lucifan killed them. All but one."

Chapter 1

For Cyrus, only two things were certain. Firstly, that his mother had not given him a surname, and secondly, that it did not matter. What mattered was that he and his mother were alive, healthy, and together. Everything else was an ever-shifting river of uncertainty, and he was okay with that.

He considered it a virtue to be carefree and forgiving. As a child, he'd grown up scared of a lot of things, including the future, but worrying hadn't helped one bit. As he'd grown older, he'd realized that actions spoke louder than words, and so the only way to change anything was through action.

The way he saw it, one had to adopt such an attitude, something bordering on blitheness, in the Forest of Angor. If not, one could not survive. The land here was covered in huge trees, which were older than elves, and filled with all manner of dangerous creatures. Warring centaurs, stoic elves, wandering treants, scavenging kobolds, thundering bugbears, harpies, hippogriffs, and perhaps the most dangerous of all—werewolves.

Cyrus would know. He was one of them.

Yet, despite how crowded Angor felt, it was densely wooded, and that meant there were a lot of places to hide out of sight. Cyrus and his mother, Belen, had such a place, a small camp built by Cyrus and a few of his elven friends. It was modest and spartan. Cyrus called it home and meant it.

Their 'house' was a small lean-to he'd built against a wide tree, with its leafy bed and raised earthen platform to keep the rain out. Their 'kitchen' was the little fire pit he'd made with stakes set up on either side for roasting meat and vegetables. Their 'storehouse' was the small garden of fruits he'd started just to the south. He'd also made a scouting post in a nearby tree with a rope ladder, a well-trodden and defined path that led the short distance towards the elven village, and small stools they used for seating. The only thing he'd made that he didn't like was his mother's cage.

She didn't like it either.

Belen stared at it now, rubbing her eyes from lack of sleep. The mind didn't rest like it needed to when one shifted into a werewolf, so although Belen had done nothing all night but nap and groom her black fur, she still looked exhausted this morning in her human form.

"Just two more nights, Mother," Cyrus said, checking over his backpack to make sure he had what he needed. "That's all."

"I know, I know," she replied, yawning and stretching. "If you really must insist that we sleep in that thing, you should build a bigger one. This one is too small for the both of us."

"Well, it wasn't supposed to be for us both," Cyrus replied. "I didn't think I'd have to join you in there, not until the first night, when you got lonely and clawed at the cage. However, I think it's fine. And besides, a bigger cage just means more weak points. You've almost escaped twice already."

Belen huffed.

"Twice," she mumbled. "Twice over what? More than a year? I'm safe now, Cyrus. You don't have to worry about me so much. I'll have you know I was a warrior before I was turned into a werewolf, and besides that, I'm your mother. It's my job to worry about you, not the other way around."

Cyrus slung his pack over his shoulder and gave his mother a wink.

"Yet here we are," he said. "I'll be back shortly."

Belen rarely joined Cyrus on his trips to the elven village. She enjoyed her solitude these days, having finally cast off the mental shackles that had been so thoroughly latched to her from a previous relationship. Cyrus' stepfather, for a lack of a better word, was a werewolf named Ralph, and he was the alpha male of their former pack. He'd also been abusive, to put it mildly. Only through a combination of hard training and sheer luck had Cyrus been able to rescue his mother from that prison.

Well, mostly rescue her. There were still some moments where Belen would drop an odd comment that made Cyrus feel uncomfortable.

"This meat is missing something, don't you think?" she'd say. "Back at the camp, they had that herb they'd rub into the meat, do you remember? Ah, do I miss that."

"I wonder if I could meet up with some of the ladies one day, you know?" she'd said another time. "They were always so nice to me. You don't understand Cyrus, but I grew up with nothing but women. I miss female company sometimes."

Or the worst of all, the arguments they'd have over Ralph.

"He wasn't that bad, Cyrus. He had a gentler side that you never saw. You don't know what it's like, having to be the alpha male. You have to present yourself as strong and brutal."

Cyrus did his best to avoid those conversations. It seemed the harder he tried to vilify Ralph, the harder Belen tried to defend him. As time passed, she also began to forget some of the darker parts of the past, while glorifying others. He couldn't fathom it, but she did have one good point: it didn't matter. She was here now, and that's what was important.

Yet there was a second reason Belen didn't go with Cyrus to the elves. Around this time of the year, the elves had visitors, specifically the only human visitors they ever had annually, the amazons.

Cyrus didn't know a great deal about them. He knew amazons were all women and all warriors. They hailed from the dense jungles south of Angor and made a trip once a year from their home to the mythical city of Lucifan across the Great Plains. The trip took months, and Cyrus couldn't help but think that perhaps it'd be more pragmatic to just stay in Lucifan, if that place was so great. Not that he cared either way. He'd only been to Angor's edge a few times, and he hadn't heard enough about the outside world to make him want to traverse the emptiness of the Great Plains anytime soon.

Belen had been an amazon once, but her sisters had abandoned her, falsely accused of a crime she did not commit. They'd left her in the forest to be bitten by werewolves, and it was just Cyrus' luck that she'd been pregnant with him when it happened.

So, understandably, Cyrus didn't care for the amazons much either.

But supplies were supplies, and the amazons could spend as much as two weeks with the elves if they so desired. Cyrus had been running low on plants, seeds, flint, and a few other things for days now. He couldn't wait any longer, and with luck, the amazons would be gone by now.

Cyrus stopped when the smallest creek of a bowstring reached his sensitive ears. Panic flashed through him for a brief moment until a chance breeze brought a familiar scent to his nose. An arrow launched passed him and thudded into a nearby tree. He didn't even flinch.

An elf popped up from behind a bush, smiling and holding a treantwood bow. Even though he was almost one-hundred years old, the elf looked similar in age to Cyrus' sixteen years. However, he didn't have small bits of stubble growing on his face like Cyrus, and he was short by human standards. Then again, Cyrus was tall and broad shouldered even among his own kind.

Cyrus let out a chuckle. The elf laughed.

"It's so hard to catch you unaware," the elf said.

"Katar," Cyrus replied. "What are you doing out here?"

"Just taking my turn at watch. I heard a noise and assumed it was you trying to sneak up on me. Guess I was right."

"Huh? What do you mean? I just got here."

"Well, I must have heard you stumbling from far off, then. You heard me, too, didn't you?"

"And smelled you. Like bugbear piss."

Katar Phizeiros chuckled and approached, coming close enough to shake hands, but he did not extend an arm. At times like this, Cyrus had to suppress his human desire for physical touch. He got the urge to hug Katar, or pat him on the shoulder, but he knew doing so would only embarrass the elf. Just being close to someone, like this, was enough for them.

"The amazons are still here," Katar said.

"Really?" Cyrus replied, slumping his shoulders. "I thought they'd have moved on by now."

"Just tell me what you need. I can collect it and bring it back to you and Belen."

"Well, thanks for the offer and all, but I also wanted to see Ven."

"Hm, well, she'd want to see you, too."

Cyrus sighed.

"Why do you let the amazons in anyway?" Cyrus asked. "From what I've seen, they're nothing like elves. They're loud and obnoxious. They're the opposite of modest, which is the only thing elves ever wanted to see from me."

"Yes, but we only have to put up with them twice a year. We're forced to see your ugly face every week."

Cyrus couldn't resist giving Katar a shove this time, which the elf dodged with a shoulder roll. That was probably for the best. Cyrus tended to forget his own strength.

"Sorry," he mumbled.

"Eh, don't be. You've hit me with a lot worse and I survived, barely. Look, we let the amazons in because that's what Dirthzea ordered, and he's the oldest and wisest of any of us. You know it was his decree that swayed the council to let you camp out so close to us."

"Yeah, I know. It's just, well, my mother and all."

Katar frowned and raised an eyebrow. It was a mocking gesture, human in nature, to which Cyrus rolled his eyes.

"Look, Cyrus," the elf said. "I'm not going to tell you to get over your grudge. History proves that elves hold some of the longest grudges, outside of dwarves, but we also have a firm belief in justice. Now that's a tricky thing, justice, because it forces a person to look at both sides of an issue. Like, for example, it forced me to realize that maybe I'd been wrong once upon a time. That maybe a werewolf that risks his life to save mine isn't a mindless beast after all. Maybe he's more noble than some elves I know, perhaps even my own brother. So maybe, just maybe, this side of the story you've heard from your mother about the elves is only one part. Maybe there's another part that the amazons know.

"And maybe you have a chance to ask them about it."

Cyrus blinked, staring openly at Katar.

"Did Ven tell you to say that?" he asked.

Katar smirked.

"Of course not," Katar said. "But of course, Ven is always talking to us younger elves."

"That sounds exactly like something she'd say."

"Well, maybe she did, and maybe I'm not on scouting duty after all. Maybe I was sent here to give you this exact message."

"And maybe you use the word 'maybe' too much."

"Maybe."

They laughed. Cyrus scratched the bottom of his neck and took a deep breath. There wasn't much of an argument left, though. If

Cyrus ever had a mentor, it was Ven, and when she offered advice, Cyrus took it as gospel. He nodded and followed Katar the rest of the way to the elven camp.

'Ven' was short for Flinar Vensandoral, and she was old, one-armed, sweeter than honey, and the best teacher any pariah could have asked for. She taught Cyrus how to fight, how to respect and love the forest, and how to believe in himself when no one else did. It was only with her help that Cyrus was able to break himself and his mother away from Ralph's control, and so Cyrus felt he owed her everything. He called her 'Ven' because elven custom demanded that everyone be addressed by their family name, and then by their given name if needed.

Cyrus and Katar flaunted this tradition between themselves, which Cyrus always took as a sign of their growing friendship. Once upon a time, Katar had bullied Cyrus, and the memories still hurt some days, but Cyrus was too desperate for companionship to spurn Katar when the elf turned over a new leaf. It ended up being a good decision.

As for the amazons, the pair heard them before they saw them.

"Come on! Another round, let's go!"

"What, bowing out already? Admitting defeat? Can't stand the might of the amazons, can you?"

"You were the one that said it! You said it! Another round. I bet my bow on it!"

"No! You can't be serious."

"Oh, yes I am. Another shot!"

The sudden outburst of shouting ceased, and the forest was silent again. Cyrus could only assume the elves were giving their answer at normal volume, and although his hearing was better than the average humans, it wasn't up to elven standards.

Katar could hear, though.

"Huh, they're really going to do it," he said, balking. "I can't believe it. Let's hurry!"

"Do what?" Cyrus asked, but a chorus of amazon cheering roared over them.

Katar didn't answer and took off running. Cyrus sprinted to catch up. Although his stride was longer, elves were strangely light of foot and covered ground fast. Cyrus struggled to keep up.

"Hurry!" Katar repeated.

They burst into the elven village—a conclave of little hovels built right into a grove of massive trees. In the center was a small clearing, and a row of targets had been erected to one side. Opposite those targets sat a crowd of elves and amazons. The elves were stoic, watching silently as one of their own took aim with a bow at one of the targets.

The amazons were more animated.

Mouths open, eyes fixed, they leaned on each other and held their breaths. Because they were all human, the amazons were taller and wider than the elves in stature, though only one woman among them came close to Cyrus' size and height.

The elf released his arrow and it sunk deep into the target's center. The amazons groaned slightly, and the elves countered with proud silence.

One of the women stood up, and Cyrus noted she appeared the youngest of the group. The brown-green leather skirt and vest she wore seemed too big for her, and although she stepped forward shyly, she held her bow with confidence. With long fingers, she drew an arrow and set it to the string.

"You can do this, Octavia!" one of the amazons burst out, unable to contain herself.

She was quickly shushed by the others, but Octavia turned back and smiled wide enough to show her upper gums. Then she turned back and focused. Octavia took a breath and let it out, then another, and drew until the bowstring was taut. She aimed carefully at her own target, and a spark set off in her sharp eyes. From Cyrus' angle, he could see her mouth twitch at a sudden idea, and she shifted her bow to the elf's target.

Her fingers released, and the arrow shot forward, striking the elf's arrow precisely dead center. The second arrow followed along the first's shaft and hit dead center as well, forcing the first to the side. The ensuing silence was deafening until the amazons started cheering.

They leapt up and ran to Octavia, hoisting her into the air. Some danced, others threw their arms up. One was so bold as to give the elves a wink, yet another stood motionless. That woman was tall and broad shouldered, and her straight black hair fell like water about her face. She was thick, solid one might say, and imposing in her stance. More importantly to Cyrus, though, this woman held a fixed gaze on him as she ignored her sisters' cheering.

Cyrus knew this woman. She was the amazon queen, and her name was Adelpha.

"Well, well, I believe that settles it," one of the amazons said. "You said it yourself that there wasn't a chance any of us could match elven skill. I guess you didn't know the daughter of Iezabel traveled with us. That'll teach you!"

That comment was addressed to an elf named Elidin Nathok. If the elves had a standing army, Nathok would be its general, but as it stood, he was more like a well-respected elder of the clan. He and Cyrus were well acquainted as Nathok had trained Cyrus on occasion, if reluctantly. He was a tough individual, cold even by elven standards, and he tolerated a lack of modesty like water tolerates fire.

"Leda," Nathok began, "I'd ask that you and your sisters show a bit more humility in victory. This is most unbecoming."

His jaw was so firm that his mouth barely moved, yet Leda was anything but deterred. She laughed loudly and grinned. Though they'd never talked, Cyrus recognized her from past visits. He'd be lying if he said her thin waist and wide hips didn't play a part in that.

"Huh, can you believe that?" Katar said. "Nathok must have been overconfident. He should have put the targets further away. Wouldn't you say? Cyrus? Did you hear me?"

"Yes, sorry, yeah," Cyrus answered, snapping out of his trance. "Crazy."

"Nathok would have placed the targets further away if he'd been the one shooting," Katar went on, "but I guess I shouldn't be surprised he had another elf challenge the amazons. Can you imagine how mad he'd be if he'd tied with a human? Now that would be a sight. He'd have stomped around in blind rage for weeks! He hasn't been humbled like I have, wouldn't you say?"

"Yes, that's exactly what I was going to say," Cyrus replied, ducking his head and stalking off.

Katar had to hurry to catch up.

"Eager to get going, I see," he said.

"Did you see the way the queen was looking at me?" Cyrus replied as they passed behind a tree, disappearing into another part of the village.

"Cyrus, you're a werewolf. You always draw attention."

"That's not it at all. She's never looked at me like that."

"You're overthinking it. That look was really no surprise," Katar offered, shrugging. "Adelpha always asks about you."

"She does?"

"Oh yes, every visit. You and Belen."

Cyrus had avoided seeing the amazons roughly every other year. The other times were either unavoidable or unintentional, and when they did end up in the elven village at the same time, Cyrus made sure to stay away from the women. Luckily, Adelpha was the only one who seemed interested in talking to him.

Over the years, she'd tried once or twice to strike up a conversation with him, always asking how he and his mother were doing. When Cyrus' curt replies weren't detailed enough, she'd abandon tact and go for a blunt approach, flat out demanding to know that everything was going well and that they were happy and healthy. Having been partially raised by elves, Cyrus respected his elders too much to refuse to answer, but he'd never told her the whole truth either. He'd just say everything was 'as usual' and mumble some excuse about needing to leave. For a long time, he never understood why this one amazon ever bothered to reach out to him, and for a time, he thought it was because Adelpha and his mother used to be friends. Then he had asked his mother.

"Adelpha," Belen had said, shaking with rage at the name. "It was her decree that damned us to this life, Cyrus. Her own sister—blood sister—committed the crime they declared me guilty of, and all thanks to this little halfwit farmer they picked up in the Plains. She's asking about me, huh? You know why? Guilt. She feels guilty about what she did and the fact that she can never make it right. And you know what? She should feel that way. Don't tell her anything, Cyrus. We don't want her help or her pity. She's done enough for us already."

So that's what Cyrus did. Every time Adelpha tried to talk, he gave her no more than 'the usual.' He saw the guilt in her eyes. Adelpha was incapable of hiding it.

"Well, yeah," Cyrus continued now, then repeated, "but she's never looked at me like that before."

"Hm, if you insist," Katar said. "I'll have to take your word for it."

They moved through the elven village, passing from hovel to hovel as Cyrus looked for supplies. Elves divided up tasks in a utilitarian format, delegating duties on a rotating basis, ensuring everyone knew and understood the sum of the tasks involved in keeping them all alive and well. What this meant was that if Cyrus wanted herbs, he had to go to a different elf this week than he had last week. If he wanted leather straps, he had to ask last month's leatherworker who had taken over. It was a lengthy and somewhat inefficient process, but elves had time in abundance. It didn't matter if something took longer to do if the result was increased harmony for the group.

That was one of the reasons Katar stuck around. He knew the value of time to Cyrus and helped the werewolf weave through the village faster.

"Oh, you need herbs, huh?" the elf said, teasing. "Lucky you. Guess who collected them this time. She's rather good at it."

Cyrus knew the answer immediately. Katar would only ever tease him like that about one elf, Tiatha Glynynore. She and Katar were similar in age, almost a century old, but both appeared to be close to Cyrus in human years. She was also beautiful, with long blonde hair and piercing eyes. More than once, Nathok had snapped at Cyrus for getting distracted during his lessons when Glyn had passed through the village with a basket of plants in one hand and a book in the other. The older he got, the more frequently she visited his dreams. Supposedly, she and Katar had a bit of a feud, which according to Katar, was several decades old. Cyrus couldn't imagine over what though, as he couldn't picture being angry at Glyn for anything.

He also couldn't imagine going to her for herbs this morning.

"Um, maybe I'll just go see Ven," Cyrus mumbled. "I don't actually need anything else."

"Aw, what's the matter?" Katar asked, still teasing. "Afraid you'll stumble over your words again? Just saunter up to her with undeniable human confidence and give her a wink. Shouldn't be that hard. I've seen the amazons do it often enough."

Then he chuckled, and Cyrus pushed down a turmoil of mixed emotions.

Intentional or not, jokes like that from Katar were what drove Cyrus to avoid Glyn. Whenever Cyrus had tried to talk to her in the past, he'd just bumble over his words and walk away feeling like an idiot. To add to that, she talked to him like an elder would, as if he were still a child and not a young man. Of course, to an elf, anyone under a century old was basically a child. From her perspective, just twelve years ago, she'd seen him enter this village as a weepy toddler missing his mommy. Since then, she didn't appear to have aged a day. It would take more than a growth spurt to shake that image from her mind, and Cyrus wasn't up to it right now.

"Another time," Cyrus said.

"You are no fun sometimes," Katar replied. "And here I thought humans were supposed to be a humorous, adventurous race. Does the werewolf curse sap your ability to poke fun at yourself?"

"Oh, I can laugh at myself, no problem. The joke just has to be funny."

Katar froze. The two shared a look, then a grin. They walked on.

When they called on Flinar Vensandoral's home, she was sitting outside, and her eyes lit up with a warm smile as Cyrus approached.

"Cyrus," she beamed, "so good to see you, and so good that you could find time to drop by. And Phizeiros, did you know your brother is looking for you?"

"When is he not?" Katar replied, sighing. "Where did he go?"

"I think he wanted your help with archery. Practice or some such, I can only imagine. I didn't pry."

"Yes, well, he needs it. I'll catch up with you later, Cyrus."

A short nod was standard parting manner between two close elves, so it had to be enough for Cyrus, too. Thankfully, as close as he was to Katar, Cyrus was closer with Ven. He could drop the stoic veil almost entirely with her.

He waited until no elves were walking by, then quickly stooped down and hugged Ven. She patted his back once and chuckled.

"How is your mother?" she asked.

"She's fine. Lonely, I think. You can really tell when she changes at night."

"Well, I know of few races that aren't social creatures in some sense."

"Even elves?"

"Come now, Cyrus. We live in a village. Of course we are social. I was talking about creatures like bugbears. You've never heard of a pack of bugbears, have you? Let's be thankful for that. Packs of werewolves and centaurs are trouble enough for this forest, I think."

Ven had more cause than most to say that. She was one of the few to have been attacked by a bugbear and live to tell the tale, though the creature had mauled her badly. That was also the reason why she could only use one arm, which also meant she couldn't use a bow, so she'd trained with swords all her life and had passed those refined skills onto Cyrus. The elves would never agree to teach a werewolf elven archery techniques, but sword skills were apparently acceptable. It was all a perfect cascade of events, as it were, which ultimately led to Cyrus growing up well versed in a useless ability.

As if anyone needed to know sword fighting in a forest.

But Cyrus couldn't complain. He'd also learned hand-to-hand combat, and that had been the skill he'd needed to beat Ralph and win his mother's safety. Cyrus could be nothing but grateful for all that Ven had shown him.

At this moment, though, he shrugged and leaned up against the other side of the door to Ven's home. He set his pack of supplies down and then slumped to the ground, happy to take in the sun alongside his teacher. Despite Ven sitting on a low stool, they were the same height now that Cyrus sat on the ground, and he was reminded of just how much larger he was to the elven kind. From this angle, he also happened to catch how the rays fell against Ven's disfigured face, distorting and amplifying her ugliness.

He laughed. Ven had taught him many things without ever speaking, and one of those was not to judge a book by its cover.

"Have you seen the amazons yet?" Ven asked.

"Oh yes," Cyrus answered. "I arrived just in time to see one of them match an elf in archery."

"Really? Is that what all the fuss was about? I wasn't listening until I heard all the shouting. I can't believe it. Are you sure?"

"Apparently that was their best archer, this woman named—ah, wait. I forgot. No, Octavia. That was it. Yes. Kind of a strange name."

"Everyone's name is strange to outsiders. Think of your own name. Your mother was an amazon, and I think it was her intent to give you an amazon-sounding name."

Cyrus paused. He had planned to do nothing but speak idly with Ven, but she just so happened to transition the conversation into something more serious. Cyrus paused, then broached what was on his mind.

"Ven, do you believe in forgiveness?"

"You know I do."

"Yeah, but," he paused, "that's not what I'm talking about. I mean something like, do you remember when Katar and I were younger, and he'd pick on me? Then I hit him, forgetting my strength, and the village elders decided to cast me out for a while? Despite all that, you still went out to the forest to meet with me. You defied their order until Katar and I saw past our differences and the elders let me back in."

"I'm afraid I don't understand the question, Cyrus."

"Yeah, I'm bad at this. I guess what I'm trying to say is that, well, the elders were right to cast me out. Katar might have had it coming, but I understand they were willing to take his side over mine, because he was family. That's what you do for your family, isn't it? But you still came to see me. Why?"

Ven shrugged.

"You've answered the question," she said. "There were two sides to that story, and mistakes were made. However, I wasn't about to make another mistake by abandoning you in your quest and me in my duty to raise you up to be the person I knew you could be."

"And what kind of person is that again?" Cyrus asked, giving her a sidelong look.

"The kind of person who would march into a werewolf camp and fight for his mother's life. The kind of person who, when victory was in his sights, would show mercy. Also, the kind of person who, when presented with a chance to hear both sides of the story, would be an impartial judge."

Cyrus squinted. He followed the first two examples, but the last one didn't bring a memory to mind. Then he saw Ven was looking past him, and he turned the other way.

Down the dirt path leading to the village center, a large amazon woman with straight black hair had popped into view. It took a half second for Cyrus to recognize Adelpha, and it took her just as long to scan the setting and spot Cyrus. They both froze, and a flash of panic swept through Cyrus.

He contemplated running, but one look back at Ven told him that wasn't going to happen. There was nothing stern in the elf's gaze except for that singular look of anticipation and encouragement. It was a look of expectation, and it bespoke one of those moments Ven would judge him for.

There was nothing else to do.

"Did you plan this?" he demanded.

"Plan? No," she said. "Anticipate? Maybe."

He sighed and peered up the road again, looking for an escape, but Ven leaned forward into his vision.

"Remember, Cyrus," she said. "Two sides to every story. Perhaps it's time you heard the other half."

Cyrus took a deep breath and hung his head. Then he stood up, fighting the urge to run, and walked calmly towards Adelpha as she marched towards him. They met in the middle, but he looked everywhere except at her.

"Cyrus, hello," Adelpha started, sounding as awkward as he felt. "I've been looking for you. I thought you were trying to avoid me there, for a little while."

"Um, well, just a little," he said. "My mother is still doing fine, by the way."

"Cyrus, I know you aren't fond of me, but," Adelpha paused.

She glanced around, then up ahead at Ven. She sighed and put her large hands on her hips and shook her head.

"Oh fine, let them all hear," she mumbled. "Cyrus, has anyone been to visit you lately?"

Cyrus straightened. That wasn't the question he'd expected.

"Well, no," he said. "I mean, the elves do."

"That's not what I'm talking about. Cyrus, does the name Takeo Karaoshi mean anything to you?"

Cyrus thought for a moment, but it was unnecessary. He shook his head.

"Should it?" he asked.

Adelpha swallowed. It suddenly dawned on Cyrus what was different about the queen on this visit. He'd never seen her scared.

"Come with me," she said.

Chapter 2

Cyrus was not keen on following this woman anywhere. As familiar as she pretended to be with him, he didn't know her at all. He saw her at best once a year, for a minute or less, and from his understanding, this woman and her kin had caused his family nothing but harm. Despite all the manners the elves had pounded into him about respecting his elders, it would take more than a nervous glance and a strange sounding name to get Cyrus to follow Adelpha anywhere.

Thankfully, Adelpha realized this without any word on Cyrus' part. As she turned and walked away, she only got in two steps before seeing that Cyrus hadn't moved. She stopped and sighed.

"Look," she started. "I know you have no reason to trust me, but I owe Belen a debt I can't repay. The least I can do is give you a warning."

Cyrus folded his arms across his chest.

"So what is it then?" he asked.

"I'm not taking you anywhere secret, child," she said. "I just have a lot to say, and I'd prefer to say it sitting down."

"Excuse me. I'm not a child. If I was with the pack, I'd be running with the hunters by now. I rescued my own mother from the prison you abandoned her to, and I won't be ordered around by a stranger."

In a flash, Adelpha's face turned bright red, her hands balled into her fists, and a lengthy vein pulsed against the skin from within her neck. Her whole demeanor changed so rapidly that Cyrus was caught off guard and he swayed back a hair.

However, though Adelpha fumed and a thin wail of anger escaped her lips, she held it together. With immense visible effort, she pushed down her rage and took a long, calming breath.

"That was not meant as an insult," she said, straining the words with eyes closed. "It just slipped out. I know you're not a child. If you were an amazon, we'd consider you a woman of age. Could you please just come with me? This is about keeping you and your mother safe."

"Well, um, thank you for that, but I'm just going to be honest here—I definitely don't feel like following you now."

"I swear upon my mother's grave, boy, you have no idea what is going on or how serious this is. This is not a suggestion. You need to come with me, right now. I'll have you know I'm working really hard to talk some sense into you rather than beat it into you."

Cyrus scoffed and tightened his arms across his chest.

"I'd like to see you try."

He expected an actual outburst this time, but Adelpha seemed to have passed that hill and instead fizzled out with a grunt. She shook her head and buried her face in a palm, taking deep breaths. She looked ridiculous.

"And I thought I was headstrong at that age," she whispered. "Alright Cyrus, if I talk to you right here, will you listen?"

Cyrus had to fight back an immediate reaction to say no. He'd been told what to do and how to do it for so long, literally all his life, that seizing the power to steer a conversation was difficult to resist—even if it steered the conversation to a dead end.

However, they weren't alone in this part of the village, and it finally pierced Cyrus' adolescent brain that this entire conversation was drawing negative attention. Sure, Adelpha looked ridiculous, fuming in place, but so did he by causing it. Cyrus glanced over his shoulder at Ven, searching for confidence. The elf wasn't watching, but he knew that she was listening.

And that changed everything.

"I, um," Cyrus said, turning back and slumping his shoulders. "I'm sorry. I didn't mean to be rude. We can go somewhere to sit, if you like. I can't stay long, though. I need to get back to my mother."

That last part was a white lie. Belen was independent in her own right, and she often went whole days alone as Cyrus scouted the forest for food. However, if Adelpha knew the truth in the matter, she didn't show it. She took a deep breath and smiled graciously.

"Thank you, Cyrus. I'll try to be brief."

Before they left, Cyrus stole another glance at Ven. She was watching now, and she gave Cyrus a wink and a smile. Warmth spread out from his heart, even as his stomach did flips while he followed his woman to a carved log on the outskirts of the village.

They sat down. They looked at each other. Silence ensued.

"So," Cyrus said, drawing the word out. "This, what was the name?"

"I don't know where to begin," Adelpha confessed. "If you don't know whom Takeo Karaoshi is, then it's clear your mother never told you anything about where you came from, or why you're different, and I don't want to intrude on that, but I have to."

There was no clarification on Adelpha's part on what she meant by different, neither was there a need. It seemed everyone and their mother knew what made Cyrus different from other werewolves, and that was that he could control himself in that form. All other werewolves lost themselves when they changed under a full moon. They turned into the animals they appeared to be and rampaged across the land, killing indiscriminately.

Cyrus, though, retained his human mind mostly. He could think clearly, logically, and act on that. A werewolf let loose in an elven camp would have to be put down with arrows. Cyrus, though, could walk casually throughout and ignore the impulse to rip and consume flesh.

That's why the cage back at his camp was for Belen, and not him.

Cyrus had tried to pry the cause from his mother once or twice, but she only said she'd tell him when he was older. He'd tried to ask the other werewolves, but they didn't know. Cyrus did know, from his stepfather, that Belen had sent him away when he was young, and that he returned different, but where he went and why was never revealed. After a while, Cyrus lost interest in the mystery. What did it matter? Whether it was due to a birth defect or a divine curse, what difference would that knowledge make? The reason was nothing more than an idle curiosity of his, and he couldn't see why Adelpha was making such a big deal out of it now.

"Why don't you just tell me whom this Takeo person is?"

Adelpha huffed and hunched forward, staring at her feet.

"That's exactly what I'm trying to do, Cyrus," she said. "Listen, a long time ago, when you were just a couple years old, if that, Belen sent you away."

"Yeah, I know that. Ralph never let me forget it. He told me my mother didn't want me."

"Did Ralph mention that you were sent off with two men? That you were dragged across the Great Plains and halfway up the Khaz

Mal Mountains, in the hopes of finding an angel that could cure your werewolf curse?"

Cyrus went still. Admittedly, most of what Adelpha said had gone over his head, except for one thing.

"There's a cure? Could my mother be cured?"

"No," Adelpha answered, frowning. "Look at yourself. Clearly not. But those two men did find the angel, and that angel did the next best thing to a cure. It gave you control. The two men brought you back to Belen, and then they disappeared. I never thought I'd see them again."

Adelpha paused as if this should weigh heavily on Cyrus. He spoke out to move her along.

"Okay, so they're back, then, aren't they?" he said. "That's what this is all about, and this Takeo person is one of them. Why should this concern my mother or me, exactly? What about the other guy?"

Adelpha paused and drew fingers through her loose hair. They flowed through the straight strands like water, giving the woman a level of fragility she otherwise lacked with her intimidating stature. Despite all the confidence Cyrus had shown in challenging her to a fight, he was glad she didn't. Adelpha put off an aura that said she could handle herself. It didn't sit well that she grew more nervous as the conversation drew on.

"The other man was a knight from Lucifan named Sir Gavin Shaw. He and Takeo loved the same woman, a sister of mine called Emily Stout. She was one of the women to falsely condemn your mother, and that mistake weighed on her so heavily that, when she died, the two men did their best to honor her memory by carrying out her last wish: to help Belen in any way they could. As it turned out, helping you was Belen's only wish, so that's what they did. After they brought you back, Takeo and Gavin went east, far east, back to Takeo's homeland. There, Takeo killed him."

Adelpha's gaze poured into Cyrus, full of meaning, as if what she said should make him gasp. Cyrus swallowed but stared back with a blank expression. Adelpha continued.

"Listen, Cyrus. My sisters and I spotted Takeo just a couple weeks ago on the Great Plains, and he is not the same man he was when he did your mother a favor. He's an emperor now, of Juatwa, commanding armies of loyal samurai, and he's started wars across the world. There are stories about what he's done, from burning down cities to slaughtering innocent children. People call him The Dark Lord. For whatever reason, he was traveling alone along the southern end of the Great Plains. Like us, he was skirting the forest edge trying to evade the werewolves during the full moon. He didn't ask to travel with us, and I didn't offer, but he made his purpose clear: He's looking for you."

Cyrus' eyes popped wide. His first thought was about his mother, sitting idly by herself back at camp.

"What? Me?" he stuttered. "Why me?"

"I don't know," Adelpha admitted, relieved to hear panic in Cyrus' voice finally. "I asked, but he wouldn't say. So, I lied and said I didn't know where you were, but surely that will only delay him. I've never trusted him."

"But he's traveling alone. That's good, right? If he wanted to kill me, wouldn't he have sent his armies or something?"

"Takeo Karaoshi is a dangerous man, Cyrus. I've heard rumors that he marched into not one, but two, castles in Juatwa and slayed the reigning lord upon their very throne. We met him at night, and he appeared almost out of thin air and then disappeared just as fast. If he'd been anything less than cordial, I would have put him in the ground—with arrows, from a distance. However, I never got the chance, and I feared if we missed the shot, he might slay all of us.

"Listen carefully. If and when you meet him, I want you to be cautious. Don't test him. He claims to be just passing through, and maybe he's telling the truth. Do you understand?"

Cyrus stood up and grabbed his supplies. This time when he looked into Adelpha's eyes, he shared her meaningful gaze. He wasn't sure he could trust her, or anything she'd said, but the fear that it could all be true outweighed the consequences of it being a lie.

Then another memory, a recent one, slipped across his mind. He remembered Katar, smiling and saying he'd heard a noise in the forest and thought it was Cyrus.

"I have to get back," he said.

"Yes, you do."

He turned to run but paused.

"Thank you," he mumbled, then hesitated further after she nodded. "Um, can I ask you something?"

"Of course."

"My mother," he said. "Why were you so quick to condemn her?"

Adelpha's eyes fell.

"That's a fair question, Cyrus, but it's a long answer. It'll have to wait. I'd rather not keep you."

Cyrus hesitated a moment longer before deciding she was right. He took off at a light jog, not wanting to draw unwanted attention. Elves maintained high expectations regarding manners, and he didn't want to offend anyone unduly. However, once he passed the elves, he broke into a dead run.

The small camp that Belen and her son called home lay a respectable distance away from the elven village—more specifically, it was far enough away that the sensitive elven ears couldn't hear Belen's howling at night. That was further than Cyrus would have preferred to feel safe, but there wasn't any choice. Their entire existence out here was only allowed by the elves' good graces, so good neighbors they had to be. As for the safety part, the elves had been good enough to help Cyrus build his cage and also provided him with the location of their nearest treetop hideaway.

Yet it also meant he was running for some time.

The silence weighed down on him the further he went, hearing only his ragged breathing and his heavy pack tossing wildly about. He hoped to hear something as he got closer, but Belen had no reason to make noise without Cyrus there. The loudest she ever became was either cleaning dishes, chopping wood, or cutting vegetables. Cyrus would have to get awfully close before he heard anything.

Which is why he panicked when he heard his mother laugh.

Cyrus stopped, so did the laughter. Then another laugh came, and Cyrus knew the truth.

"He watched me," Cyrus said. "He watched and waited until I left. Damn, how? I should have smelled him or heard him. I set up tripwires that should have made sound. How could he avoid all of that? Who is this guy? Could it be someone else? It's okay, relax. Mother is alive and laughing. Don't panic yet. Nice and slow."

Cyrus took a deep breath, steadying his heart, and took up a casual stroll towards the camp. As he got closer, the conversation materialized.

"Oh, it is so good to talk to someone again," Belen said. "Human, too. The elves, they just can't carry on any conversation worth having. It's like they abhor gossip. I can only talk about the weather so many times before I start preferring the company of trees."

"Huh, I didn't know the bar was so low," came the reply, quiet yet assertive. "You must be terribly lonely out here."

"I am," she sighed, "but don't tell my son. He does his best, and it is nice talking to him, but I grew up in a clan. First it was the amazons, then the werewolves. I'm just not used to this much isolation. Cyrus tries so hard to make up for that, but two people isn't a village. It's just not the same. That said, I'm going to miss him."

A lump jumped into Cyrus throat. He quickened his pace.

"Have you considered going back to the werewolves?" the other voice asked.

Cyrus was close enough to make out that the voice was distinctly male, and it carried an accent Cyrus had never heard.

"Oh, Cyrus would never allow that. I think it'd kill him."

"I see. Well, that seems a shame. What harm could a visit do, really? However, we can ask him ourselves. I think I hear him approaching."

"Really?" Belen asked. "I don't hear anything."

Cyrus had been trying to watch his step. As best he could tell, he shouldn't have been heard, but the second that he'd been noticed, Cyrus dropped the façade. He took a deep breath and marched into view. A strange man was pacing the camp's edge, examining the large cage. Belen was seated by the fire, stirring a small pot of vegetable stew mixed with yesterday's broth. She beamed at Cyrus' approach, a warm glow in her cheeks that he hadn't seen in a long while. She swept her auburn hair aside and turned to introduce their guest.

Cyrus hadn't known what to expect when he saw this man, but what he did see caught him off guard. For one, he was dressed strangely in something like a woman's dress. Cyrus also didn't

expect this man to be on the shorter side for a human male, or so
wiry. He had a slim athletic build that spoke of emphasis on speed,
but he stood still enough that Cyrus sensed the man was quite
durable. A number of scars peaked out from the man's clothes, and a
more evident one stained his left cheek. His hair fell black and
straight to shoulder length, not unlike Adelpha's, but his eyes were
blacker still. All light seemed to die out in those eyes, which homed
in on Cyrus with careful attention.

Cyrus understood in a moment that he was being watched with
a fighter's gaze. Every flick of Cyrus' wrist and shift in bodyweight
was being calculated in those eyes. Nothing he did would be missed
if he did not hide it well. Cyrus couldn't even bluff that he wasn't
worried. It was clear this man saw through it all.

And at his side was a single sword, long and thin, slightly
curved. Its handle was black, and the sword was sheathed in black
wood.

"Cyrus you're back!" Belen said. "Takeo, you remember Cyrus,
of course. Cyrus, allow me to introduce you to Lord Takeo
Karaoshi. Oh, a lord! It's still so strange to say. Anyway, Cyrus,
he's come back, just like he promised."

Cyrus said nothing. He stared at Takeo's hand, where it rested
carefully on the pommel of his sword.

Chapter 3

Lord Takeo Karaoshi bowed, lowering down with stark formality and confusing Cyrus. At first, he thought the man had dropped something and was stooping down to grab it. Then when Takeo bent back up and looked expectantly, it suddenly dawned on Cyrus that this was a form of greeting. He'd never seen anything like it. In fact, he only caught on at all because the elves nodded at each other, and a bow was a lot like an overdramatic nod.

Cyrus panicked anew, thinking he was being rude, and attempted a bow. It came out like an awkward stoop, but Takeo didn't seem to notice.

"Good day, Cyrus," Takeo said. "It's been a while. You've really grown, haven't you? You probably don't recognize me."

Cyrus shook his head. The man turned back to the section of the cage he was examining. His eyes scanned up and down the strong wood and plentiful knots used to keep the strength of a werewolf contained. His left hand glided up along the craftsmanship, admiring it as far as Cyrus could tell.

"I didn't think so," Takeo continued. "To be fair, I don't recognize you either. You were much too young last we met, hardly old enough to be called a child. Now, you're a man, aren't you? And quite tall, it seems. Your surprise is warranted, by the way. Your mother tells me she never mentioned that I'd be coming back."

"She never told me about you at all," Cyrus corrected, darting a glance at Belen.

Belen scoffed and waved the look away. She went back to stirring the pot as nonchalantly as ever.

"Oh, I had my reasons," she said. "Be honest, Takeo, there was never any guarantee you would return. I thought it better not to get Cyrus' hopes up. I decided to take matters into my own hands while you were gone and had the elves train him from an early age. You'll be happy to know that Cyrus is no novice farmer like Emily was. He can handle himself. He even beat the alpha leader of our old pack!"

Belen smiled and chuckled, enjoying the chance to brag about her son. Neither of the men joined in.

Takeo continued to inspect the cage, though it was clear to all that the man was just finding something to idle away the time. He didn't appear eager to talk after that first exchange of pleasantries, and Cyrus took that opportunity to slip towards the fire and sit next to his mother. He brushed a hand over hers to garner her full attention.

"Mother, what is this about?" he asked.

"Oh, it's quite a long story, my son. You see, it's thanks to Takeo that—"

"I know," Cyrus said, then thought quickly as his mother's eyes raised. "I, uh, overheard the elves talking about it. This man, he took me when I was young to something called an angel? Is that right?"

Belen scowled.

"Damn elves," she said. "One would think they could keep a secret with the way they emphasize privacy, but no. Seems they're a bunch of hypocrites. What a surprise."

"It's really not their fault," Cyrus hastened. "I was eavesdropping. But why is he back? Sorry, why are you back, uh, sir—lord? I didn't mean to talk about you like you aren't here."

Takeo waved a hand.

"I take no offense," he said. "On the contrary, I don't mean to intrude on your conversation. Please, carry on as if I weren't here."

Belen and Cyrus looked at each other again. Then Belen's eyes fell back to the stew. She stirred the boiling pot, releasing nervous energy.

"You don't know why he's back," she said. "Well, at least one part of the story remained hidden. You see, Cyrus, after Takeo brought you back to me, I asked him a favor. I asked that he come back when you were older, when you turned sixteen. In amazon tradition, that's when a girl comes of age."

"To do what, exactly?" Cyrus asked.

"To give you the chance at a better life," Belen said, pleading at the same time. "The chance to be something more than a diseased outcast. Takeo is knowledgeable, and he's a lord now! Can you believe our luck? You should be grateful that he's taken time out of his royal duties to come and get you personally. Just think of all the amazing places you'll see when you finally leave—"

Cyrus pulled his hands away from his mother's, and Belen choked on her next words. She dropped the stew ladle and scrambled for Cyrus' hands, grabbing them, and pulling them to her. The urgency in her grip stopped Cyrus from turning away.

"I'm not leaving you," he said.

"Cyrus, listen to me," she begged. "This camp, this forest, this place you call home—it's a prison. A massive, cold, unforgiving prison where the werewolf kind were banished long ago to live out their days in isolation. Why do you think we're out here, huh? Because we want to be? No, Cyrus. We're outcasts, but you don't have to be. You, with your angel-gifted control, could join the world and have a chance to do something worthwhile."

Cyrus went to shake his head, but Belen lifted a hand to his cheek, and he stopped.

"You know what I hate most about the amazons?" she continued. "It's the fact that I miss them. I hate not being one of them anymore. I used to be someone, Cyrus. I had followers, power, and women at my command. I used to travel every year to the greatest city ever built and mingle with travelers from all over. That was life, Cyrus, a real life. Not this trapped existence of stagnation. There's no hope for me, but Cyrus that life could be yours, and more."

"Mother, I—"

"Stop it!" Belen shouted, but she did not get angry. Her voice returned to normal. "Listen, this has been my dream for you since you were born. I'm sorry to put this all on you so suddenly, but it's time. Do you think it was easy for me, huh, to send you off when you were so young, so vulnerable, barely able to talk? No, Cyrus. It tore me apart. However, I knew it was the best for you. And when you came back, I was happy to see you, but also heartbroken for what it meant. Your place is not here, trapped and forgotten. You can have the life you deserve. Don't worry about me. I will not have your life ruined, your best years snatched away, to take care of an old woman who's not worth saving."

Hot tears came to Cyrus' eyes. He brushed them off.

"How can you say that?" Cyrus said. "Of course, you're worth saving."

"Stop crying," Belen commanded, though her voice was shaking. "Don't cry for me. Do you hear? Stop it."

Her command did not help, but Cyrus closed his eyes and took deep breaths until he could push his emotions down. It pained him to admit, but he'd always been a sensitive child. The elves said so; the werewolves said so. It must be true. Abandoned by his mother, abused by his stepfather, never knowing his real father, always treated as an outsider, Cyrus hadn't exactly grown up with any sort of emotional stability. He'd been eager for love, to feel wanted, for as long as he could remember, and it'd been painful learning to love himself before anyone else would. He still struggled with it, but finally everything was coming together. He'd rescued his mother from the captivity of his abusive clan, he'd become a somewhat acceptable member of elven society, and he'd even begun exploring the forest and engaging with the other races. Yet now he was being told it was all for nothing.

Belen sighed.

"Good," she said, seeing Cyrus bring himself back under control. "You're getting better at that."

"Yeah, well, I've had a lot of practice," he replied, sucking mucus to clear his nose. "Between you and the elves, and all."

"You're a man now, Cyrus. You even beat Ralph, remember? Although I hated to see it come to a fight, I was proud of you, do you know that?"

Pride seeped into Cyrus' heart. His cheeks grew hot, and a few more tears found their way out of him. Belen gave him a smile.

"It's time, Cyrus," she continued. "You're ready for this."

"No," he started. "I love you too much."

"Cyrus—"

"If I may," Takeo interjected.

The two werewolves jumped. Still holding hands, sitting close enough for their knees to bump, they turned to the samurai who was standing next to the cage.

"I don't mean to intrude, but I might be able to help here," he said. "Belen, I have to apologize, but I haven't been completely honest with you. You believe I'm here because I promised to return when Cyrus came of age and take him away. I've been lying by omission of the truth, unfortunately. The fact that I'm here now, at the right time, is a matter of coincidence. I'm actually here because

34

I'm seeking the angel, Ephron—that very same angel I brought Cyrus to so long ago."

Belen blinked, stunned.

"You are?" she said.

Takeo shrugged apologetically. Cautious relief mixed with hope flooded Cyrus' heart.

"I've spent the past few months up in the Khaz Mal Mountains looking for Ephron, but I can't find him. I'm not sure why. Angels are supposed to be easier to find if you've seen them before—something about their aura—but it's not working for me. I need help. Cyrus, who has seen and felt the angel's presence, could be that help. Even though he was a child, he may be able to feel the angel's presence where I have failed. That's why I'm here.

"So let me explain why this is a good thing. Here's my proposal: Belen, it's clear you want your son to leave this place, yet it's also clear Cyrus isn't keen on leaving. Let's compromise. Cyrus, why don't you accompany me for this short quest of mine? It shouldn't take more than six months, and if you want to return home at the end of it, you can. In this way, everyone gets what they want. Cyrus, you will have made your mother happy by giving the world a chance, yet you will not be banished. I will get what I want, and you and I will also establish a sort of relationship. Even if you return home, you can always leave again. You can come and go, actually, like the amazons do.

"Everyone wins."

Belen and Cyrus met each other's gaze again. They stared in silence, thinking it over, but Belen made up her mind faster. She squeezed Cyrus' hands, drawing his attention.

"He's right," she said. "Six months, that's easy. I have everything I need, and the elves are close by for protection. You don't have to worry about me. Okay? You don't have to worry."

"You keep saying that—"

"Cyrus, you forget that I got along just fine for many, many years, before I raised you. I am your mother, do you hear? That means you do what I say."

"I thought I was a man now," Cyrus replied, raising an eyebrow. "Doesn't that mean I get to make my own decisions?"

"Only if they are the right ones! Listen to me. Is this about my happiness? That's why you want to stay? Well, do you know what would make me the happiest of all? If you were to leave with Takeo, that's what I want. Like he says, give the world a chance."

Cyrus wanted to argue that point, but he stopped. By chance, he caught a glimpse of Takeo, and they locked gazes for a second.

However, it was a long second. Those black eyes drew Cyrus and seemingly everything around him in, watchful and calculating, yet also cold to the core. In a flash, Cyrus felt like he was peering into Takeo's soul, and a chill ran up his spine.

"When you meet him, I want you to be cautious," Adelpha had said. "Don't test him."

Cyrus' eyes fell to Takeo's sword, and how the man's hand rested so comfortably on that weapon. Cyrus thought about what else Adelpha had said, how she chose not to challenge him, despite outnumbering him two dozen to one. Then Cyrus' eyes drifted back to Belen, and he understood what to do.

"Okay," he said, reluctantly. "I'll go."

They left that night. Takeo was quite insistent that he'd been delayed long enough, and Belen seemed all too certain that her son might change his mind if given the chance. Cyrus resigned himself, submitting to the will of his elders like he'd been taught since birth. However, truth be told, that habit was getting more difficult to adhere to, day by day. Rebellion stirred within, and he couldn't help but feel the desire to challenge his upbringing.

But not yet. Tonight, he would make his mother happy.

When Cyrus left, there were no heartfelt tears of goodbye. Growing up, during his time with the elves, Cyrus would often go a month or more without seeing his mother. That was just normal, as if he had two homes. They had spent more time together at this camp than they ever had before in Cyrus' memory. So, he hugged her, held her close, and promised to return, but only Belen's eyes were moist on departure, and those tears were clearly of joy.

Cyrus didn't take much. There wasn't much to bring: provisions, a few small traps, a waterskin, the clothes on his back. He didn't have a bow. The elves had never trained him in archery, and out of respect for them, Cyrus had avoided using one. The only weapon he had was a longsword given to him by Ven as a present. It had never been used.

The most direct route out of the forest went by the elven village, and Takeo offered no objection when Cyrus took them that way. They stopped on the outskirts when they were challenged by a sentry, and Cyrus asked her to pass a message along to Nathok and Katar. He wanted them to look out for his mother while he was away.

The journey out of the forest took a couple of days, the first two nights of which Cyrus changed into his werewolf form. He had hoped that Takeo would get unnerved at the sight, but the man didn't so much as blink. He sat calmly, patiently, studying the way Cyrus grew in height and mass, howled and snapped, and sprouted fur, teeth, and claws. Cyrus tried to make a show of holding back some inner monstrosity by growling and drooling, like any other werewolf would do when unleashed by its curse, but Takeo just reclined against a tree trunk and rested his hand on his sword.

"Fascinating," was all he had to say.

In the morning, Cyrus changed tactics.

"I think it will be safer if we move at night," he said.

"That is fine with me," Takeo replied.

"The going will be—wait, it is?"

The man blinked.

"Oh okay, well," Cyrus stumbled to get going again. "It's just that, well, I'm sort of awake at night when I shift under the full moon, so it's convenient for me to move then. Also, I can see pretty well in low light, but I thought that, as a normal human, you might have issues with that and, well, you see . . ."

Takeo blinked again.

"It'd be even safer if we didn't stop," Cyrus pressed. "If we traveled all day and into the night, we could get out of the forest faster. Time is important to you, right?"

"I'm fine with this."

Cyrus balked.

"You are, huh? So, when will you sleep? Uh, I mean, well, uh, that's good. You know, I grew up in these woods, and I can move rather fast through them, even in the dark. You're not going to slow me down, are you?"

Takeo blinked once more. Cyrus swallowed.

"Okay then, well, follow me, I guess."

They did as Cyrus suggested, and Takeo had no trouble keeping pace. In fact, when they finally did make camp, Cyrus fell asleep first. He awoke some hours later to Takeo tapping him gently on the shoulder.

"We should keep moving," he said. "You've led us into centaur territory. It would not be wise to linger here."

"Yes, yes, I know that," Cyrus replied, shrugging off fatigue. "Wait, how could you possibly know that? Did you sleep at all?"

Takeo stared at him. Cyrus sighed and got up.

Chapter 4

The contrast between the Forest of Angor and the Great Plains stood stark across the landscape. A thick grove of tall, green trees came to an abrupt halt along a dense line of yellow grass and rolling hills. Cyrus had been out this way a handful of times as he'd explored the forest throughout his life, venturing into the Great Plains for fleeting moments just to see what it was like. What threw him off the most wasn't the way one could see off into the distance or how dry everything was, but the constant wind that blew strongly. The Great Plains was noisy, Cyrus concluded, and he preferred the quiet solitude one found in the forest.

If Takeo agreed with this, Cyrus never found out. In fact, Takeo was a man of few words, and it had unnerved Cyrus how the man could say so little in their days together. Not that Cyrus needed to talk. He'd spent a lot of time in the forest alone, so he'd grown accustomed to keeping to himself. However, it just felt rude to say so little. Takeo didn't ask Cyrus a single question until they neared the forest's edge when the weeds of the Great Plains began to sprout about their feet and reach for their waists.

"So, I can't help but notice you carry a sword," Takeo said. "Are you any good with it?"

Cyrus jumped at the question disturbing the entrenched silence between them.

"This thing?" Cyrus replied. "I think I am, but I'm not really sure, to be honest. I only ever trained with Ven and a few other elves. It's not like the werewolves use swords or anything. Growing up, sword training felt more like a hobby rather than a skill."

"Hm, so you've never used it to fight for your life. That's dismaying."

Cyrus furrowed his eyebrows but didn't turn back. Takeo's tone couldn't be flatter if he tried, yet it carried a weight to it that was difficult to describe.

"Look, I know how to fight," Cyrus replied. "I beat my stepfather in an alpha fight, and I took on a bugbear once, stupidly. I didn't win that one, but well, I don't know, that's gotta count for something. And besides, I didn't train with swords as small as this one. Ven liked to test my strength by having me fight with huge swords that you'd have to hold with two hands. They were made out of wood strapped with iron bands."

"You think the sword you carry now is small, huh?" Takeo said. "Are you aware that sword is in the style of those carried by the Knights of Lucifan?"

Cyrus thought for a moment.

"Lucifan? No, but that makes sense," he said. "I don't know what knights are, but I heard about Lucifan. Ven said this was an old sword in their arsenal. I guess that's where they got it from. I thought it was strange. The sword she carried was thinner and curved. Actually, it looked like yours."

Takeo faltered a step, which Cyrus only caught because the man's foot made the slightest noise crunching a fallen leaf amongst the growing weeds. That was a relief to hear, honestly, because the way Takeo had moved up until that point had been uncanny. No normal human should be capable of such stealth as this man was, especially in an environment as tricky to navigate as the foliage-strewn ground of Angor.

"Really?" Takeo said, with a twinge of intrigue. "A katana?"

"Oh yeah, that's what she called it. I remember now. She said it was from the far east. That's where you're from?"

"Did she say how she got it?"

Cyrus paused. It took a moment to push Takeo's rudeness aside and answer his question.

"It was a gift, I think," Cyrus said.

"From whom, did she say? How long ago was this gift received?"

Cyrus stopped. They'd just passed the threshold between Angor and the Great Plains, with trees at their backs and grass at their feet. This was as good a place as any for which Cyrus had planned all along.

He turned and faced Takeo.

"You seem awfully interested in this sword," Cyrus said.

Takeo stared back, unflinching. Cyrus drew in a breath.

"It was a gift, but she didn't say from whom—or she did, and I forgot. It was some years ago. All I remember is the sword was from a human who visited the forest. They might have been lovers."

"How long ago?"

"I don't know," Cyrus replied, scoffing. "It couldn't have been that long, though. Ven started training with swords after the bugbear attack, so perhaps, maybe fifty years? Sixty? Something like that. You're not that old, so why does that concern you?"

Takeo flicked his gaze to the sword handle sticking out from behind Cyrus' back. The sword was strapped beneath Cyrus' pack, where it was easiest to carry, because he wasn't used to having a sword attached to his hip.

"We'll have to spar one day," Takeo said. "If you trained under this elf, I wouldn't be surprised if I found your style of combat familiar."

Takeo started walking again, brushing by Cyrus and out into the sun-drenched grass of the plains. Cyrus steeled himself and planted his feet.

"Actually, if you want to spar, this is the only chance you'll get," he said.

Takeo stopped dead, as if time itself had frozen. The wind lapped around his robes and his hair, but he could have been a statue otherwise. Cyrus drew himself to full height.

"This is as far as I go," Cyrus continued.

Takeo turned his head first, swiveling it about with ill-concealed ire until his pitch-black eyes fell, full force, on Cyrus' tall form. Then Takeo's body followed, and all the while, the gaze between them grew more intense.

"Excuse me?" Takeo said.

"I'm sorry I couldn't be honest with you before," Cyrus offered, trying to be courteous. "It's just, my mother; I didn't want to upset her by denying you right then and there. If it's all the same to you, I'll probably lie when I get back and say it was your idea to break our arrangement. I think she'll take that better than if she knew it was my idea. I don't know why she wants me to charge off into the unknown with some stranger, but I'm not interested. Despite what she says, we're happy, and that's what life is about, right? Being happy. That's all any of us can hope for, and I'm happiest when I'm with her. Plus, the friends I've made among the elves, perhaps Angor isn't much, but it's home and—"

"I don't care about your mother or your home," Takeo cut in. "We had a deal."

Cyrus' gaze fell. He remembered Adelpha's words, but he knew this was the best decision. Better to challenge this dangerous man here, close to home, then out in the middle of some unknown land. Also, he wouldn't kill Cyrus if he truly needed him.

Cyrus folded his arms across his chest, raised his head, and stood firm. Takeo still hadn't moved an inch, yet Cyrus noted that at some point, the man's hand had come to rest on his sword again.

"About this deal," Cyrus began. "I'm not buying your story. Something's not right. You claim you've been searching for this angel for months and found nothing and that it's easier to find an angel if you've been around them before. Well, it sounds like you've been around this one plenty, so why can't you find it? Personally, I think either you're lying, and you've never been around an angel, or that angel is avoiding you.

"See, I've been warned about you. Only rumors, of course, but they weren't kind rumors, and they appear to have some truth to them. My mother said two men took me when I was little, yet only one of you is here now. What happened to the other? Why don't you just ask him for help to find this angel? Surely he'd be better suited than me."

Takeo closed his eyes and wrinkled his nose, as if Cyrus' words brought such annoyance as to cause physical pain.

"Don't try to bait me," Takeo said. "Clearly you know the answer."

"You killed him. What for? What did he do to you?"

Takeo raised a hand and rubbed his forehead. The hostility melted away, and Cyrus relaxed a hair until Takeo began to stalk towards him. Cyrus readied himself, but Takeo stopped, having closed the distance just enough to talk easily through the wind.

"I don't have time for this," he said. "Listen, let's not complicate things. My reasons for needing you are too great for you to comprehend. All I need are a few months; that's all I'm asking, and you'll make your mother happy. Plus, you'll never see me again. You can go back to watching over your depressed, small, outcast family, and you'll never lie awake at night, wondering if I'll want revenge for breaking our deal. I hope those rumors you heard spoke about how dangerous it would be to offend me."

Cyrus felt like he balanced on a knife's edge. A sinking feeling welled within him, not unlike when he had faced off against his stepfather time and time again. Like then, he could sense how his actions would have repercussions beyond his own physical pain, yet also like then, he couldn't ignore what felt right. He thought about the one time he'd lashed out in anger, and how he'd been treated like the monster he shifted into each full moon. He thought about the kind of man he wanted to be, and how it mattered most in moments like these.

Cyrus shook his head.

"No," he said. "I won't help you. That angel is avoiding you and having me around won't change that. You're desperate, that much is clear, and I won't be stuck with you up in some strange land when things get even more dire. I'll have no part in that, and neither will my mother. As sad as she might be if I return to her in a few days, she'll be even more sad if I die searching for this angel, just like your friend did. So, excuse me, but we're done here. Thank you for helping my mother once upon a time. I wish things could have been different between us."

Cyrus didn't turn his back and walk away, but he did backpedal a pace to add some finality to his words and some space between them. Takeo did not follow. He shook his head again. Cyrus kept his attention on the man's sword.

"I wish things could have been different, too," Takeo said.

Then he flew at Cyrus faster than an arrow, his free hand extended into a fist with such speed that it was a blur to the eye. Cyrus, staring at the sword, had been unprepared, and his heart got in half a beat before the fist connected with his chin and his world exploded. He lost consciousness for the second it took for him to hit the ground, where his head bounced hard enough to wake him back up. As his vision flashed in spotty patches, he heard footsteps approach and the sound of knuckles cracking.

"I had a feeling this would happen," Takeo said. "Now we'll have to do this the hard way. Maybe I'll have better luck convincing you when you wake up."

A hand pushed into Cyrus' back and grabbed a fistful of clothes, lifting him almost effortlessly, and Cyrus flailed to life, swinging wildly at the man. The hand dropped him, and Cyrus rolled away, backing against a tree and stumbling to a stand. A few more blinks were required to see normally again. He beheld Takeo, fist raised once more and eyes wide in shock.

"How are you still awake?" Takeo demanded. "That blow should have leveled you."

"And how can you hit so damned hard?" Cyrus stammered, working his jaw to make sure nothing was broken. "I haven't been hit like that since a bugbear smacked me. Are you even human?"

"Nevermind," Takeo said. "We can discuss this later."

"Wait!" Cyrus yelled.

Cyrus threw up his arms, but Takeo ignored the gesture. He flew at the werewolf with fist raised, but Cyrus was ready this time. He dodged, and the fist slammed against the tree like a club. Bark and splinters exploded, but if the pain bothered Takeo, he didn't show it. Cyrus twisted just like Ven had taught him and countered. He hit Takeo once in the stomach, then followed it up with a full force punch into the side of the man's head.

Cyrus knew he was unnaturally strong. Something about the way his human and werewolf forms bled into each other. He could smell things no human should be able to, could move silent as an elf, and he was twice as strong as his physicality suggested. He put all that strength into his attack, hitting Takeo with a blow that he felt certain would kill a lesser being.

Takeo groaned and hit the ground. A momentary panic swept through Cyrus, thinking he'd killed the man, but another moan escaped Takeo's lips from the ground.

"Oh, good," Cyrus said, breathing a sigh of relief. "I thought you died for a second. Now you listen to me. I want you to leave this place and—"

Takeo roared—literally roared—and launched from the ground. Cyrus yelped and caught Takeo by the wrist, but not before the man's fingers wrapped around his throat. Cyrus' feet left the ground as he was lifted into the air and slammed against the tree.

Then Takeo changed.

He grew in height, adding more than a foot and raising Cyrus higher with every inch. Whiskers sprouted from his face, his ears moved to the top of his head and morphed into a triangular shape. His nose became a short snout, his teeth turned sharp, and orange fur with black strips covered his entire body. The last thing to pop out was a long, thin tail that swished about in furious movements. Takeo snarled.

"What are you?" Takeo demanded, in a voice that had grown considerably deep, yet had an undeniable feminine quality.

"What? What am I?" Cyrus gasped, kicking his feet and trying to pull back the iron grip at his throat. "What in the world are you?"

He—no, she—the thing snarled and raised Cyrus an inch higher. She was taller than Cyrus now and clearly stronger.

"No human should be able to hit like that," she roared.

"I'm a werewolf," Cyrus offered, struggling for air.

"I visited the werewolves," she said. "I fought a few of them, too. That's how I found you. None of them were this strong. Answer me, what are you?"

Cyrus' eyes began to flutter. Air was difficult to come by.

"Put me down," he begged.

"No."

"Please?"

She cocked an eyebrow and tilted her head to the side. Cyrus brought up his knee swiftly into her gut and lower ribs.

A muffled cry escaped her lips as her head came down, and she lost her grip on Cyrus' jugular. They both collapsed to the ground, with her moaning and him coughing.

"I'm sorry," Cyrus said, voice recovering first. "I tried to ask nicely."

Despite his opponent still struggling for breath on all fours, he got up and moved to put part of the tree between them. He watched her carefully, arms up in case she lunged again. Then he thought better and dropped his pack, pulling out the sword. The metal rang as it cleared the scabbard.

"Now look," he continued. "I don't know what you are, but clearly I'm not as easy to handle as you thought. Just what in the world are you? You're not Takeo Karaoshi, are you?"

The thing, whatever it was, touched her jaw tenderly, but seemed to recover quickly. She gave Cyrus a hateful glance, then sighed and stood up. She brushed her robes off, now a bit small on her enlarged figure.

"No," she said, but offered nothing else. "I'm not Takeo Karaoshi."

"So, what are you, then? Who are you?" he asked, then continued when she held silent. "Listen, the way things stand right now, there's no chance I'll help you. Whatever you are, you've lied to me, attacked me, and now you're withholding information. The only reason I haven't run yet is that I'm not about to turn my back on you. Now start talking, or you better be prepared to use that sword."

The creature stood still for a moment, taking in Cyrus and his hostile stance. Her eyes were yellow now and had somehow become more watchful. Her hand fell to the black sword at her waist, where she pulled the entire thing free—sheath and all—and held it out. Then she snapped it over her knee and dropped the pieces to the ground.

It was hollow inside the sheath.

"You pretended to carry a sword?" Cyrus whispered.

"My name is Emy," she said. "I'm a rakshasa, and I'm not good with swords."

"A raka-what?"

"A rakshasa," she repeated, putting her paws on her hips. "Our kind hails from Savara. It's a large desert across the ocean, east of here, though I haven't been there in a while. But that's not important right now. What's important is that you understand there are forces at play far greater than you or your little mother-son relationship. I'm trying to accomplish something that could very well save the world from destruction, and I need your help to do it."

Cyrus blinked three times in quick succession. Then he fully relaxed and let his sword drift to the ground. Then he burst into laughter.

His voice echoed off the trees, loud and full-bellied. He stopped suddenly, seeing his laughter had no effect on Emy as she stood stoic and completely serious. Then he laughed harder.

"Wow," he said, pausing to grip his stomach. "Okay, I did not expect you'd be crazy, too."

"I'm not crazy," she replied flatly. "I said before that you wouldn't be able to comprehend my reasons. It's not my fault that you're stupid."

"Oh, and an insult, too. Well, now I can't wait to help you. Is this how you normally interact with people? Lie, then attack, then insult? I don't know what kind of manners are acceptable in Savara, but let's just say you're lucky I'm still bothering to talk to you."

"And you're lucky I found you first."

Cyrus paused. It didn't take a genius to pick up on that threat. Emy stayed quiet, baiting him, and he had no choice but to take it.

"What do you mean, found me first?" he asked.

"I'm not the only foreigner probing these woods," she said. "A henchman of the Dark Lord, accompanied by a large group of mercenaries, is out here, too. The henchman's name is Aiguo Mein, and he's as clever and merciless as his master. He first started tracking me when I landed in Lucifan, and I thought heading for Angor would put him off my path, but he didn't hesitate an inch. He's here, and he'll burn this forest to the ground if he has to."

Cyrus took this in quietly. That was a lot to take in, let alone understand or believe. However, he thought for a moment about how this creature had disguised itself so that his mother couldn't tell the difference and had timed its visit to extinguish all suspicion. There was something telling in that. Maybe whatever this thing had to say was worth listening to, if tempered with a large dose of skepticism.

"Alright," he said. "You can talk, and I'll listen so long as you keep your hands where I can see them and this tree stays between us."

Chapter 5

"I'll give you the short version.

"I don't know if you've heard, but Lord Takeo Karaoshi did not earn his title honorably or by birth. He cut his way up the ranks of the royal caste in Juatwa, personally killing no less than three shogun and probably a half dozen lesser lords and ladies. Juatwa is driven by a warrior culture, so his prowess and infamy inspired a religion of sorts among the common ranks. Rather than unite to destroy him, those in power either ignored his rise or attempted to bend him to their will. When his power became too great, they chose to placate him rather than risk losing their privileged positions. Now he's Emperor of Juatwa, the first in an age, and he's set his sights on the world at large.

"Juatwa is dense with humans. Its lands are lush and bountiful, easily feeding the largest army this world has ever seen. It's allowed him to invade multiple places, starting wars on at least three fronts and, from what I can gather, preventing anyone from uniting against him.

"Where I come into all of this is simple: I want to kill him. Like many, apparently, I knew him personally. Takeo killed my father— my surrogate father anyway. Perhaps he killed my real father, too; I'll never know. Now, normally, Takeo wouldn't waste time tracking a single individual, but I'm a rakshasa. Takeo has a personal hatred for my kind, an understandable fear of our potential, and a personal vendetta against me. He hates me so much that he sent Aiguo out with one purpose: to find and kill me.

"You're probably wondering what this has to do with you, now, right? Well, let me ask, have you heard of a thing called a colossus? No? Eons ago, when there were five angels and they ruled Lucifan peacefully, they created three massive statues that could move and defend the city. I do mean massive, by the way. You should see the one that remains. It's taller than some of these trees.

"However, times have been rough. Some time ago, probably around the time you were born, an army attempted to invade Lucifan, and that one colossus beat the army back, thanks to the control a human had over it. An angel gave her that control, and now I'm seeking the same thing.

"No one knows if that last colossus is alive or dead, active or inactive, and we may never know until Takeo's army comes pouring into Lucifan. However, if I can find that last angel and convince it to give me the colossus, then I can use it like that girl did. I can put a stop to Takeo's armies, and him, too.

"So, you were right. I've never met an angel, and all my attempts to find it have gotten me nowhere. I can't sense it, and it can fly, traversing the Khaz Mal Mountains like a dragon. However, although I disguised myself, I didn't lie outright to you. I need a guide, someone who has seen him before. I need you. However, more importantly, the world needs you. Unfortunately, whether or not you think any of this concerns you is irrelevant.

"Takeo's war is not coming for you. It's already here."

Cyrus took this all in silently. He watched Emy's eyes for signs of dishonesty, or nervousness, or any hint that she wasn't being entirely truthful. His search came up empty.

"Alright, that sounds serious," he said. "However, you've got a problem. I already know one thing for certain: that you're a very good liar. If all this were true, why not just tell me from the start? Why trick me with the disguise? Can you disguise yourself as anyone?"

Emy stood still a moment, then slowly morphed into the exact image of Cyrus himself. He blinked in astonishment, and she shifted back.

"It helps to see the person as I'm doing it, but thankfully I have a good memory," she replied.

"All of your kind can do this?"

"As far as I know."

Cyrus shook his head. There was something frightening about that, and his feelings of distrust towards this creature intensified. Then he remembered how wrong that was, how so many had hated him for the exact same thing, being born different, and he pushed the feeling aside.

"As for your first question, I only approached as Takeo to gauge your mother," she continued. "I'd never met either of you, but after seeing how happy Belen was to see Takeo, I knew I couldn't change into my true form. Then you were so resistant to leaving, and I felt stuck. If your own mother couldn't get you to leave, imagine how little chance I stood if I were a complete stranger. So, the precaution became a lie, and I figured there'd be no harm in it when all was said and done.

"See, I don't even need you for six months, Cyrus. Half that time will do. In three months, we could find the angel, and we could split up. You'll have done your part in saving the world, and then you can go home."

Cyrus hung his head.

"Emy, right?" he asked.

"Yes, just Emy," she answered. "I don't have a last name, like you, I suppose. My kind isn't big on family names, or families in general."

"Well, Emy, we've got more problems," he said. "You said it yourself, how excited my mother was to see Takeo. You've said a lot of terrible things about him, sure, but I've only heard those things from two types of people: those who condemned my mother to a life she hates, and you, who, well—enough said. I've yet to hear Takeo's side of this story, or even my mother's. On the contrary, she seems to think quite highly of him.

"On top of that, let's think about this angel. According to you, you've been searching for it, and it's been avoiding you. For me, that's reason enough to stop right here. I don't know you or this angel, and I'm damned sure not going to help you hunt him down if he doesn't want to be found.

"But you're in it deeper than that. You say this Aiguo Mein, an agent of Takeo's, is in this forest? And he's out here looking for you, wants to kill you, and you expect me to get involved? What do you think will happen then? If he's willing to burn the forest down to get to you, you'll need to remember my entire family, blood or otherwise, exists in that forest. And I'm supposed to put them in danger for you, someone who lies and attacks me?

"I'm sorry to say, Emy, but we are finished. Good luck on finding this angel. If your purpose is truly worthy, I'm sure you'll find him eventually."

Cyrus didn't move. He kept his gaze locked with Emy, watched as her gaze turned slowly from hopeful to angry. Her eyes filled with malice, as if Cyrus himself had murdered her father. He paid attention to her feet and shoulders, looking for the subtle shifts in weight that would foretell another attack.

Yet her body remained calm. For all the anger in her eyes, her arms remained lax, and her shoulders slumped.

"I wasted months coming here and finding you," she said.

"No, I think that's a lie, too," Cyrus replied. "You seem smarter than that. I'm getting the sense that this whole trip out to fetch me was just a perk. If I came with you, great, but your real intention was to throw Aiguo off your trail. And you didn't concern yourself at all with whether or not that would put my mother and me in danger."

Emy didn't respond, but she did go perfectly still for the faintest second. Cyrus caught it and scoffed.

"Wow," he said. "You're no hero at all. You're just as bad as you make this Dark Lord out to be. You'd better get out of here before I decide to find Aiguo and tell him exactly where you're headed."

He made that comment absentmindedly, as his thoughts darkened into panic over what he had left behind. Yet, as he worried about Belen, he noticed Emy's head drop and her gaze fall to the ground. The anger passed from her face with a flash of shock, but soon a clear look of shame followed.

"I need to go," he said.

Cyrus backed away, keeping Emy in his sights lest his exit lift whatever spell had fallen over her. She didn't move, but when he got a short distance away, she did speak up.

"Don't seek out Aiguo," she warned. "Whatever you think of me, whatever doubts you have, don't go looking for that man. And if he finds you, run."

Cyrus paused, regarded her, and decided she was right. He'd avoid all outsiders for the next few months, at least. Then he took off into the woods at a light jog, which he hoped would be fast enough to prevent anyone or anything from following him without being noticed.

Next, he contemplated how to break the news to his mother that all her dreams and planning had been for naught.

* * *

Cyrus made good progress through the forest. Youth aside, he'd always had a fair bit of stamina for a human. He could only guess part of this came from his werewolf form. Also, Cyrus was familiar with this side of the forest. In fact, he was familiar with everything a couple days walk outside the elven village, his old werewolf village, and the entire swath of land between them. He'd spent a lot of time traveling around these areas, alone, as a child, so he could take the quicker routes he had avoided with Emy lest she learn his every secret.

Unfortunately, shortcuts could only help so much. Time and distance held supremacy, and since the full moon had passed, Cyrus had to sleep at night. He climbed up into the trees when he could or found a rock or bush to crawl under. He slept on his stomach in the hopes that would prevent a snore from leaking out. He worried that Emy had decided to follow him.

Besides that, and his mother's safety, there wasn't much else to worry him. Cyrus had made peace with this forest long ago. Although there were no borders drawn, the many hostile races of Angor lived together in relative peace by maintaining rigid and well-understood territories. The elves stayed on their side, the werewolves had theirs, as did the centaurs, the treants, and the kobolds. These unwritten rules were obeyed even by less intelligent creatures, such as bugbears and hippogriffs, which avoided the southern half of Angor every full moon and the centaur territories in general.

But not Cyrus. As a lone wanderer from a young age, he'd somehow grown up in a way that made the rules not apply to him. Freely traveling between the elves and werewolves, he'd stumbled onto a lone kobold once and saved it from being a hippogriff's meal. Since then, he'd never had an issue with kobolds, because they avoided him and his trespassing as if he didn't exist. Once, outside elven territory, he'd been captured, but they'd been too perplexed to do anything other than question him. Miraculously, they'd let him off with nothing but a warning to keep to himself. He'd obeyed out of fear, until one day the centaur leader had sought him out and asked what news he'd heard of the elven and werewolf worlds. Naïve as Cyrus was back then, he'd told him, and that had been that.

This is all to say that Cyrus didn't run into any trouble until he reached the elven village. The shortest route back to his camp led through it, so he figured why not drop by and let the elves know that there could be a dangerous creature wandering about—one that was quite strong and could change its appearance at will.

But he never got the chance.

A sentry probing the tree tops spotted Cyrus first, but rather than let him pass, the elf plunged from the skies to the ground on her hippogriff mount. Hippogriffs were fascinating creatures, beautiful as they were deadly. They had two wings, four legs, and a long wide neck that ended in a head with a sharp beak. A colorful array of feathers covered their entire body except for that beak and the sharp talons at their feet. Cyrus had always wanted to ride one, but never thought he'd get the chance. Like archery, it was forbidden fruit to a werewolf like him.

"Cyrus," the elf shouted out, bringing her hippogriff to a stop. "You're back? How? Why? I was told—nevermind. There isn't time. Get on."

The elf leapt from her mount and pinched the hippogriff on the side of the neck. The beast let out a shrill squawk, but then went docile and stooped down.

Cyrus froze. His momentary disbelief and excitement quickly extinguished by a cold dousing of fear.

"My mother?" he started.

"Get on," the elf repeated. "She won't hurt you; I gave the command. She'll take you back to the village. Just hold on tight."

Cyrus swore. Bile rose from his stomach and his body flashed hot with sweat. He climbed onto the hippogriff and mumbled a 'thank you' before the elf pinched the hippogriff again and the beast took to the treetops. Cyrus clutched the reins and took in the sensation of flight while completely submerged in dread. It wasn't how he'd always dreamed this moment would be, but there was something undeniably thrilling about soaring through the air. He'd underestimated how fast it would go, though, and the hippogriff dove down into the elven village in no time. He spotted Nathok striding towards him at a pace Cyrus had only seen once before when he'd really screwed up. Flashbacks of childhood fear washed over him as he realized just how angry Nathok was likely to be at seeing Cyrus on a hippogriff.

That was until Cyrus hopped off and he saw the regret in Nathok's eyes.

"Cyrus," the elf started, shocked. "You're back. Did our scouts find you?"

"Scouts? No, I walked back," Cyrus replied. "You were looking for me? Why? What happened?"

"Listen," Nathok said.

Then he paused and placed his hand gently on Cyrus' shoulder. Cyrus' eyes fell on that hand, the hand that belonged to the most cold, distant figure he'd ever known, and a tide of terror washed over him. His throat clenched.

"My mother?"

"She's alive," Nathok said.

Relief flooded through Cyrus, but only for a moment.

"Alive, but captured," the elf continued.

"By?" Cyrus demanded.

"Ralph," Nathok answered.

Cyrus breathed as hard as the rapid twists of emotion would let him. He felt lightheaded but thought that if he sat down, he'd jolt upright again. It wasn't good news that Belen was back with the old werewolf clan, but it was far better news than what he had feared.

As he tried to take everything in, he realized how much attention he was drawing. The hippogriff had put him down in the clearing in the village's center, and the elven population that was normally so mindful of privacy now watched him carefully. He saw ill-concealed looks of pity and worry on their faces. In some slight way, it was nice to see that they cared.

He also noticed the amazons were gone.

"What happened?" Cyrus demanded.

"Katar can explain best," Nathok said, then turned on the others. "Where is Katar? Has anyone found him yet?"

As if on cue, Katar came soaring into the village from the southern end on the back of a hippogriff. The elves must have sent for him the moment Cyrus came into view. Katar spotted Cyrus and put his mount down nearby, vaulting off at the same time. All his momentum came to a sharp halt, though, when he met Cyrus' gaze.

Whatever he saw there made Katar deflect his gaze and draw his body inwards.

"Cyrus, I'm so sorry," Katar started.

"What happened?" Cyrus demanded, loudly this time. "Is she okay? What happened?"

"Your mother broke free of the cage," Katar explained, summoning the courage to meet his friend's gaze. "On the second night, the last night that she turned into her werewolf form, she broke the cage somehow. I think she must have worked on it the first night you were gone, while in her werewolf form. It shouldn't have broken so easily."

"But if it was only one night, she shouldn't have gotten far."

"Yes, yes, please, Cyrus, let me explain," Katar continued. "I thought the same thing. When I went to check on her in the morning and found the cage breached, I went searching for her immediately. When a quick scout of the area came up empty, I got my brother and some others involved. We expanded our search, particularly to the south. In her werewolf form, she would try to rejoin her pack. That made the most sense. We figured she couldn't get far, and that we would find her and bring her back. Our village is not so close to the werewolves.

"But we didn't find her. We searched and searched, looking further south, and I worried she was dead. I thought maybe a bugbear got her or something. Then, well, something strange happened. Your werewolf clan sent a messenger. They said they had her, and that they wanted to talk to you."

"What?" Cyrus balked. "Me? Why me?"

"I don't know," Katar said. "We haven't had a chance to reply. Before you came back, Nathok was trying to come up with a reply that would stall them. Cyrus, they must have been looking for her. They must have travelled north, both in human and werewolf form, to find and bring her back. Whatever they want with you, Cyrus, they're awfully set on it."

Cyrus tried to discern the reason. This was all Ralph's doing for sure. As the alpha male, his word was law, so there was no way the clan had done this without his direction. On top of that, Ralph was the only one with a motive to go to these lengths. No one else cared about Cyrus or Belen, but Cyrus had embarrassed Ralph in front of the entire clan when he'd challenged and beat the old man.

But still, to wait so long? Belen and Cyrus had been living peacefully for a while now. Why wait for this exact moment? It wasn't like Ralph could spend a lot of time scouring Angor, waiting for the moment Belen broke free. Another element had to be involved, and Cyrus could only think of one.

"Emy," he whispered.

"What was that?" Nathok asked.

"That man that I was with wasn't a man at all," Cyrus explained. "It was this creature called a rakshasa. She called herself Emy, and she said that there was a group of foreigners hunting her through the forest. She also said she fought or talked with my werewolf clan, I think, to find me. I don't know, but this is all connected somehow. Maybe Ralph wanted answers to why some stranger was looking for me and attacked his clan or demanded something. Either way, I don't think they were looking for Belen. They must have been searching for me, but when they came across her, they decided that was the next best thing.

"I have to go."

A grave silence suspended over the group. Katar's gaze was intense, and he looked to Nathok, but the old elf was holding his tongue. Katar spoke up.

"Cyrus, maybe there's another way. Let Nathok send his message to delay them. Belen surely told them you're gone; perhaps that will be enough for them to set her free. They must think you'll be gone for several months."

Cyrus shook his head.

"No," he said. "Ralph's not like that. My mother, she's not like that. They won't let her go, and I don't think she'll have the strength to leave. This is my fault. I left her, and I'll get her back. I've done it before."

"This won't be like last time," Katar continued. "Last time, Ralph fought you fairly because he thought he would win. Now you've beat him, embarrassed him. He won't stick to the rules, and you're not considered part of the clan anymore. Right? Haven't you told me that before? You can't go alone."

"We can't interfere," Nathok broke in. "Having Cyrus and Belen take shelter nearby is one thing, but to actively encroach upon werewolf territory and involve ourselves in this dispute could disturb a centuries-long peace."

His voice was stern, yet with the slightest trace of regret. The rest of the elves in the village watched unabashed now, listening with their superb hearing upon the conversation that had taken a turn that involved them. More than a few breathed a sigh of relief at Nathok's decision. Katar wasn't ready to give up, however.

"Isn't that a decision Dirthzea should make?" Katar asked.

"Dirthzea will agree," Nathok replied.

"Well, as individuals, I should be allowed to make my own decision—"

"This is not up for discussion," Nathok cut in. "Elves are allowed free will in every capacity except for situations where an individual's actions will have negative consequences for the group. Then it is the Council of the Elders' decision, and you will not take any action until the council has convened. Is that understood?"

"We can't just let him go alone to certain—"

"IS THAT UNDERSTOOD?"

Silence ripped through the village. Cyrus had never heard Nathok raise his voice before. Judging by the way his heart skipped a beat, he hoped to never hear it again, and judging by the enveloping silence, the rest of the village agreed.

Katar's gaze fell to the ground.

"Yes, sir," he mumbled.

"Good," Nathok continued, then turned to Cyrus. "Now then, as we've established that no elf will accompany you beyond our border, we can begin to discuss available options. Katar is correct that it may be best to play dumb and wait until we've sent your old clan a reply. However, I can understand your desire to act. I get the sense you won't listen to reason, and I don't find that surprising, given your humanity."

He put an emphasis on the last word and cast a glance at Katar. The young elf lowered his head.

"She's my mother," Cyrus said.

"I know," Nathok continued. "And everyone knows what that means to you, even Ralph. I'd wager that's why they didn't hesitate to take Belen, because they knew we elves would stay out of it, yet you would come, nonetheless.

"However, that doesn't mean you have to go alone."

Chapter 6

Cyrus got to ride a hippogriff for the second time in his life that day, and he hoped it wouldn't be his last. The journey south to his old werewolf clan wasn't a short one, and he and the elves figured there wasn't any time to waste. Still, the hippogriff couldn't take him the whole way. It dropped him off about halfway, then flew home without an inkling of the severity of the situation.

From there, it would be a full day's travel, but the journey would be longer still because Cyrus had to sleep at some point. He managed to squeeze in a couple hours under a tall bush and called it good. Stressed as he was, it helped to know what was coming. Cyrus knew his werewolf clan, his stepfather, his mother, and all the surrounding territory. He didn't know what Ralph wanted from him, but one unknown was better than any number greater than that.

"It will all work out," he tried to convince himself. "Just keep calm, stay alert, and have faith. The elves won't let you down. Katar won't let you down. He owes you."

Cyrus had picked up the habit of talking to himself as a child. It helped break up the silence of the forest and dispel the shroud of loneliness that hung in the air. It steadied his nerves, too, which was helpful.

He made the best time possible, taking the most direct routes. He didn't move quietly or cover his tracks; he didn't worry about stumbling into a stray bugbear. He trudged and jogged and climbed when necessary. He didn't stop until he reached the edges of his old werewolf camp.

That's when he heard singing.

"I once knew a girl," the words drifted on a chance breeze and then were lost.

Cyrus went rigid as a tree. That wasn't what he expected. He waited to see if the wind would change again and bring him anything else, but it held steadfast against his back.

"Easy," he whispered. "Take it easy."

Cyrus grimaced and crept forward.

There should have been sentries at some point, either standing in the open or hiding in the brush. Cyrus knew the usual spots, so it bothered him to find the normal locations vacant. Cyrus expected to hear the camp's usual daytime noise at any moment, from pots clanging together to children laughing and adults shouting. He caught a whiff of smoke, though, which was good. There was always a fire going in the camp where the people were cooking something or other.

"Her skin was like water," the singing continued.

Cyrus stopped again. He was close enough to the camp now to hear better. He recognized the song and also the singer: Ralph. It had to be. No one else sang those words, which the old man had called a 'sea shanty'—whatever that meant. According to Belen, pirates liked to sing them, and Ralph had been a pirate in his pre-werewolf days.

Cyrus waited again, but Ralph had either stopped singing or lowered his volume. It was a strange feeling to hear Ralph's voice because, on one hand, Cyrus' anxiety increased at hearing his old tormentor's voice, but on the other hand, he was relieved to at least hear something. The previous silence and lack of sentries had made Cyrus nervous to the extreme.

He crept forward again, scanning the area for sentries and assuming that they were hiding damned well in new locations and waiting for him. That would make the most sense. Then the wind took a sudden shift and filled Cyrus' nostrils.

There it was! Smoke and cooked meat. The scent of charred skin, dripping fat, and burnt hair brought the slightest twinge of normalcy to Cyrus' stressed nerves. Out of reflex, his mind tried to determine the meat, but it wasn't coming to mind. He inhaled again, listened for any sounds, and searched his memories. Nothing came up. He didn't know what this meant.

Or perhaps he did? He'd smelled this meat once before, not so long ago. On the night he'd challenged Ralph for Belen, Cyrus had pushed the old beast into the campfire. Ralph's hair, skin, muscle, and fat had all been charred just an arm's length from Cyrus' nostrils. That's what he smelled now, burnt human flesh.

And as this realization struck him, Cyrus' blood went cold, and his stomach flipped over.

Then Ralph could be heard again, only he wasn't singing this time. He was crying.

The wind drifted away, taking the smells with it, and left Cyrus with a cold chill running down his spine. He took two deep breaths and tried to think, but fear paralyzed his mind. Sweat accumulated on his forehead and under his arms. Then he remembered why he was here and steeled himself. He couldn't let anything freeze him up. Belen was depending on him. Cyrus took another breath and dashed to the village clearing.

He was not prepared.

A scene of destruction greeted him. Where once had been a bustling village of tents, families, and storehouses, now only a smoked wreckage remained. The tents were either shredded or burned down, the storehouses knocked over and their contents strewn about. Yet it was the bodies that caught Cyrus' attention.

They were everywhere. Stabbed bodies, burned bodies, cut bodies, in a single glimpse he saw severed heads, pools of dried blood, and flesh charred black as night. Smoke drifted from piles of ash where the flames had long since died out, yet smoldering embers lurked within. The bodies were stacked in piles all around and were turning to carrion, filling the camp with the vile smell of decay. It was a wonder that the sheer volume of meat hadn't attracted a bugbear or two by now. The smoke was clearly masking the scent.

In the middle of the massacre was Ralph, alone, naked, and tied to a tree. Even with his head hung low, Cyrus could tell it was him, judging by his bright red hair, his leathery skin hardened by sun and age, and his build thick from a lifetime of throwing punches. He seemed only dimly aware that he had company.

"Cyrus?" Ralph whispered, lifting his head and peering through the hair that fell over his eyes. "Is that you? I must be dreaming again. Water! Can anyone hear me? I need water."

But there was no reply. Not a single body moved, and neither did Cyrus as he gazed in shock over the scene. His body was numb, except for his stomach, which flipped over and over again. An urge to vomit seemed to be welling there, but it was held in check by sheer disbelief. All around him, Cyrus saw familiar faces, kids he had grown up with and parents who had given him advice. Most of them had avoided him as he'd grown up, probably because of the way Ralph treated him, but that didn't mean they had been unkind.

Cyrus gaped and blinked. He couldn't think. He couldn't react. Despite his previous promise not to lockup, his body was frozen. He didn't know what to do. Slowly but surely, horror was working its way through him, but it hadn't reached his mind just yet.

Nothing in his life had prepared him for this.

"Bastard kid," Ralph muttered, slurring his words in delirium. "Of course, it'd be you I see. Should have killed you when I had the chance. This is all your fault. Always was. I had no choice. Did you hear me? Not my fault."

Cyrus couldn't hear him. Through the paralyzing shock, one thought filled his mind. Before panic could take over or despair render him frozen again, he rescanned the bodies and severed heads for a familiar face. This purposeful movement restored a twinge of consciousness, and tears welled in his eyes.

"Not her," he begged, unable to finish the sentence. "Please, don't be. . ."

"Wait," Ralph said, blinking. "It's you, isn't it? It's really you."

Cyrus couldn't summon the strength to face his lifelong tormentor yet. To do that, he might have to acknowledge that somehow, someway, Ralph had been spared while everyone else had died. It wasn't fair. It didn't make sense. It couldn't be true. Belen had to be alive, and he would find her.

Cyrus closed his eyes and turned away, shutting away the scene of bodies. Tears poured down his cheeks and his chest tightened at the magnitude of carnage in front of him, yet he knew what he had to do. Cyrus let a wave of nausea sweep over him, then took a deep breath and turned back. He went to the first corpse pile and slowly, respectfully, pulled one corpse after another off the pile. As each new face was exposed, his hopes and fears grew exponentially.

"Please don't be here," he mumbled, fighting not to break down.

"Hey! Cyrus!" Ralph shouted, then struggled uselessly against his restraints. "It's you. It's really you! Get me out of here."

"Where is she?" Cyrus demanded, screaming, unable to turn away now that he was directly addressed. "What happened here?"

"Never mind that, boy. We don't have much time. Get over here and untie me, or we're both dead."

"What happened?" Cyrus demanded. "Tell me!"

"You idiot! Are you even listening to me? Huh? Damned child
is what you are. You got dirt in your ears? I can tell you later, but
right now, you've got to untie me, and you and I need to run as far
away as we can. We can find another clan, you and I, you know?
Even the elves at this point, I don't care, but just get over here and
fast. Why are you just standing there? Listen to me, damn it!"

Cyrus didn't move. Ralph's anger heightened, but then he
dropped his head in defeat.

"You're not going to untie me, are you?" Ralph sighed. "Can't
say I'm surprised. You always were an ungrateful little coward. All I
did for you, all I provided for you and your mother, and you can't
even summon the goodwill to save a poor old man's life. They'll kill
you, too, and good riddance."

Once upon a time, words like that had cut deep. Ralph was a
living monument to hypocrisy. It used to keep Cyrus up at night,
thinking about how Ralph would call him a coward while he
proceeded to beat his helpless wife and stepchild. It used to boil
Cyrus' blood to be called ungrateful by a man who'd done nothing
but cause agony and strife. However, Cyrus' skin had toughened
under years of such verbal abuse. Cyrus shrugged off Ralph's
comments like rainwater, and Cyrus felt no need to correct him. He
had come to expect that Ralph would always play the victim, no
matter the reality.

"Where is she?" Cyrus demanded.

"Oh, I'll tell ya," Ralph chuckled. "Oh boy, yes, I'll tell you.
Not going to free me, huh? Well, you'll see. You want to know what
happened, eh? I was right! That's what happened! I told that whore-
scum mother of yours this would happen. Stupid wench wouldn't
listen, and she sent you away. Now look? Her wicked ideals caught
up to her. They caught up to us all. She did this. She and you, little
Cyrus.

"I still remember that black-eyed samurai and blonde knight
who took you away. I should have killed them both, but I showed
mercy. Stupid, I was, and I should have known better. Then what
happens? That samurai comes back asking for you. We told him to
piss off and tried to throw him out, we did, but he was stronger than
he looked, so I told him where you were. Then he left, and I thought
that was the end of it. Then that vindictive bastard sent his

henchmen next, the coward. A whole damned army shows up some days later, looking for that samurai, and you, Cyrus. Don't know why. What could anyone want with a little piss-sack like you, huh?

"I told them where you were, too, but they drew swords on us! Can you believe that? They took hostages and demanded we head up north and pluck you out of elven protection. Well, the lads and I weren't keen on this, so when the full moon turned, we went hunting for the bastards. You know what we found? They'd killed the hostages and fled into the trees. We couldn't get to them.

"When we shifted back into humans, they took more hostages.

"You see, I didn't have a choice? So, we did what they asked. They said we had until the next full moon, or they'd kill us all. Their leader, he was some faceless, soulless human if I ever met one. I ain't scared of much, but that man meant business. I knew he'd kill us if he didn't get what he wanted. So, I thought it was our lucky day when we found Belen stumbling about the woods.

"So, we bring Belen back with us and send a messenger to the elves, intended for you. She starts blathering on about how you and that samurai had already left the forest. Headed for Khaz Mal, she claimed. She didn't seem at all worried when she met this warband's leader and he explained that he served this Takeo fellow. Well, I thought that was that. You and Takeo were gone, so there was nothing left for these outsiders but to get out of Angor. The lads and I wanted him dead for the hostages they'd killed the first time, but at this point, we were just happy to survive. But then their leader, he said he agreed with me and all, but he . . . then he . . ."

Ralph paused. His cold exposition shattered as fresh memories tore at the fragments of his sanity. Tears came to his eyes, and they came to Cyrus', too. Ralph closed his eyes, and Cyrus took another look around and understood the story before Ralph could continue. Cyrus choked up and suppressed the urge to break down again.

"He didn't even spare the children," Ralph stammered. "It don't make no sense. Why? All he said was, 'Kill the animals,' and then screams. So many screams. All my lads, they didn't stand a chance."

Ralph sobbed, and Cyrus hung his head and squeezed tears out of his eyes. Even without the scene of carnage, Cyrus had always found it difficult not to cry when he saw others do so. It was something he hated about himself, something the elves picked on him for as a child, and something his mother had tried countless times to berate out of him. When he saw others feel pain, or joy, he felt it, too, intensely. Yet, at this moment, Cyrus understood his tears had little to do with Ralph. They fell all on their own at the sight of such needless slaughter.

Ralph was right. It didn't make any sense.

"But they spared you," Cyrus said, hoping.

"Aye, lad, that they did," Ralph answered, sucking hard to stem his tears. "Weren't no secret either. Their leader, that wicked fellow, said he wanted to see what one of our kind looked like under the full moon. You know what that means, huh? It means those hostages, the ones he'd killed first, he'd done that while they were still human. He never meant to spare them, or us. Vile bastard. He said they'd wait a couple weeks to see if you or that other fellow came back, and then they'd execute me when their experiment was over."

"But if they were waiting for me," Cyrus pressed, "then they'd have spared her, too, right? Where is she?"

Ralph raised his head until their eyes met. The look said it all, but Cyrus couldn't accept it—wouldn't accept it.

Then a cruel smile slithered across Ralph's face, and Cyrus' heart plunged into ice.

"She's over there," Ralph whispered, and pointed with his gaze.

Cyrus turned slowly. It was difficult to move. His body flashed numb, and his breathing slowed. A stack of bodies lay next to where the meat racks had once been. None of the bodies had been completely burned. It was as if the killers had trouble getting the wet, dense wood of Angor to burn, so they'd given up. Sticking out of one mutilated mound of flesh, blood, and blackened skin, was a hand that looked somewhat familiar to Cyrus.

Pain and horror flashed through him. Through immense effort, he forced himself to approach, his limbs fighting him every step of the way. His ears rang, and his heart beat irregularly as shock and fear gripped him.

He reached the pile and lifted the body that covered Belen. A shudder went through him as he recognized her and then pulled her into his arms.

Belen's left arm and leg were charred black, the skin wrinkled and shedding off as she was dragged from the mound. Her auburn hair was singed and curled on one side and caked together with a combination of dried blood and ash on the other. Her body was stiff and cold, and her belly swelled with rot. A thin line cut across her neck with near surgical precision. The skin was black where the blood had been stained with a mixture of dirt and soot. Her eyes stared lifelessly into the sky, as hollow and empty as her gaping mouth, forever frozen in surprise.

"Mommy?" Cyrus whispered, tears pouring from his eyes.

"She didn't deserve what happened to her," Ralph said, "but at least she went quickly. She was in their hands when he gave the order, so she didn't get the chance to run like the others. No screaming, just one quick strike to the base of the neck. Saw it with my own two eyes, I did. She bled out in moments."

Cyrus didn't hear a thing. He couldn't breathe. He buried his head into Belen's neck as he collapsed into her and wept.

There were no words. There was nothing he could think to say, or even think at all, as anguish ripped through him and strained his will to breathe. He held her close and, without thinking, rocked her like she used to do to him when he was a child. His attempts to suck in air only exasperated his cries, and the moans that escaped his lips became a haven for the floating ash circling the camp.

Nothing seemed real. This couldn't be happening to him. He'd done so much. He'd planned so much. He'd saved her. They'd been safe and sound, just like they'd always wanted.

"Mother, no," he mumbled out before another wave of sobs wracked him.

His pain was so great that even Ralph couldn't bring himself to say anything. The old man hung and shook his head.

"I'm so sorry," Cyrus whimpered, completely unintelligible to anyone but him. "Mother? Don't go. You can't. Mommy, I'm sorry, I shouldn't have left. Mother, I . . ."

The wind shifted at the same time Cyrus sucked in a breath of air. He hadn't intended to do anything but continue to weep, but a distinct scent drifted into his nostrils and brought a chill to his mind. His tears stopped for an instant in sheer surprise until he sniffed again to confirm, and then the tears continued to run.

As he held and rocked Belen's corpse, he looked out to the forest and steadied his voice enough to shout.

"Come out!" he yelled, voice cracking. "Stop hiding."

Ralph lifted his head.

"Huh?" he said. "Who are you talking to, boy? Ain't no one here but us. They made their camp out of earshot, they did."

Cyrus didn't answer, couldn't answer. He just cried and held his mother and told her over and over how much he loved her in a way she'd never let him do in all the years he'd known her. She'd always wanted him to be strong and brave and tough, and he'd always felt like such a disappointment because none of those things had described him. Not until that day, that night, when he'd marched into his old werewolf camp and won her freedom. Now this had happened, and he was a failure again.

Then, from out of the trees, Emy emerged in her rakshasa form.

"What? What is that?" Ralph stammered. "Cyrus! Hey, Cyrus! Look out! It's coming right at you."

Emy walked up to Cyrus, stopping just short of arm's reach. Her shadow fell over him. Cyrus gazed up at her for a brief moment, though his vision was obscured by tears and ash. Emy's face was emotionless, but something lurked behind her eyes.

He had countless questions. Why was she here? How did she get here? Why was she hiding? But only a single word escaped his lips.

"Why?" he begged.

"It's Aiguo's way," she said. "I'll have to explain later, though. Aiguo is close by, I'm sure of it. Let's leave, and you can mourn her afterwards."

Cyrus looked down at his mother again, or what had once been his mother. Leave her? He couldn't fathom the thought. He'd left her once before, and this was the result. Yet, he also knew—even if he couldn't admit it, he knew—that she was truly dead and there was nothing that could be done for her.

"Cyrus!" Ralph shouted. "Damn it, boy. What is that thing? Do you know it? What is going on?"

Emy glanced at Ralph and hesitated. Then she dropped her gaze to Cyrus and lowered her voice.

"We should kill him before we go," she said. "If we don't, he'll tell Aiguo we were both here. If he dies, he can't talk, and Aiguo won't know if one or both of us returned. It'll give us an edge."

"What did she say?" Ralph called out. "Cyrus, what's happening?"

Cyrus had heard, but Emy didn't seem interested in waiting for a response. Either that or she didn't care what he thought. Emy stepped away and walked calmly towards Ralph.

"Hey, hey!" the man snarled. "You, back away. I said piss off! Cyrus. Cyrus! Help me, Cyrus. I don't like the look in her eyes."

Emy opened a palm and extended her claws. Ralph's eyes went wide. Cyrus still hadn't moved.

"Stop!" Ralph yelled. "Help! Help me! Damn you, thing, whatever you are. Huh, you want a piece of me, huh? Cut me loose, you coward. Then we'll see who's tougher, huh? You scared? Scared, I said! Cyrus. Cyrus! You just going to let this happen? You pathetic, worthless, useless sack of shit! I should have killed you. Every time I hit you, I should have hit you harder. And your mother, if I'd known, I'd have killed her myself."

"Stop," Cyrus said.

Emy hesitated just one pace from Ralph. She looked back.

Cyrus blinked to clear the tears from his eyes, if only for a moment, and swept the stiff hair from his mother's face. He took in her open mouth, her cut throat, her ash-covered hair, and tried to remember all the times he'd seen her alive and happy, as rare as those were. That's what he would remember, he promised himself. Not this moment, not this pain if he could help it. Then he did what his mother had taught him to do and wrapped up all his pain and put it into a box. He closed that box and tucked it away for another time, when he was alone and he could let it out. He'd have to, or one day, it'd force its way to the surface.

He planted a final kiss on his mother's forehead and lowered her gently to the ground.

"Be quick," Emy instructed. "We've wasted enough time already."

Cyrus ignored her and walked up to Ralph. His movement shook the old man from his stunned state.

"What's this?" Ralph stammered. "You? Going to kill me? You wouldn't. Cyrus, I raised you. I fed you. I let you sleep in my tent—the alpha's tent. You had a place of respect and honor as my stepson. Damn it, boy! I fed your mother! I kept her warm! You kill me, you're nothing but a coward, and scum, just like that whore mother of yours. Never gave me a child, she did, but she spread her legs back in Lucifan now, didn't she? Whore amazon, just like the rest of them, and look what popped out."

Cyrus stopped a pace away from the bound man. He took a breath, wiped his eyes, and reached towards his pack. When he drew his sword this time, the ring of the metal as it cleared its sheath took on a grave tone. Cyrus held it high overhead, the tip gleaming in the sunlight.

Ralph trembled, but then anger consumed him. He scowled and glared at the blade.

"Going to do it, eh, little Cyrus?" he taunted. "Well, go on, then. You never were grateful for anything I ever did. Always running and crying and sniveling. You only beat me the once by cheating, you little brat, now look at you. You think this will make you a man, huh? You ain't a man, Cyrus. You never will be. You'll always be a little pissant coward who can never measure up. Ah, getting mad, eh? 'Bout time. I see it in your face. That's it, get mad! Now you go ahead and strike down a helpless, bound, widower who ain't done nothing but tried to raise you best he could. Do it, you bastard. I said do it!"

Cyrus felt his anger rise. He sensed it down in his gut, raging alongside memory after memory of Ralph's fist connecting with his face, with his mother's face, and all that anger boiled up and out. Cyrus gave a shout and swung.

Chapter 7

The sword passed right through the ropes in one clean blow.

The tension around Ralph's body went instantly slack, and the unprepared man tumbled to the ground. He caught himself on his hands and knees, and his hair fell around his face like water. Right alongside his head lay the tip of Cyrus' bloodless sword.

Ralph froze.

"Let's get one thing straight," Cyrus said. "You don't control me, not anymore. I buried the last of your influence over me when I beat you in front of the clan. I spared your life then, and I'm doing it now, but not because you deserve it. Killing you won't bring her back, and it won't erase all the terrible things you've done.

"I'm letting you go because, for once in your life, you're right. Only a coward would kill a bound old man. I also know that if our positions were switched, you'd kill me. I don't know what kind of man I want to be, Ralph, but above all, I never want to be like you."

Ralph didn't move at first. His eyes drifted to the sword resting just a hand's width from his face.

"We can't let him live," Emy cut it, calmly, as if she were explaining the difference between wet and dry. "I've explained this already."

Cyrus risked a glance at her, his gaze unflinching. She didn't back down, though. Cyrus decided against trying to intimidate her. Logic and reason seemed to be all this creature understood.

"If you want me to go with you," he said, "you'll let him go."

Emy took a deep breath, prepping to counter, when her eyes popped in a sudden thought. Her ears perked up.

"Wait, this could work," she said. "He'll run away, and Aiguo will waste days tracking him down. That delay would work in our favor. Alright, I agree."

"You don't get to—" Ralph started.

Cyrus kicked him in the side, and Ralph hit the ground with a groan.

"That you did deserve," Cyrus said. "Now run, and don't you ever come back."

Ralph scrambled to his feet, standing defiantly for the single moment it took him to realize that he faced a tall, clawed creature with murderous intent on her face and a slightly less-tall, sword-wielding stepson with less-severe murderous intent on his face. Then Ralph swallowed his pride for the first time in his life and ran.

He got to the edge of the werewolf camp when a dagger darted out of the trees. Its silent charge ended when it struck Ralph in the neck, spurting blood into the air. Ralph whirled from the force and then collapsed, kicking for a few brief moments until too much blood had flowed out from around the thick blade. He didn't even get the chance to scream.

Cyrus' eyes went wide, and he gaped in astonishment. Shock overwhelmed him until Emy grabbed him and drew him close, putting her back to his.

"Damn! Damn it!" she snarled. "How? I didn't see or smell them. Where are they? Do you see them? Watch out. Watch out!"

Cyrus regained control over his body as Emy pushed against him. They both moved a step as another dagger flew from the woods, barely missing her. The sudden brush with death snapped Cyrus fully out of his trance, and he pushed back against Emy. He scanned the treeline.

"You see anything?" he stammered.

"No," she growled, ears flattened. "I don't see them, smell them, or hear them. It's not possible."

"They killed him," Cyrus stammered. "Just like that, they killed him."

"Nevermind that," Emy said. "Just keep your eyes open. Where are they? How are they hiding? The smoke? Aiguo!"

Laughter echoed out from the woods. They were surrounded.

"I'll be honest, I didn't think you'd let him go," a lone, disembodied voice shouted from the darkness. "Alright, boys and girls. Looks like we've lost the element of surprise. Let's give 'em a show."

Two dozen figures materialized out of the shadows around Cyrus and Emy. They were the oddest assortment of humans Cyrus had ever seen in his life. Some were dressed in the same robe-like attire Emy wore, wielding long curved blades. Others wore tightly fitted black clothing, covering their mouths, and wielding shorter versions of that sword. Yet still others had loosely fitted dregs of clothing, exposing their chests or midriffs, and they carried large, heavy, two-handed swords that were thicker at the top than the bottom.

All had weapons drawn. Most were smiling.

One man stepped forward. At first, nothing seemed distinct about him, and Cyrus almost missed the movement altogether. The man was middle-aged with a wiry, average build, a firm jaw, and black-brown hair. Cyrus glanced over him once, only to completely forget the man existed, and then saw him again on the second pass. It was strange. Cyrus closed his eyes and seemed to forget the man a second time.

But then that man smiled, and Cyrus understood whom he gazed upon.

"Well, well, well," Aiguo Mein said. "We finally caught you."

The assemblage of warriors laughed. Emy swore.

"How?" she demanded. "I can't smell you. The smoke isn't that strong here. How?"

"Oh, on the contrary," Aiguo replied, grinning wider. "You've been smelling us this whole time. Now, the fact that you didn't hear us. That's the real miracle."

Cyrus took a deep breath. All he smelled was smoke, too. Then it struck him.

"They didn't just rely on the camp smoke," Cyrus said. "They covered themselves in it before coming here. It's an old hunter's trick."

"Right you are, lad," Aiguo answered, though his eyes never left Emy. "That's what one has to do when you're hunting a beast. You see this creature here; she is a tricky one and has abilities that make her tough to catch. Not infallible, of course. Let this be a final lesson in human superiority, eh? This has been a long time coming, I must say, and I'm going to enjoy this. I'm going to make a rug from your skin, girl, and I'm going to do it while you're still alive. I'll tell the story to Takeo, for his pleasure, so my lord can smile every time he wipes his feet on your remnants when he goes to take a piss in the morning."

The warriors laughed louder this time, and Emy hissed. With her back pressed to his, Cyrus could feel her hair stand on end and her body tremble with fear.

"I don't know if we can survive this," Emy whispered.

Cyrus ignored her. He'd ignored most of the conversation, actually. He was still under a level of shock from his mother's death, the sudden death of his stepfather, the death of his old werewolf clan, and his entire world falling to pieces around him.

But now there was this man in front of him, smiling and making threats, and Cyrus focused on that one thing just enough to bring a slim moment of clarity to his thoughts.

"You," Cyrus said. "You're Aiguo Mein."

"Ah, so you've heard of me?" Aiguo said, then made a shallow bow. "That's Lord Aiguo Mein, by the way."

"You killed my mother."

Never in his life had Cyrus spoken words so coldly. It stunned even himself, and silence fell over the warriors. They looked to their leader in time to see Aiguo's smile fade. The man folded his arms behind his back and stood up straight.

"Cyrus, isn't it?" Aiguo said. "Yes, I've heard of you, too, but let me tell you a bit about myself. I'm a simple man who enjoys simple pleasures: a bit of drink, the love of a woman, and, of course, unadulterated power."

His warriors chuckled again. The sound grated Cyrus' nerves.

"Now, I get my power from my lord, Emperor Takeo Karaoshi," Aiguo went on. "He's soon to be your lord, and the world's, just so you know. So, when our lord tells me to go forth and bring back the head of a fugitive, I obey. I do not ask questions, I do not doubt, and I do not blink. That fugitive is right behind you, Cyrus, and she's to blame for your mother's death.

"Let me guess what happened. This creature here, this criminal, she came to you disguised as Takeo, am I right? She convinced you to leave your mother, perhaps for good, on the pretense of a lie. That's their way, Cyrus, these rakshasa creatures. Liars and manipulators, the whole lot. She intentionally put your mother's life between her and me, knowing full well what would happen. She knew whom I was, what I would do, yet she did not care. She sacrificed your mother to slow me down, and if you're not careful, she'll sacrifice you, too. Think about that."

Cyrus didn't take his eyes off Aiguo, but he did tilt his chin back towards Emy. The rakshasa lowered her head.

"I," she started, catching herself. "I thought the elves would protect her. You did, too. Don't listen to him."

"Then why did you come back here?" Cyrus demanded of her. "To get here as fast as you did, you would have had to come directly after we split up. Why?"

"I didn't come for you or her," Emy replied. "What you said, about throwing people in my way, it hit home. I realized you were right. I came back to warn your clan about Aiguo. I got here too late, unfortunately. How did you get here so fast?"

Cyrus ignored her. In turning to glance at Emy, his eyes had caught sight of Belen's half-burnt corpse lying on the ground. Fresh tears came to his eyes, and a numbness spread through his body as his knees went weak. It took some effort to push the agony down, yet he couldn't take his gaze off her. As he spoke, his voice cracked.

"You killed her," Cyrus whispered, yet Aiguo heard him in the silence of the camp. "You didn't have to, but you did. I—I don't think I can forgive you for that."

Aiguo sighed and his shoulders slouched. He rolled his eyes, and his hands dropped free from behind his back. His hand came to rest on his sword.

"Fine, fine," Aiguo mumbled. "If you think I'm responsible, then that's your call, Cyrus, as ignorant as that viewpoint is. However, what's done is done, and you're standing between me and the goal I've been after for too long. Look around, boy. If you run with her, even if you break out of this circle, we'll hunt you down and kill you both the same. You're outnumbered, and we've been sleeping and eating well these past few days. I'll wager neither of you is well rested, at least not enough to keep up the pace I'm going to set.

"Forget your mother if you want to live, Cyrus. Leave that conniving creature at your back to her fate and forge your own path. If you like, I can take you with me to meet the lord himself. Emperor Takeo would be pleased to see you again, no doubt. He told me a bit about your history, and I think he has fond memories of you.

"However, he never said I had to spare your life. Step away from that creature now, or I'll be forced to gut you alongside her. Think of your mother. Would she want you to die so needlessly?"

He grinned again, and his minions, too. Cyrus clenched his jaw so hard his teeth threatened to shatter. Emy swallowed down a dry throat.

"Cyrus, listen to me," she began to whisper.

"No!" Cyrus boomed out. "No, you listen to me. All of you! You dare bring up my mother like that? First you kill her and then you—you . . . mock me with what she would want? What sort of sick, twisted person are you? If you're the kind of person Takeo trusts, then I don't want to meet him. I wish I'd never met any of you, and I swear, very shortly, you're going to wish you'd never met me."

The group of warriors whistled and laughed.

"Oh-ho," Aiguo chuckled. "Big words for—alright, you're actually pretty big yourself. Not going to lie. However, a word of advice, if you're going to utter such big words, you shouldn't carry such a small sword."

His warriors roared their laughter this time, but Cyrus was too angry to feel embarrassed. He was tall and well-muscled, but the sword he carried did seem small in his hands. It had once been used by elves.

"All of you," Cyrus said through clenched teeth. "All of you are outsiders here. You haven't lived here, survived here, fought here like I have. You are isolated, alone, and outnumbered. I won't guarantee you'll die, but some of you will never make it out of here alive. It won't bring my mother back, but it's what you deserve.

"As for you, Emy, I don't trust you yet, and I don't know if I ever will. I'm not taking your side, but I'm damned sure not going to follow these people. However, you have no choice but to trust me. Got that?"

Emy swallowed again, and Cyrus felt her nod. Aiguo, meanwhile, lost his smile. A snarl formed.

"Enough with this," he roared. "Kill them."

The war party shouted a battle cry and charged. An assassin beside Aiguo drew another dagger and flung it. The move was so quick that the blade would have ended Cyrus' life if he hadn't started running at the exact same time. He heard the blade whirl by his head, and his body flashed cold at the near miss. Cyrus ducked his head and bolted toward the thinnest point in the coming line of death—a narrow line of three foes. His mind struggled to figure out how he was going to break free in the few precious moments available before the melee.

Another dagger aimed at Emy materialized in the air just as she fell into step behind Cyrus. Rather than dodge, she raised her hand and willingly took the blade through her palm. Without pause, she yanked the dagger free, spun it in mid-air, and then flung it at one of the assassins in their way. The man dodged but not quick enough, the blade taking him in the shoulder and spinning him about. Cyrus took the opportunity and barreled into the man, sending him crashing to the ground a pace away.

Two assassins remained, blocking their exit. Only a second or two remained before the others would close in, and Cyrus could spare no time to be tactical. His only hope was to focus on one and pray Emy's injury didn't keep her from engaging the second.

Cyrus closed with his opponent at full charge, sword pointed like a spear. The man stepped aside at the last moment and swung to cut Cyrus down, realizing a hair too late that the move had been a feint. Cyrus shifted his bodyweight to slam directly into the man, like a battering ram of muscle, bone, and speed. Cyrus' werewolf-aided strength flung his opponent into the air, where the man gave a frantic yelp before crashing to the ground.

And Cyrus never lost a beat. He kept running at full speed and thus never gave Aiguo's other minions the chance to close on him. Only then did he risk a glance back. Emy was less than a pace behind. In her right hand were the bloodied remains of what looked like a human throat, while her left hand was pressed against a deep gash along her right shoulder. She'd taken a sword blow to end her opponent's life quickly, and Cyrus could hardly believe it. He thought he might have to carry her as they dashed into the forest, yet her breathing held steady. In fact, he realized her wounds were hardly bleeding.

Strange.

"After them!" Aiguo shouted. "Go, go! Don't let them escape."

Cyrus and Emy dashed through the shelter of the trees while echoes of battle cries chased after them. Cyrus made a sudden hard right, and Emy followed without question. Cyrus bounded over shrubs and rocks, anticipating them before he could see them because he knew these woods better than anyone left alive, and again Emy mimicked him perfectly.

Their new path brought them dangerously close to the enemy, running alongside them instead of directly away, and a thrown dagger cut along Cyrus' back. He clenched his jaws to fight down a yelp of surprise and pain, then jogged left, putting another row of trees between him and Aiguo's expert knife-thrower.

The target lay close—the chosen spot—and Cyrus held his breath as he reached the imaginary point of safety and then dashed over to the other side. He breathed a sigh of relief but did not slow his pace. No one suspected a thing, not even Emy.

The enemy pursued with reckless abandon through the forest foliage. The foremost foe was an eager, younger man with a short, curved sword in one hand and a dagger in the other. His eyes narrowing in on Emy's back, a wicked grin staining his face, and it was the grin he died with as a tree branch dropped from the sky and crushed him into the ground.

The trap was sprung.

Two treants came alive on either side of the invisible path Cyrus had run through. Humanoid in shape but four times the height, they instantly dominated the battlefield as their thick timber-like limbs swung out to block Aiguo's soldiers. The charging warriors gave a frantic yelp as one of the treants flung a massive hand sideways, sending two would-be assassins into the air. The other treant made a kick, barely missing his target, who dodged by throwing himself to the ground only to die a moment later as the same treant stepped on him. A terrified scream escaped his lips before he was crushed.

The warriors were quick to counter, swinging swords and throwing daggers that meant nothing to the treants. Sword blades meant for carving human flesh mattered little to solid wood. Among the mayhem, Aiguo's voice rang out even as the entire scene faded from Cyrus' view.

"Fall back!" he shouted. "Go around! Right—no, left! After them!"

Cyrus silently thanked the treants and hoped for their safety. He dashed at full speed deeper and deeper into the forest with Emy at his tail. They ran for some time before their pace proved just a tad too much and Cyrus had to stop to catch his breath.

"Treants!" Emy called out in amazement. "Those were treants, weren't they? I've never seen one before. How did you know they were there?"

She wasn't breathing nearly as hard as Cyrus, and the werewolf had to wonder at that. What sort of creatures were these rakshasas anyway? And it looked like her wounds had stopped bleeding, too. He couldn't believe it. The bleeding should have worsened with such physical exertion.

"The elves," Cyrus said. "The treants and the elves have a sort of alliance. The elves asked the treants to watch out for me."

"But—"

"We can talk later. We're not safe yet. Treants are slow, and Aiguo will figure that out soon enough. He'll skirt around them. We don't have much time. Follow me."

Cyrus pressed on, and Emy stayed silent, showing wisdom. Cyrus was not a commanding person, but she understood that Cyrus was doing his level best to save their lives. Questioning him would get her nowhere.

He led them due north, traveling as fast as he could while obscuring their trail. Between twigs and brush and leaves and mud, moving through the forest without leaving any evidence was a skill only mastered by a few of the elves or those who could fly. However, with some caution, any person could select paths that were difficult to trace, and Cyrus knew those paths well.

The methodical trail-finding and path-foraging brought some semblance of routine to Cyrus' mind. He found it easy to distract himself as he ducked branches, traversed brooks, and scaled boulders. However, when darkness fell and his body was exhausted, he found a place to hide and laid his head down to rest just a pace from Emy.

She agreed to take the first watch, though he didn't offer any input. When Cyrus closed his eyes and the forest disappeared, all he saw was charred skin, ash-covered auburn hair, and hollow eyes.

He went to sleep crying.

Chapter 8

Cyrus woke sometime in the early morning with the soft glow of the sun rising in the distance beyond the trees and a firm, furry hand cupped over his mouth.

Emy held a finger to her lips as she pressed her face close to Cyrus. Urgency filled her eyes, and her ears twitched at sounds too quiet for Cyrus to notice. All Cyrus knew was that he didn't remember falling asleep in the first place, and for a moment, he thought it was still evening. His first thought was that Aiguo had somehow, impossibly, caught up to them.

"We need to leave," Emy whispered, barely audible despite being so close. "Centaurs. Follow me."

Relief swept through Cyrus, though his sigh was muffled against Emy's grip. He raised a hand and took her by the wrist, pulling her away.

"Did they see us?" he whispered.

She shook her head.

"Okay, that's good," he said. "Stay down and trust me."

He stood up.

Emy suppressed a hiss and flattened against the ground as Cyrus exposed himself and gave away their position. Cyrus scanned the trees and found a half-dozen centaurs some distance away. They also found him and stopped searching the area as they homed in on him. They carried shortbows, which Cyrus guessed could reach him from this distance.

Cyrus prayed he'd made the right call, raised one arm, and waved.

"What are you doing?" Emy whispered. "Are you insane?"

"Just stay down," Cyrus replied through pressed lips.

The centaurs broke into a gallop towards him at first, but then slowed to a canter as they closed the distance. A younger centaur led them; his vibrant hair, both on his body and growing from his head, flowed in the morning mist that lingered in the air. He had a bulk to him, however, that spoke of a warrior breed, while he carried himself with a calm collection. Cyrus kept his gaze on that centaur and nodded respectfully, and not just because he knew him.

The centaur nodded back.

"Cyrus," the centaur began. "I thought those were your tracks my scouts found. However, I also thought surely that couldn't be so, as there are two sets."

"Chav'ha, believe it or not, I'm glad to see you," Cyrus replied. "I hoped you'd come in person."

"I was left with little choice. Our normally quiet forest has become a hive of activity lately. Word spreads fast in such a crowded place. Armed invaders probing the woods, werewolf clans being attacked, the elf tribes meeting among themselves; it's enough to worry a centaur sick."

Cyrus sighed and hung his head. Nervous energy pulsed through him, mixed with lingering regret and anguish. It didn't help that centaurs were physically intimidating creatures. They were tall, fast, and heavily built. Coupled with a history of violence, it was little wonder their territory was rarely infringed upon.

But desperate times called for desperate measures.

"Chav'ha, I'm going to be honest. I have nowhere else to turn to."

"Is that why you're hiding in that bush?" the centaur continued. "However, you can't possibly need my help. That wasn't our agreement. You remember that, I presume? You were younger then, Cyrus, but surely you can recall trespassing on our lands once before? I explained to you then that this wasn't acceptable, yet I let you wander off with a warning. Most trespassers don't get that. If you need help, I believe the elves have that responsibility."

"I'll never make it to the elves," Cyrus answered.

Chav'ha paused. His exterior remained cold and unyielding, a practiced stance he'd adopted from years of standoffs against older, jealous members of his tribe. Cyrus knew a bit about Chav'ha's history from the elves. Chav'ha had partly inherited, partly fought for leadership of the centaurs after Chav'ha's uncle, Lok'har, had been killed and left no heirs.

"What troubles have you brought to our home, Cyrus?" Chav'ha asked.

"If you know about the dead werewolves, then you know whom I'm running from," Cyrus answered. "Something about my past, something about when I was a child. It's not important. What matters, or at least what matters to me, is that they killed my mother.

It's a group of marauders, for lack of a better word, sent by some foreign ruler who calls himself the Dark Lord. Apparently, I have him to thank for the way I am and for the life I've had. It's a sick joke to realize my entire life is being driven by someone I've never met. Now this warband has murdered my mother and is coming for me.

"There's a good two dozen of them, dressed and armed like I've never seen. The elves sent me south on a hippogriff, but that's where everything went wrong. The treants did what they could to get me free, but they're too slow to help anymore. I need to get out of Angor, Chav'ha. That's it. I'm going away, and to be honest, I'm not sure I'll ever come back.

"Wait, please, let me finish. I know you don't owe me anything. I also know that centaurs and werewolves are more enemies than most races in the forest. However, that doesn't change my situation. My life is in your hands."

Chav'ha listened patiently. At the end of Cyrus' speech, he glanced left and right to those near him. Cyrus didn't know what position this put Chav'ha in, but Cyrus had heard that centaur politics were a brutal affair, both mentally and physically. Like werewolves, only the strong were considered worthy of leading, though that was mixed with a bit of heritage, too. One had to both possess and spill the right sort of blood to stay on top of the social hierarchy.

This should have meant Chav'ha was ruthless. This should have meant that Cyrus had walked himself and Emy into certain death. Yet, Cyrus couldn't help but remember that warning he'd received once from Chav'ha, and all the humility that had gone into it.

Cyrus trusted his gut.

"Your mother, you say?" Chav'ha said.

A lump swelled in Cyrus' throat. He nodded.

"Outsiders," Chav'ha said, spitting the word. "Who does this Dark Lord think he is that he can just walk into this forest and slay whom he wills? My uncle never would have stood for that. He was the sort of centaur who would summon an army to snuff out such imperious actions; such was his hatred for others. Of course, it was that exact hatred that eventually killed him and his sons and so many of our fellows. I have resolved to be a different sort of leader. It is lucky for the centaurs I lead that I am not my uncle. However, it sounds to me like this entire thing is between you, the werewolves, and this Dark Lord. I'll not spill a drop of centaur blood over it. We will keep to our borders, and you to yours.

"Now, listen very carefully to me, Cyrus. If you pass through our lands as a shortcut away from these invaders, I will consider you exiled from my goodwill. You had best never return to Angor, for if you do, I will give my soldiers permission to shoot you on sight.

"As for these invaders, so long as they keep out of our territory, I have no quarrel with them. However, if they attempt to cross into our borders, we will repel them with extreme prejudice. If they want to find you, they will have to skirt the edges of our lands like anyone else. It shouldn't be a problem for them. I imagine if they wanted to leave the forest, it would only delay them by a week or so.

"Now, was any of that unclear?"

Cyrus hung his head and sighed. When he closed his eyes, they moistened as emotion swept through him. His nose warmed, and he had to blink away a tear.

"Thank you," Cyrus whispered. "Thank you so much."

"What was that?" Chav'ha asked.

"Nothing," Cyrus said, speaking up, but keeping his head lowered. "I understand."

"Good," the centaur concluded. "Now, since I know an enemy approaches, my warriors and I will head back to our village for reinforcements. As powerful as we are, it'll take more than six of us to make sure these invaders understand whom they're dealing with. As for you, Cyrus, I suspect you'll be gone by the time we come back?"

Cyrus nodded.

"Good," Chav'ha concluded, nodding back. "This is farewell, then. You've been an interesting anomaly in this forest, Cyrus. I trust I'll never see you again."

Chav'ha and his warriors galloped away before Cyrus could reply, riding quickly out of sight. Once they were a little beyond earshot, Emy finally stood up from where she'd been hiding perfectly still. She had altered her shape to make herself smaller, a little shorter than an elf, with fur that was black, brown, and green. She shifted again now, back to her normal height and fur color.

"Question," Cyrus spoke before she could. "How small or large can you grow, exactly? Could you get as big as a treant?"

"That was a huge risk you took just now," Emy replied, a low growl escaping her throat. "You should have warned me this was your intention."

"Why? So you could run off? Aiguo would have just gone after you then, and I don't want your death on my conscience. I have enough of that already."

"I wouldn't have run off," Emy snarled, "but perhaps I could have thought of a better plan than flinging ourselves at the hooves of callous and intolerant creatures. If any of them had seen me, they'd have killed us both, wouldn't they?"

"Why do you think Chav'ha didn't press me about those two sets of tracks? I knew right then that I'd made the right call."

Emy paused, but her anger didn't lessen. Cyrus continued.

"And just so we're clear, those callous and intolerant creatures are the only reason we'll get out of this forest alive. Also, let's establish who gets to trust whom between us. Let's establish whose life is destroyed right now. My mother is dead. I'll say it one more time, just because I haven't received a word of sympathy from you—my mother is dead! Aiguo is right about one thing. He may have given the order, but you share the blame, just like I do. The only reason I haven't run off is because, well, I don't really know. I don't want to see you dead or skinned by that man's hands. I don't even know why. Your presence has done nothing but hurt me, but if Aiguo wants you dead, then that's reason enough to keep you alive right now.

"So, until we're out of this forest, it would be helpful if you would let me make the decisions about where we go and why. It would also be nice if maybe, just maybe, when I save your stupid life, you say 'thank you' instead of 'that was an unnecessary risk.' Hm?"

Cyrus was shaking with rage by the time he finished, and he had to break eye contact to calm himself. It took Emy several moments to reply.

"You're right," she whispered. "You're completely right. I've been cruel. I'm sorry for the loss of your mother. She didn't deserve what happened to her, and none of this is fair to you. Thank you for what you've done for me. However, I never said you took an unnecessary risk, just a huge one. All I wanted was to be informed."

"Noted," Cyrus mumbled.

Emy had spoken honestly, but the words hadn't comforted Cyrus on anything more than a superficial level. None of what she said numbed the pain in his heart. On top of that, he was now on the run—a fugitive—though what his crime was, he could not say. He felt like a leaf caught in a violent storm, tossed about by forces far greater than he could comprehend.

However, choices had been made.

"Well, we better get going," Cyrus said.

"Yes." Emy nodded. "Every moment counts. Thank you again, Cyrus. I assume we are heading through centaur land?"

"You catch on quick."

"Please," Emy said, brushing the compliment off. "An akki could have caught onto what Chav'ha was really saying. While we run through his lands, never to return, he'll cover our retreat. Aiguo will be forced to take the long way around, buying us several days of time. I'll admit that, although you took a big risk, it paid off. You've saved our lives, for now."

"I'm sorry if I said anything harsh to you," Cyrus went on. "I didn't mean to be rude."

That wasn't honest. Cyrus didn't feel sorry for anything he'd said, but years of conjuring up a submissive attitude under both the elves' and his stepfather's dominions had instilled a desire in him to admit wrongdoing even when he felt innocent. That was how he'd survived.

"You weren't," Emy replied. "But if you were, I deserved it."

The werewolf paused. He hadn't expected that response. He also didn't know what to make of it yet. He mumbled a thank you out of habit and took off through the forest, Emy in tow.

They made good time and didn't run into any centaurs along the way, despite traveling through their lands—another gift from Chav'ha. By running directly to his camp and summoning warriors, the centaur leader had not only prepared himself to greet Aiguo but had also drawn soldiers away from finding Cyrus and Emy along their direct path out of Angor. Thinking back on it now, he realized just how many ways that young centaur had helped him. Cyrus didn't feel worthy of it.

Those thoughts soon faded, though, replaced with memories of Belen dead in his arms. He thought over and over about how he had failed his mother, how he'd left her to die, even if that had been her order. It was of little comfort to remember that at least she had died quickly, believing that her son had finally fulfilled her lifelong dream for him.

Even if it had been a lie, Cyrus wasn't with Takeo; he was with this . . . this thing, this rakshasa. What exactly was a rakshasa anyway? Some shapeshifting, tall, strong, fast creature that also healed unbelievably quick? Already the wounds that Emy had taken yesterday had faded into pink lines as if they'd been there for months. Her continued stamina implied her blood loss had been little more than an inconvenience. Also, Cyrus had evidence that Emy could hear better than him, and possibly smell better, too.

Frightening, that's the word that came to Cyrus' mind. Abilities like that rightfully instilled a sense of fear in others. Like bugbears, with their unnatural speed and massive size, ruled Angor between full moons, so must this rakshasa creature surely have some place in the world where she ruled as the most feared thing in the land.

If not, then Cyrus shuddered to think what else might inhabit the lands that Emy hailed from.

And maybe that was the other reason Cyrus had never wanted to leave Angor before now. Maybe the unknown was more than a little bit scary, and Cyrus' life had been scary enough growing up. Maybe it had been nice to have some peace and quiet and a sense of safety, if only for a time.

Now here he was, trudging through centaur territory, running for his life and the life of another, orphaned in reality rather than just in his mind.

He just wished he knew what he had done to deserve this.

Chapter 9

They made it back to the Great Plains in two days. They arrived in time to see a roaming thunderbird in the distance, scanning the wide-open skies for prey. Massive, dark thunder clouds were conjured about the beast as it soared on magnificent wings. Occasional bolts of lightning shot down to the ground, echoing out a boom that broke the sound of wind rushing by and tall, yellow grass rustling about.

Cyrus had heard many stories about thunderbirds but had seen precious few. His mother, werewolves, and even the elves were not immune to the sense of awe and wonder those creatures instilled. They were the only reason Cyrus ever travelled to view the Great Plains. He felt a sort of kinship with them. Like them, Cyrus had roamed his domain alone and somewhat untouchable. He wasn't powerful, like them, but thunderbirds gave off the impression that they didn't really have a land to call home. They had merely adopted the Great Plains because it suited them, as Cyrus had adopted the forest.

Of course, he wasn't alone anymore, and as they broke free of the shadowed trees, Emy reminded him of that by speaking.

"We have two options," she said, sparing the thunderbird little more than a glance. "We can either make a direct cut across the plains towards the mountains, or we can skirt the forest edge due north. The first is the most direct route, but likely easier to track. By doing the second, when Aiguo breaks free of the forest, we could possibly throw him off by making our path harder to follow. We should consider each carefully. Our lives depend on it."

Cyrus drew in a deep breath and sighed.

"You're not good at taking in the moment, are you?" he replied.

"Huh? What do you mean?"

"Well, we just got done doing the whole run-for-your-life thing," Cyrus answered. "We're in the clear for at least a few days, so maybe you could give me a moment to absorb, well, everything that's happened to me. I get that we'll have to make a choice on where to go eventually, but I have more important things on my mind right now."

"Like what?" Emy demanded. "What could possibly be more important than staying at least one, if not two or more, steps ahead of Aiguo?"

"I'm hungry."

Emy narrowed her eyes at Cyrus in a way that suggested she'd never, in her whole existence, seen anything as dumb as him. Cyrus, for the first time in days, cracked a smile.

"Come on," he said. "Think about it. We can't rely on our rations forever. We'll have to hunt and forage eventually, and the plains are scarce. We might as well scour Angor while we can for something decent to eat. You said it yourself that we should consider our options carefully. Why don't we do both at the same time?"

Emy blinked and deflected her gaze.

"I," she started, "I suppose that makes sense."

They didn't find any game, but Angor had a lot of fruits and nuts. There were edible roots and plants, too, if one knew what to look for. A sense of normalcy returned to Cyrus' life as he went about trying to come up with a decent meal from what he could scavenge. Feeling eccentric, he gathered firewood and water, too, and set to work cooking for his guest, as it were. When he served Emy, he got a kick of satisfaction as her ears perked up at the scent of the food. By the size and frequency of her bites, she enjoyed it immensely.

"It'll be dark soon," she said with a mouthful. "We should put the fire out."

"It's a small fire, and we're in tree-cover," Cyrus replied. "This is actually the best time to have a fire because the smoke will be hard to spot in the fading light. Let's just enjoy a hot meal for once. Twice, if you have room for seconds."

"Seconds?" Emy stuttered.

Cyrus tilted the small pot toward her. She hesitated only a moment before scooping more out. Then she leaned back against a tree and ate, tension flowing out of her as she did so. Between the evening breeze and the crackle of the fire, Cyrus forgot his sadness for a short while.

He was glad to have company, or rather, he was glad not to be alone.

"Now, about our direction from here," Emy started.

Cyrus shook his head.

"I can see you're not easily distracted," he muttered. "Fine, sure. Talk away."

"Is this not important to you?" Emy replied. "You saw what Aiguo did. You know what he's going to do. Neither of us can afford to be distracted."

"No, no, I may have helped you out of Angor, but let's be clear whom Aiguo is after. He wants you. I can walk away right now, right back to the elves. I can go right back to where I was until you walked into my life and screwed everything up. And now it'll never be the same."

Emy's demeanor quickly lost the hostility that it had gained. She remembered what Cyrus had lost so recently, but that was of little help to Cyrus, who was more than annoyed that she could forget so soon in the first place. A moment of silence passed, and then Emy tried a different approach.

"But Aiguo is still out there," she said. "Don't you want, well, revenge?"

"Will that bring her back?" Cyrus replied. "Will that put my life back to the way it was? What good is revenge when the damage is done, huh?"

Emy blinked, then went wide-eyed.

"You can't be serious. Everyone wants revenge."

Cyrus shrugged, which was an honest reply. He was too busy drowning in another pit of self-loathing to think of what he wanted.

"If you really mean what you said, then you're an interesting creature," Emy said. "I'll give you that."

She sighed and let the silence pass between them undisturbed. Cyrus didn't want to admit it, but he knew Emy was right. He couldn't leave now. He couldn't imagine going back to the elves and putting them in danger. What if this Takeo person changed his mind and came for Cyrus? The elves could be caught up in that, and Cyrus owed them too much to put them at risk. It was better to stay with Emy, until he came up with a better plan, or any plan at all.

However, he couldn't do it. To think up a new plan, he would have to admit that his old life really was over. That his mother truly was dead. That she had been killed because her son had gone back on his word never to leave her side.

"Cyrus," Emy began again. "I know you don't owe me anything. In fact, the way the scales balance right now, I owe you in a way that can never be repaid. I would know. I've lost a parent, too. He was killed by Takeo's own hand, right before my eyes. I know that is of little comfort, but still. What I want you to know is that although I've lied about many things in our short history together, I never lied about your importance to me. I need to find the last angel, and I can't do it without you. I've tried. Now, you could be right that maybe the angel is avoiding me on purpose, and if that's the case, then I accept that. However, the Khaz Mal Mountains span a massive range, and it's far more likely I've been looking in the wrong place.

"Help me, Cyrus. Angels, from what I understand, are the embodiment of goodness, and one played a part in what you are today. Perhaps he can help you again."

Cyrus blinked. She was right about that. The angel, for whatever reason, had granted his mother's wish to change Cyrus in ways no one had thought possible. Did the angel remember him, he wondered? If given the chance, would the angel help him again?

He didn't know, but finding out sounded better than his other plan, which didn't exist.

"Alright, I'll go," he whispered, eyes on the dying flames of his small fire. "However, I just want one night more in the forest. Besides, it's getting late and—"

Emy's right ear perked then flipped back, and her eyes dilated. She held up a hand for silence, and Cyrus immediately obeyed. He didn't hear anything, but he had seen enough to trust in her abilities.

Emy kicked dirt over the fire, killing the struggling flames. Cyrus dumped what remained of their food over it, too, and began to stow what they had gotten out of their packs. Fortunately, they hadn't settled in for the night, so it didn't take him too long.

"Voices," Emy explained after a moment.

"Not close, then, if I can't hear them," Cyrus said.

Emy shook her head, then crouched and motioned for him to follow. They crept away from the thinning treeline along the Angor and Great Plains border and disappeared into the sea of tall, wavy grass. Cyrus lost track of where they were, but he dared not peek out because the sun hadn't quite set yet. His dark hair would be easily seen against the yellow background of dancing weeds.

Also, he heard voices in the distance. More specifically, he heard laughing, high-pitched and female. Considering that it was almost impossible that Aiguo had gotten out to the plains this quickly, it didn't take long for Cyrus to guess what group of women would be out in this desolate terrain, travelling loudly and unafraid.

Cyrus grabbed Emy's tail to get her attention. Her tail jerked in protest, and she whirled around with a half-snarl on her face. Cyrus grimaced.

"Sorry," he whispered.

"Do not," she growled, "touch my tail."

"I'm sorry," he repeated, cheeks growing hot. "I just wanted to say that I think they're amazons."

"I know that. I'm taking us away."

"What? No. We should go to them."

"Go to them? Why? The last time I met those amazons, I got the sense they were itching for a fight. I don't think they'll look too kindly upon a creature like me."

"You don't know that," Cyrus replied. "And besides, their leader, she warned me about Takeo. I need to return the favor and let her know about Aiguo. They need to know what happened."

Emy paused.

"First the centaurs, now the amazons," she grumbled. "You seem to know a lot of people. Unfortunately, we can't compromise on this one."

"What? Why not?"

"I was still disguised as Takeo the last time I met those amazons. I have a bad feeling about what they'll do once they find out I tricked them. I don't think they'll take it as nicely as you did."

"You haven't given them a chance."

"This isn't the sort of thing you take a chance with."

"Let me rephrase this. I'm going to warn them. You can stay hidden—"

Emy's right ear twitched, and her hand flew over Cyrus' mouth, silencing him. Her eyes went wide. Only then did Cyrus realize that the amazons had stopped talking and laughing.

"What is it, Octavia?" one of the amazons asked.

Cyrus could barely make out the voice over the gusts of wind, but he heard clearly enough through the gaps. Emy likely heard all.

"I thought, no," came the reply. "No, I certainly heard something."

"Out here? Are you sure?"

The slightest creak reached Cyrus' sensitive ears, and it dawned on him that Octavia had her bow out and an arrow drawn. No wonder Emy had reacted with urgency. She still held her hand to Cyrus' mouth, as if he might speak at any moment.

"Whomever you are," Octavia shouted, "now's your chance to come out in peace. If you wait, my sisters and I are going to let loose a volley. We've got arrows to spare."

Emy's ears flattened, and her gaze into Cyrus' eyes turned into one of pure loathing. She dropped her hand.

"Damn you," she said.

Cyrus failed to suppress a smirk and stood up.

As expected, he found some two dozen amazons in a small camp atop one of the rising hills of the plains. They weren't as far away as he had expected, and he assumed the shifting winds were to blame for that. Apparently, his hearing couldn't be relied upon here as strongly as it could in the forest. Only Octavia was standing with bow drawn, but the others were reaching for their weapons until Cyrus showed himself.

He was swiftly recognized, followed by a wave of shock that swept through the amazons. Adelpha bolted up, towering over her sisters.

"Cyrus?" she called out. "What are you doing here?"

"And who were you talking to?" Octavia followed up, relaxing her strung arrow.

Cyrus looked down at Emy. She glowered before standing up, too, and then a second wave of shock went through the amazons.

"What is that?" Octavia asked, redrawing her arrow.

"I've never seen that before," another said.

"It's a rakshasa," Adelpha answered, breathless with disbelief. "How in the, wait, Cyrus, is that really you? Octavia, keep that bow up. These creatures can appear as anyone. We could be looking at two of them."

"It's me!" Cyrus called out, hands going up. "Adelpha, it's me. Just a few days ago, you pulled me aside and warned me about Takeo, remember? No one else would know that."

Adelpha narrowed one eye at Emy and kept it there. Emy gazed back, but her attention was entirely focused on that bow, Cyrus could tell. The tension balanced on a knife's edge, and Cyrus couldn't take it anymore. There was no need for any of this. He stepped between Emy and Octavia's arrow and advanced, arms raised.

Adelpha pushed the tip of Octavia's arrow down.

"Cyrus, what are you doing out here?" Adelpha asked. "And what are you doing with that creature?"

"Hey," one of the amazons whispered none too softly. "That creature is wearing a kimono. Isn't that the same one Takeo—"

Adelpha held up a hand for silence. Her lack of surprise revealed that she'd already come to this conclusion, and the mood about her sisters darkened. A number of heads lowered and eyes narrowed in Emy's direction.

Cyrus, meanwhile, did not pause. He approached Adelpha with arms still raised, struggling to bring words to his lips. He wanted to answer Adelpha's question but doing so meant speaking aloud the images running through his mind. He knew it had to happen, yet the task was not easy. When he came close enough for the fading light to illuminate his features, Adelpha saw the lines of sadness creeping about his lips and eyes. Her hard stare softened with concern.

"Cyrus?" Adelpha asked again. "What happened? Where is your mother?"

Tears. He couldn't stop them. He hated them, but he always seemed powerless against them. Now he stood before Adelpha. She frowned and leaned toward him, arms drifting out as if aching to hug him. Or maybe that's just the way he wanted to see it. All he knew was that he didn't want to carry this burden.

"She's dead," Cyrus whispered.

Adelpha and the amazons gasped. Cyrus' tears came hard then, and he covered his face in shame at the emotion. Adelpha flung her arms around Cyrus, and without thinking, his arms went around her, too. Adelpha's hand drifted over his head, and she held him close. He couldn't take it anymore. His knees went weak, and she guided him down to the ground. There, finally, Cyrus let loose all the agony he'd held inside for days.

In the distance, Emy watched with head hung.

Chapter 10

Cyrus sat there for some time, and although he didn't feel better just yet, he knew that one day he would. For the first time since he'd held his mother's corpse, he felt like he could walk again, rather than stumble forward without falling.

He told them everything—well, almost everything. He really only wanted to tell Adelpha, but before he could stop himself, he began describing what happened while all the other amazons were in earshot. No doubt Emy wanted to intervene, but that would mean coming closer to the group, and she did not seem willing to move from her distant location. In fact, she seemed to be slowly inching away, watching the amazons, their hands, and their bows. One could hardly blame her, especially when it dawned on the group that Emy had not only deceived them but in doing so had led to this tragic event. Only Cyrus' swift explanation of how Emy had returned to save him stopped the amazons from drawing arrows.

That was until they all learned that Takeo's henchmen were on Cyrus' trail, then they reached for their bows all the same.

"Looks like we'll be doubling the watch tonight, ladies," one of them said. "I call the first shift."

"So eager," another replied. "I'm jealous."

"No," Cyrus cut in. "No, we—Emy and I—will keep going. I only wanted to warn you, that's all. It's not your responsibility—"

"Let me stop you right there," Adelpha replied, her voice full of maternal command. "You're not going anywhere, Cyrus. You want to talk about responsibility? I'm the queen of the amazons, and that means it was my decision that doomed Belen to suffer for a crime she didn't commit. Now I've failed her again by playing a part in what led to her death, and I will not fail her thrice by leaving her son to be hunted down. No, Cyrus, you are my responsibility, and you are staying with us. In fact, I hope this Aiguo fellow comes looking for you. He killed one of us, our sister—our lost sister—and that means we have a score to settle."

A cheer went up among the amazons, silencing the protest that hung on Cyrus' lips. He hadn't expected this sort of enthusiasm. Perhaps Adelpha felt responsible for Belen's death, but that didn't mean her sisters should. The younger one, Octavia, for example, would have been a child when that decision was made, so why should she have to risk her life? But she had cheered, too, so the decision appeared unanimous.

However, one problem remained.

"Thank you, Adelpha," he said. "Thank you all, actually. I never should have been so afraid of you while I was growing up, yet I can't accept. Emy and I, we're not going the same direction as you. You're headed for Lucifan, and we're headed for Khaz Mal. We can stay the night, but in the morning, we'll have to part ways."

Adelpha cocked her head in disapproval and glanced at Emy. The rakshasa's refusal to come forward was surely noted. Cyrus felt bad for Emy, honestly. Sure, she had brought this on herself by being deceitful, but she'd had her reasons, and she had come through in the end. Didn't that count for something?

"You're determined to stay with this creature," Adelpha said. "Why? She's already lied several times, to all of us. Who's to say she's telling the truth now? And besides, have you considered that maybe it isn't such a good idea to lead her to an angel?"

"I'm not sure what's a good idea anymore," Cyrus replied. "My last good idea didn't go so well. However, it's not really about her right now. I feel lost, and maybe this angel can help me with that. Emy brought up a good point; it was the angel that made me this way, and that was my mother's wish. It seems only fitting that I should know why."

Adelpha put her hands on her hips and sighed.

"Well, I suppose that makes sense," she said. "And I guess you couldn't stay with us forever, anyway, being a man and all. However, I don't see why you have to make for the mountains just yet. You can reach Khaz Mal from Lucifan just as easily as you can from here—in fact, more easily. In Lucifan, you can get supplies for your journey, and you'll have a chance to lose your pursuers, assuming we don't kill them first.

"I can't command you to do it. All I can do is ask. Please Cyrus, come with us. Let me see you pass safely through Lucifan, not just as a favor to you, but to repay my debt to your mother."

Cyrus made his decision quickly. Adelpha made good points, and he didn't want to be alone again. Emy didn't quite count as company, not yet, and it wasn't hard to persuade Cyrus with such simple things as kindness and concern. His mother had always told him this was his weakness, one among many, but he could live with that. As much as he loved his mother, she been wrong about almost everything.

"Okay, I'll stay," he said.

He had to pause while a cheer went up among the amazons. They really were a tight-knit, enthusiastic bunch. A smile cracked along Cyrus' lips. He'd always dreamed of being a part of something like that, and now here was his chance, if only temporarily. Though, perhaps their eagerness for a fight was a little overzealous.

"But that means she has to come, too," he added and flicked a thumb at Emy.

The amazons went quiet, eyeing the rakshasa before turning their attention to Adelpha. Their queen glanced between Emy and Cyrus with a hard stare. Cyrus had a feeling it was all for show, though. The way he saw it, if Adelpha didn't trust a rakshasa, then the last thing she wanted was for Cyrus to charge into the unknown with one. She'd made it clear that she and her sisters were willing to fight. To refuse Emy would show fear, and that just wasn't in Adelpha's blood.

At least, that's what Cyrus thought. He hoped he was a good judge of character.

"You there," Adelpha called out. "So, Takeo's hunting you, huh?"

Emy took a moment to reply.

"Yes," she said.

"Why?"

"He hates my kind," Emy replied. "But more importantly, he blames me for the death of his friend, a knight named Sir Gavin Shaw."

"Blames you?" Adelpha balked. "I'd heard Takeo killed Gavin personally."

"He did."

Adelpha placed one arm across her chest and rested the other on it, lifting a hand to touch her chin.

"Emy, was it? That's an awfully familiar sounding name."

"My father gave it to me—surrogate father—and your suspicions are correct."

"Really? Then you must be aware of the sheer morbid irony in giving a rakshasa that name."

"Yes, I'm aware of that, too. I can assure you, however, that there was no malicious intent or dark humor involved in giving me that name. My surrogate father was too kind and simple for either. You may have heard of him. He was an ogre named Krunk. Takeo killed him, too."

Adelpha raised an eyebrow.

"Emy, do you believe in the phrase the enemy of my enemy is my friend?"

"Heard it, but I don't believe in it. I watched many, many people make friends with Takeo that way, and he killed them just the same."

Adelpha smirked.

"They do say you rakshasas are clever creatures. How about you tell us your story? It sounds like Cyrus hasn't heard it, and if you two are going to travel together, then you'll have to tell him eventually. There's no time like the present."

Emy stood motionless while she thought.

"It's a long story," she said.

"We've got a long journey," Adelpha replied.

"Do you promise to believe me?"

"No, but I do promise to listen."

Emy held Adelpha's gaze for a moment before looking to her feet. When she glanced up again, she locked eyes with Cyrus, and in a flash, he saw something he should have seen all along.

She was afraid.

Of course, she was afraid. Why hadn't he seen that before? She was alone, and a group of assassins were chasing her across the world. She trusted no one—incapable of trust, it seemed. Why hadn't Cyrus realized this sooner? That's why she'd disguised herself at every opportunity. She lived in a constant state of fear.

Cyrus knew what that was like. He'd been there before under the abusive tyranny of his stepfather.

So, when he returned Emy's gaze this time, she saw in his grey eyes neither resentment, begging, nor distrust.

She saw acceptance.

"Okay," Emy said, never lifting her eyes from Cyrus. "I'll talk."

* * *

"For your benefit, Cyrus, I'll start from the beginning: the short version, for now. We can discuss the details later.

"Adelpha probably knows this part, but Takeo Karaoshi left Lucifan for Juatwa just a few years after you were born. He took with him an ex-knight, a viking, an ogre, and a broken heart. His one and only love, an amazon named Emily Stout, died in his arms when a rakshasa led a massive army to assault Lucifan.

"It cannot be understated the depths of Takeo's love for this woman. Distraught over her loss, he blamed the entire world for her death, and in his madness, decided the world itself needed to change to atone for this loss. He claims he wants to make a peaceful world, a unified world, one in which all power and law is confined to a single individual: that individual being him. He believes that in such a world Emily would have survived.

"Unfortunately, he's chosen to complete this goal the only way he knows how: through death and conquest.

"Takeo and his group stumbled upon me before he had any real power, but he terrified me, nonetheless. He always has. The way he looks at people can only be described as lifeless, as if he's dissecting the best way to kill you at any moment. I tried to overcome this when I was younger by learning from him and seeking his guidance. I thought, like Gavin and many others, that he was simply misunderstood and that his true nature could be conjured out. I was naïve.

"Takeo killed Krunk, my surrogate father, first. Like me, he was an outsider, hated and feared for a nature he could not control. When everyone else looked at me as an object to be either feared or used, he looked at me as the scared little cub I was and cared for me. After his death, I knew that I would not rest until Takeo had paid for his treachery. Unfortunately, the Dark Lord knew it, too.

"See, in my efforts to try and win Takeo over, he'd made a show of taking me under his wing and training me. He never trained me with swords, and I should have understood why—what a fool I

98

was—but encouraged me to 'hunt' him by stalking and changing like a rakshasa does. In this way, he learned my every move. He can identify me even when disguised. All my training had ever done was to nullify myself as a threat to him. He knew from the beginning that we'd end up as enemies, and he abused my trust to gain the advantage.

"Everything came to a head when Takeo took total control. With every increase in power, Takeo's methods became more and more twisted and desperate. Takeo's surviving friends, Gavin and Nicholas, resolved to flee with me and another refugee of Takeo's wrath. In a horrible tragedy, Takeo killed Gavin and Gavin's wife before they could flee to safety. It was only thanks to Nicholas that the rest of us escaped. Takeo kept Gavin's daughter as a trophy of the friendship he'd betrayed, and I pray for the girl's safety every night.

"Nicholas had us transported by ship to Lucifan. There we split up, all going our separate ways. It was my suggestion, hoping that by doing so, I'd have a greater chance of throwing Takeo off my scent. He only wanted me, but all I did was slow him down. At first, I was afraid he'd come for me personally, but I shouldn't be surprised he sent Aiguo. Aiguo has served two rakshasa lords and knows my kind well. Plus, he's as ruthless and cold hearted as Takeo would want anyone to be towards me.

"Like I said, that's the short version. I'm one of the many orphans Takeo has made and will continue to make until he is stopped. The only difference is that he sees me as a threat, and for that crime, I must be eliminated."

Cyrus shook his head. Everyone but the sentries were gathered around that dying campfire and listening intently. Adelpha watched with fingers touched to her chin.

"Is he really that cruel?" Cyrus asked.

"I can answer that," Adelpha cut in. "That angel you want to find, he had brothers and sisters once. Perfect beings of pure good. Takeo helped assassinate them."

"I watched him choke the life out of his own commander to seize power," Emy said.

"Is it true that he burned down a whole city after infecting it with a plague?" Adelpha asked.

"He did that after I left, but yes," Emy replied.

"Disgusting." Adelpha swore. "How does anyone follow that man?"

"Oh, his inner circle is no better. His closest confidants practice cannibalism as a rite of passage. Takeo does nothing to discourage this. It's a well-known fact that he's done it, too."

"I heard he killed his wife on their wedding night, the day he was crowned Emperor," a voice called from the crowd.

"His pregnant wife!" someone yelled.

Cyrus' mouth fell open. He glanced from Emy to Adelpha to the others, stunned that not a shred of doubt showed on anyone's face. He shook his head again in disbelief.

"He sounds horrible," Cyrus said, "but you all knew him personally, apparently. How did anyone not stop him sooner?"

Silence followed. Adelpha's gaze fell to the dying flames. Emy's eyes fell slower, along with her head. A few of the amazons looked apologetic.

"The enemy of my enemy is my friend," Adelpha said, shrugging. "In the Battle for Lucifan, Takeo fought alongside us to repel the invaders. At that time, everyone was willing to look the other way. In fact, you might even say some of us held hopes that Takeo could become a force of good in the world. I certainly hoped so since Emily, one of our sisters, had fallen in love with him. When she died, out of respect for her memory, I washed my hands of Takeo and let him go off in peace. You must understand, I had no way of knowing that he would develop such a thirst for global domination. He was just a wandering ronin back when I knew him."

"You also must understand that Takeo is not so easily killed," Emy explained. "He is cunning and tenacious, a walking manifestation of human willpower, which has seen him through situations that would kill any lesser man. It's easy to get intimidated by his aura of dominance. Easier, even, to be lured in by his promise of a peaceful world."

"You talk like he's a god," Cyrus said.

"His followers certainly think so. Not only is Takeo a skilled tactician, he's perhaps the best fighter in the world—I am not exaggerating. My father told me stories about how Takeo faced down a hydra on his own and beat the beast back into the ocean."

"What?" Adelpha balked. "That really happened? I thought that was just a rumor."

Emy shook her head slowly.

"Damn," the amazon queen replied, blinking. "Though I suppose I shouldn't be surprised. I watched him kill a minotaur with a single blow and disable a gunslinger with nothing but a sword."

"Oh, but it gets worse," Emy pressed. "Those are all things he did while he was still, well, normal. Have you heard about his sword?"

Adelpha glanced at her sisters. Hesitation spoke louder than words. This was a rumor she didn't want confirmed.

"I've heard he, um," Adelpha started, "traded his soul for strength and speed. They say that his sword makes him faster than the eye can see, and that it breathes fire when he swings it."

Emy nodded. Adelpha's head fell.

Cyrus felt the color drain from his face. In the silence that followed, he searched face after face in the crowd for some ray of hope or shared disbelief. All looked grave.

"And this man, assuming he's just a man," Cyrus cut in, "commands an army larger than the world has ever known?"

Emy looked into the flames.

"Do you see now why I have to find that angel?" she said.

Chapter 11

Cyrus lay awake for half the night staring up at the stars, thinking.

He used to do this often, early in his life. He'd had a lot of time for reflection in the solitude of constant travel. The only difference was that the forest canopy blocked out most of the stars, so staring up back then had been merely symbolic. Out on the Great Plains, the sky overflowed with constellations, painting a vast and complicated web that made Cyrus feel small and insignificant.

He saw it as an analogy for his life.

In the sudden and tragic anguish that had befallen his world, Cyrus hadn't had the time or inclination to consider that he and his mother weren't the first victims here. His steadfast focus on his mother's safety hadn't allowed him to grasp what Emy had been saying all along about how Takeo had killed her father. And that Gavin's daughter, whomever she was, now lived under the care of her parents' murderer. How horrible was that? Cyrus didn't want to think about it. If even half of what Emy and the amazons said was true, then Takeo was a truly vile person.

But did that mean Cyrus wanted to oppose him?

That seemed like suicide. Like the stars above, this Dark Lord was both vastly and immeasurably powerful. How could anyone so small and insignificant as a young werewolf stand against him? Surely, the entire world would fall before what was to come. But what could Cyrus do? Return to the forest and hide among the trees with the elves? Would Takeo's thirst for domination stop at Angor's border?

He shook his head. He knew that answer.

"No," he mumbled into the darkness.

Cyrus couldn't take that risk. Thinking of the elves and all they'd done for him, and the treants, and the debt he owed the centaurs, Cyrus couldn't take the chance that the Dark Lord would spare them.

Yet he couldn't commit. As he lay awake, staring into the darkness above, he couldn't conclude that everything Emy said and did was right. The idea of following her blindly into the unknown made him feel uneasy. She had this mysterious aura, as if she was hiding something, always hiding something. Even as she'd spilled her guts to Cyrus and the amazons, and Adelpha agreed with her, one got the impression that Emy was keeping facts hidden. He realized, in that moment, that his reluctance to travel with Emy had only been partially rooted in his desire to stay in the forest. The other part had to do with her.

However, he couldn't leave her. Where else would he go? Emy's suggestion that he seek out this angel still seemed the best choice. And besides, it wasn't like traveling with her to the angel meant he had to be with her forever. He could cross that bridge when he came to it.

And sometime after that, Cyrus finally hit the right combination of exhausted and satisfied. He fell asleep and didn't wake up until Adelpha nudged him in the morning light.

"Up, up, up," she commanded. "The morning is the best time to travel out here. It's the coolest time of the day."

Cyrus was good at following commands. Between the elves and Ralph, Cyrus had little practice in challenging authority. He practically leapt off the ground and started packing his things. Adelpha chuckled.

"You're not much like your mother, are you?" she said in passing.

"What does that mean?" Cyrus replied, more sternly than he intended.

Adelpha hesitated, but when she saw Cyrus deflect his gaze, she realized neither party had meant offense. Adelpha forced a half smile.

"Just a memory," she said. "If I had roused Belen like that, she would have yelled and argued with me for the rest of the week."

"Really? That doesn't sound like my mother."

"Oh. Hmm. Well, people change as they age. Just trust me when I say that few could rival Belen's ferocity once upon a time. It's a good thing you didn't inherit that. Good to see she left something better in you. Now, hurry and finish packing, and I'll introduce you to the ladies. You might as well learn some names since we're going to be traveling together."

Cyrus paused, realizing Adelpha had not mentioned bringing Emy along. He hesitated, wondering if he should bring this up, but decided against it. He felt awkward enough as it was.

As the group got on the move and Adelpha paraded him around, Cyrus couldn't help but feel like some sort of traitor. Just a short time ago, he'd thought of these people as enemies. His mother, at least, had hated and rightfully blamed them for her situation.

Or had she? Hadn't she said something about loving her time with the amazons? Cyrus dimly remembered that conversation. What would his mother say if she saw him now? Would she be distraught to see him taken in by the people who betrayed her? Or would she be happy to see her son leaving the forest like she had always wanted, surrounded by hardened warriors who could help protect him? He hoped it was the latter.

"And this is Leda," Adelpha said, "one of my best friends. She and I have been making these trips together for a long time."

She gestured to an amazon similar in age to herself with small ears, wide hips, and a warm face. Leda smiled, slowing her pace slightly as they traveled up a steep hill.

"It's good to finally meet you, Cyrus," Leda said, then winked. "I must say you've grown up to be a handsome man."

"Um, uh, thank you?" he replied.

"Oh Leda, you're embarrassing him," Adelpha said, whirling Cyrus away. "You must forgive her. Leda doesn't know how to talk to a man unless she's teasing him or flirting with him. The way she's going, she'll have just as many children as her mother. Oh, speaking of which."

Adelpha rushed Cyrus down the hillside and directly towards an older woman, heavy set and thick chinned. She beamed at Cyrus as he approached.

"This is Hanna," Adelpha explained, "Leda's mother and, in some ways, our grandmother on this journey."

"Cyrus, dear, how are you feeling? Not well, I imagine. Listen, I knew your mother for longer than anyone else here. If you ever need to talk about her, I'm available. I'm a good listener, I promise."

"Hanna," Adelpha scolded lightly. "I'm sure what Cyrus needs is a distraction right now, not reminders."

"Oh, you know I only meant to help. I'm everyone's mother, remember?"

"Practically," Adelpha said with a scoff, then whispered none too quietly to Cyrus. "I swear, if there is anyone addicted to childbirth, it's this woman right here. She's had more than a dozen children, honest. Every year she swears she's only coming to Lucifan to support us and see a few of her sons, yet without fail, she walks away pregnant. Can you believe that?"

Cyrus stomach flipped. This was not a conversation he was prepared to have.

"Oh, stop teasing, Adelpha," Hanna laughed and gave the queen a push. "As if you're any better. Will you and Abe even leave the bedroom this time?"

Both ladies laughed loudly, and Cyrus looked at the ground wide-eyed. Never in his life had he talked about anything so intimate so quickly. He couldn't believe he was the only person embarrassed right now, and for that reason, he felt even more embarrassed. Had his mother been like this?

"Enough of that," Adelpha giggled, wheeling Cyrus away again. "I've saved the best for last. Let me tell you something. Normally, this group that travels to Lucifan is a much younger crowd. It's a long, hard journey that has a tendency to get lively. Most ladies get their fill of it after a few years and stay home where things are much quieter. Younger women tend to have the appetite to explore the big city and meet potential suitors, if you know what I'm saying. I know many consider this a taboo subject, but really, this is an important trip for our society because it prevents us from getting stagnant. Strong warriors are our typical prey, but our women are encouraged to go where their hearts take them. Do you understand what I'm saying? If you don't introduce new breeders into a pool of animals, they eventually interbreed to the point where—"

"You know, I don't think I need to hear all—"

"Of course, of course, what am I saying? To the point, then. The youngest woman on this trip is actually about your age. Also, like you, this is her first trip to Lucifan. I think you two will get along great."

Adelpha finished her sentence right as they walked up to the girl in question, and it turned out to be someone Cyrus already knew, sort of. She was the one they called Octavia. As the two approached, Octavia smiled, exposing her upper gums.

"This is Octavia," Adelpha said with grandeur, "our little archer prodigy, just like her mother was. Her mother, Iezabel, was unmatched with a bow. Let me tell you, she could pin a fairy's wings together while it was zooming by, and Octavia here has put to rest many bets on whether that skill was passed down the line. Many of us think her father must have been a pirate captain who had a good aim with his pistol—in more ways than one! Haha! Do you get it? Really, it just goes to show what going to Lucifan can do for—"

"Hi," Cyrus said to Octavia and thrust out his hand, trying to cut off Adelpha as quickly as possible. "I'm Cyrus. I, uh, I saw you match that elf in archery back in Angor. That was impressive."

Octavia looked at the outstretched hand shyly before taking it. They shook lightly, and Cyrus matched her smile. A gust of wind blew her hair into her mouth, and Octavia swept the strands back over her ear.

"Oh, you saw that, huh?" she said. "I was a little embarrassed, to be honest. I knew that the elf was under a lot of pressure, but at the same time, I couldn't let my sisters down. Do you think he was upset?"

"If you're talking about Nathok, I wouldn't worry. He's always upset. My friend and I used to joke that Nathok had a good time once, but he decided the experience was too horrible to relive."

Octavia laughed. Cyrus' smile grew.

"I'll just leave you two alone," Adelpha said.

She gave her own chuckle and stepped away, joining Leda in the back of the group. The two older women began to whisper and giggle. Unfortunately, her absence left a void that wasn't so easily bridged.

For several moments, Cyrus and Octavia searched the wide-open plains in awkward silence. Cyrus worried he was making her uncomfortable and contemplated finding some way to leave, but he also worried she'd take offense, especially after Adelpha had made such a forceful introduction.

"I, uh, I wouldn't worry about her," Octavia finally said.

"Who? Adelpha?" Cyrus replied.

"Yeah, she likes to think of herself as some expert matchmaker, I've been warned. The other girls told me about it, how she likes to find men for the younger girls, to 'guide' them. They warned me not to feel pressured to take her advice just because she's our queen and all."

"Oh, that's good," Cyrus said. "Because, well—"

"You don't have to worry about me," she jumped in. "I'm not looking for a suitor, actually. That's not why I'm here. I'm not ready for children."

"Oh wow, yeah, me too. I wouldn't want to—I mean, not that you're not pretty! You're pretty, in your own way. Uh, wait! I didn't mean it like that. I was just saying, trying to say was—"

"Cyrus, right?"

"Yes?"

"Maybe we should talk about something else."

Cyrus let loose a sigh of relief.

They let a comfortable bout of silence pass between them this time, and Cyrus took in what little scenery there was. The Great Plains was boring and unashamedly so, the way Cyrus saw things, but it had its moments. Sprinkled among the endless rolling hills of dancing yellow grass, one saw not only thunderbirds but also the behemoths they hunted. Behemoths were massive, slow-plodding creatures that traveled back and forth across the plains, eating grass and causing small quakes in the ground. Each of their four legs were as wide as a person with arms outstretched, and the males had a curiously large horn on the front of their low-slung heads. Despite their size, Cyrus wasn't afraid of them. Not only were they slow moving and generally docile, unlike bugbears, but they were also kind of funny. Because of the way their eyes sat, a behemoth had to shake its head side to side as it walked to see straight. When combined with the way their squatty legs kicked about as they walked, the behemoths appeared to dance as they moved.

"Hey," Octavia broke in, "do you want to invite your friend over?"

Cyrus drew his attention away from the herd of behemoths in the distance to Emy, plodding equally slow, somewhere close to the back of the amazon group. Judging by her pace, she was trying to get the amazons to pass her, but always a few would stop, so that Emy was never truly by herself. After a time, she gave up.

"Um, I wouldn't call her my friend," Cyrus said.

"She looks angry."

"Well, can you blame her?" Cyrus said, then whispered. "Adelpha made a rather clear statement by showing me around and not her."

"Yeah, but that was Adelpha's choice," Octavia whispered back. "We can do whatever we want. Invite her over."

Cyrus paused and narrowed one eye.

"You seem awfully intent on this," he said. "What are you after?"

"What? Can't a girl be nice? Look at her. She could clearly use a friend. She looks miserable. Besides, I'll bet she's great company. You heard it yourself that she's traveled all over. I'll bet she's got some great stories."

"Interested in the world at large, are you?"

"So, what if I am?" Octavia replied, straightening up, though she was nowhere near Cyrus' height. "Stop being a jerk and call her over."

Cyrus didn't need to be persuaded. He knew he was being difficult, but there was something fun about teasing this girl. He, too, felt bad that Adelpha had so clearly defined who was welcome and who was not by excluding Emy, and he'd wanted to rectify it.

"Emy," Cyrus called out. "Come over here."

The rakshasa swiveled her attention slowly towards the pair, who smiled and waved. Emy's expression did not change.

"What?" Emy shouted back.

Cyrus blinked. Of all the responses he expected, that was not one of them. He looked to Octavia for guidance, but she appeared as baffled as he did. Fortunately, Cyrus wasn't at a loss for words. He had a fallback response for times like these.

"Please?" he called out.

The situation could not have been more awkward as the other amazons attempted unsuccessfully to let this exchange go unnoticed. Cyrus and Octavia cringed under the social pressure, but curiously enough, Emy seemed impervious to the cocked stares the older women were sharing among themselves. It wasn't that Emy was ignorant, of course. She was far too observant for that, which meant she simply didn't care.

However, in Cyrus' life, he'd come to find that a well-intentioned 'please' had a certain amount of power over everyone. It seemed Emy was not immune to this, as she hesitated but eventually caved to the plea. She changed direction, picked up her pace, and caught up with Cyrus and Octavia.

"Yes?" she said.

"Oh stop," he replied. "I know you heard us talking."

"What? She did?" Octavia said with a jump. "But the wind was going the other way. Is your hearing really that good?"

Emy failed to suppress a prideful smirk. Cyrus leapt at the opportunity to build on that.

"That's not all she can do," he said. "I watched her get stabbed with a sword just a couple days ago. Do you see a wound?"

Octavia scrunched up her face in skepticism.

"Plus, she's strong," Cyrus added. "She picked me up one handed with ease."

"Not with ease," Emy corrected, but her smirk remained.

"Wow," Octavia said in awe. "Your kind must be incredibly respected where you come from."

"Feared, actually," she said, the smirk disappearing. "My kind is being hunted to extinction in Savara, and that was before the Dark Lord showed up to finish the job. For all I know, I'm the last rakshasa left alive."

Octavia mouthed an embarrassed 'oh' and looked at her feet.

Cyrus realized this was going to be a very long journey.

Chapter 12

Things grew more awkward when the next full moon came. The amazons knew about Cyrus' condition, of course, but that didn't mean Cyrus wanted to endure the attention his forced shapeshifting would draw. He already felt enough like an outsider as it was. A sense of shame always came over him whenever he changed in front of non-werewolves. His old clan and the elves never spoke about the werewolf form as anything other than a curse, and so that's the way Cyrus envisioned it, as something to hide.

It didn't help that, as the night approached, more than a few amazons watched him carefully. Cyrus mumbled an excuse to Adelpha that he wanted to sleep somewhere else tonight, out of sight. She hesitated but agreed.

Cyrus went out far enough into the tall grass to disappear into the darkness. The moon was hidden behind clouds, but its power remained. Cyrus underwent his change and stayed low, knowing that sleep would not come and that the night would be long.

Among the many new smells that filled his nostrils, an old one crept up into his senses and made his ears perk. He rose to a crouch and peered above the weeds. Emy's figure approached against the background of the amazon's small campfire.

He growled.

"Sorry, I know you asked to be alone," she said. "Trust me, it wasn't easy to convince Adelpha to let me walk out here. I'm sure the only reason she did is because you're out here, changed, so they figure you can handle me, and maybe you can."

Cyrus whined and snorted. The trouble with being a werewolf was that a lot more than one's outsides changed. Cyrus didn't just become taller and more muscular, his muscles became denser. His ears picked up new sounds, his heart beat faster, and his body had trouble controlling its temperature, so he had to pant. Also, his vocal cords became restricted, and he couldn't speak like a normal human.

"Listen," she continued. "I know how you feel in this form; I've watched you. Maybe I don't know what it's like to be a werewolf, but I know what it's like to be looked upon as an animal. You're embarrassed, lonely even, am I right?"

Cyrus closed his mouth and swallowed a mouthful of drool. Then his tongue rolled out again because he was getting hot. This conversation wasn't helping. Not that one could call it a conversation, as only one side could speak. Cyrus pawed the ground in annoyance that Emy had waited until now to try and talk with him—to him. How rude.

"I've seen how you lie awake at night, unable to sleep," she continued. "The truth is that I haven't been sleeping so well since we joined the amazons either. I wasn't sure what you would do when the next full moon came, but I'm glad you decided to leave the humans behind. It gave me the excuse I needed to do the same."

Emy knelt down, and Cyrus growled in surprise.

"Wait, just let me finish," she pleaded and then waited for Cyrus to sit back. "I've been thinking lately about how cold I've been to you. It's . . . it's not easy to explain, but all I can say is that I'm not perfect. When I feel threatened, I get angry and defensive, and I forget the consequences my actions have on others. Afterwards, like today, I reflect and realize my mistakes, but the damage has been done. I don't know why I'm like this; part of me wants to blame Takeo and the way he treated me, but blaming others for my weakness is not within me. It's not how a rakshasa thinks, or at least that's what I think.

"I guess I just want to apologize again and to warn you that I don't know how long it will take for me to get any better. However, I'm trying. Like now. You and I, we're not like them. We'll never be like them. And I should appreciate what little kinship we share in a world full of rejection and hate."

She got on down all fours. Cyrus rose up and inched back, lowering his nose, uncertain of her intent. He liked what she had said, agreed with it on the surface, but he had trouble trusting the source. This girl baffled him. She was hot and cold, understanding, then psychotic, equal parts distant and close. He couldn't tell if she was really this unhinged or if one part was just an act.

"I thought," Emy continued, shyly, "since neither of us will sleep tonight, that maybe we could spend it together—not like civilized humans but embracing that part of us that isn't human or civilized and doesn't care about those things. It's been a long time since I hunted anything or anyone to the full extent of my abilities. I thought, or rather hoped, that maybe you'd want to do that."

Emy could have done a better job explaining, but Cyrus understood, innately, what she was getting at. His body understood before his mind.

He smiled as best he could with a long snout and canines, then nodded. Emy smiled back.

"Okay," she said. "Give me a minute to run and hide. When you catch me, we'll switch."

Cyrus barked his excitement, and Emy took off into the weeds. What proceeded next was perhaps the most competitive game of tag that had ever been played.

* * *

Over the next couple months, Cyrus learned that he had vastly underestimated the immense size of the Great Plains. He could not have dreamed, in all his years in the forest, of traveling in one direction for so long and never seeing a change in scenery. It baffled him in some regard, as he'd always considered the Forest of Angor to be this expansive plane upon which his whole world fit nicely. Cyrus had felt so comfortable in his ignorance that the outside world was not significant enough to warrant attention. The elves, after all, stayed in the forest, and they knew everything.

He quickly realized that if he could be this wrong about the Great Plains, then the world at large had a lot more in store for him.

Another mistake Cyrus made was to assume their first and only destination was Lucifan. He felt this mistake wasn't his fault, because Lucifan was all the amazons talked about, along with jokes about Adelpha's lover and children. It was only natural, he thought, to jump to that conclusion. Then a small farm with an old house and less-old barn popped into distant view, and the amazons marched straight toward it. That's when Cyrus knew something was off because all the other farms they'd spied in the distance had been avoided.

As they approached, Cyrus conjured an image he had seen often over the past few months. Although the sizes of the homesteads varied from rich to poor, Cyrus found their general construction and layout to be the same. Surrounded by row crops, a lone house would capitalize the tallest hill in the area. The house and barn would be made of the thin, fragile wood that struggled to grow in the perpetual drought that plagued these lands. Despite this shabby construction, though, Cyrus always detected a sense of pride among the people of the Great Plains. He had seen it in the humans as well as in the halflings that burrowed their homes into the sides of hills. They didn't wallow in self-pity or blame others; they just worked hard and did their best, and as far as Cyrus could tell, they were also exceptionally friendly. He had quickly decided that although the landscape of the Great Plains left much to be desired, he liked the people.

The farm they approached now had a covered back porch with a lone, dark figure slouching in an old wooden chair. Upon seeing the approaching crowd, the man raised his head and shouted something unintelligible at this distance. A moment later, three boys dashed out of the nearby barn—the oldest not many years younger than Cyrus. They stared into the distance.

"Oh, my boys!" Adelpha cried, and a massive smile spread across her face.

Both she and the boys broke into a run across the fields, meeting in the middle where they leapt into each other's arms. Adelpha enclosed them all with a wide hug and kissed each one on the forehead. Cyrus was close enough now to hear the boys call her mother, and until that point, he had been smiling along with the other amazons at the unabashed displays of affection. Then envy crept in, and he had to look away. He didn't want his pain to spoil the mood.

"William, look at you," Adelpha went on. "You're getting so tall! You'll be taller than your father, I know it."

"Not taller than Uncle, though," William, the oldest, replied and laughed.

"Oh please, no one is taller than him. And George, you're getting so strong now. Look at those shoulders!"

"I got them from you," George, the second oldest, replied with excitement, then looked confused when she and William laughed.

The youngest couldn't have been but five years old, and he had been heedlessly shouting for Adelpha's attention regardless of any conversation she was trying to have with the others. Adelpha finally caved to his cries and picked him up in a massive hug, which he returned by squeezing his arms around her neck. He let her go when she put him down and crouched to his height.

"Well, that was unexpected," Adelpha laughed. "John, I didn't think you'd remember me."

"He doesn't," William smiled. "We've just been telling him all month long that Mother is coming, so he's gotten all excited because we were excited."

John looked embarrassed and folded his arms around his back.

"Aw, just wanted to be like your older brothers, huh?" Adelpha said and kissed John's forehead. "That's okay. Maybe you'll be old enough to remember me next time."

The door on the old house swung open, and a tall, lanky man with a bearded chin strode out. He wore a long, brown trench coat and donned a wide-brimmed hat. He paused to address the figure in the chair whom Cyrus could now see was a skinny old man that bore an uncanny resemblance to the tall standing one. The little boy, John, lit up with genuine excitement and spoiled the mystery.

"Father!" he shouted and started running. "Mother! She's here! Father! Look!"

The child bounded away, and the tall man stepped off the porch, letting his coat tails flap in the breeze. He lowered his head so that his hat wouldn't fly away, but then realized that blocked his view, so he took the hat off. He smiled warmly as he approached, and as Adelpha approached him. When they met, they embraced with a hug and a kiss that banished all remaining doubts in Cyrus that he was looking at anything other than the family he'd always dreamed about.

The man pulled his lips back, but only far enough to speak, and said, "Welcome back."

"Oh, it's good to be back," Adelpha replied, grinning from ear to ear.

"How's our daughter?"

"Which one?"

"The newest one. You didn't come back last year, and you don't have a baby with you now, so that means we have a new daughter. Is she strong? Healthy?"

"Healthy as any of them. Hungry, though. Very hungry."

The man's eyes twinkled at the wonders of life and kissed Adelpha again, and when they pulled away, she nestled her head under his bearded chin. For the first time, the man looked past Adelpha at the approaching amazons. He didn't see anything of note until his eyes settled on the outsiders. Emy had altered her appearance to look like a normal human woman, but she couldn't change the gown she wore, which stood out from the usual amazon attire of green-brown leather vests and skirts. Oh, and there was Cyrus.

"Adelpha," the man said.

"Yes, Abe?"

"Who is that?"

Adelpha turned, though she knew exactly whom Abe was talking about. Before she could reply, the screen door flew open and banged against the side of the house. A massive figure emerged, taller even than Abe and so wide that it had to turn sideways and duck to fit through the door. As it stepped outside, the raised porch creaked and strained under the weight, and Cyrus balked in apprehension at what hulking monstrosity had appeared.

Then it stepped into the light, and Cyrus saw it was only a man—if not the largest man he'd ever seen. He had a huge, thick brown beard, wild unkempt hair, and in his hand, he carried an absurdly large hammer.

Also, he looked pissed when his eyes fell on the disguised figure of Emy.

"Damn it," Emy whispered and sighed.

"What?" Cyrus said nervously. "Who is that? And why does he look like he wants to murder you?"

"Nicholas," she replied. "I kind of promised I would never come here."

"Kind of promised? What did you do? And why are you so bad at getting people to like you?"

Emy glowered in reply and shook her head. Cyrus eased up, getting the sense that although an argument was approaching, it wouldn't turn into a physical fight. Emy was too calm for that.

Nicholas strode out to where Adelpha and Abe were still embracing, arriving just as the amazon group did. An all too awkward silence followed as both Abe and Nicholas took turns flipping their gazes from Cyrus to Emy, demanding answers with nothing but narrowed brows and tense shoulders.

"Well, Abe," Adelpha began apologetically. "My love, listen. That man there is Cyrus. You remember that name, don't you? Belen's son. I'll explain everything, but that other woman there isn't actually human. She's—"

"A rakshasa," Nicholas finished.

Everyone but Emy balked. Adelpha was the first to recover.

"Of course," she said. "I forgot she mentioned that you saved her. I should have known you'd recognize her—"

"Oh yeah, I know her," Nicholas answered. "I did more than save her. How do you think she got to this half of the world, huh? It only cost me my freedom. What are you doing here, Emy, and just how much trouble have you brought with you?"

A new wave of understanding swept over Abe's face. Although it appeared he had never met Emy, he certainly knew her name. As his focus was drawn away from Cyrus, Abe took in the larger picture. Emy was wanted by Takeo Karaoshi, the Dark Lord, and that meant trouble was coming. Abe's gaze fell on his three young sons then darted back to Adelpha.

"I can explain," she said.

"Please," he begged. "Please do."

* * *

The rest of the day was gobbled up by lengthy storytelling and relentless questioning. Abe and Nicholas learned what Emy had been up to, how Cyrus had been roped in, and why Adelpha and the other amazons had chosen to involve themselves. Nicholas was particularly demanding of Emy once her plan to seek the angel was revealed. He wanted to know how she'd come up with this plan and how she'd decided to seek Cyrus out, and when she said, 'Krunk,' Nicholas groaned and shook his head. Almost none of it made sense to Cyrus, who quickly realized that he had been inserted into a long and detailed history, filled with complex relationships.

He felt like an intruder.

For some time there, Cyrus thought that Abe and Nicholas were going to demand that he and Emy leave at once. When Aiguo's name dropped, Nicholas' eyes popped, and Cyrus grasped the full extent of the danger. It spoke volumes that a man of Nicholas' size would appear that worried about a name.

"I've already thought it out, my love," Adelpha explained to Abe. "There's no danger to us or our children. I'll stay here, but in the morning, Cyrus and Emy will go with the rest of the amazons to Lucifan. Aiguo will never even know they were here. And besides, you know he won't touch this place."

"Because I'm here?" Nicholas growled.

"It's sacred ground," Adelpha replied sternly. "So long as he doesn't have a reason to come here, he won't. Takeo will tolerate Belen's murder, but Aiguo will think twice before crossing this line. You've brought more danger to this house than I ever have."

"Adelpha, please," Abe cut in. "He's my brother."

"There is no sacred ground to Takeo," Nicholas replied through clenched teeth. "He's crossed every line he ever made. Trust me."

"Yes, but Emily is buried here," she said. "This is her family. You think Aiguo has been given permission by Takeo to intrude?"

"But how do you know that Aiguo doesn't have express permission by Takeo to do whatever is necessary to remove Emy's head? In that case, intruding would be considered necessary. Emy, look at me. Answer honestly, do you think you're safe here?"

Emy met Nicholas' gaze without flinching, but she did drop her eyes before replying.

"No," Emy said.

Silence followed. They were crowded around the porch while the sun dipped in the background. The majority of the amazons were setting up shelter inside the barn, while the children and the old man were inside the house. The oldest son, William, came out and lit a lamp hanging off the back of the porch, doing a terrible job of trying to stay hidden. Undoubtedly, their conversation had been overheard. They had been loud enough.

The silence, however, weighed heavy on Cyrus. He could tell by the looks he was getting from Nicholas and Abe that neither man thought Cyrus should be involved in this conversation. Adelpha had insisted he come, though. Cyrus decided to make the most of it.

"We'll go, then," Cyrus said, then continued once he had everyone's attention. "Not tomorrow, and not with the amazons. Emy and I will leave right now, tonight. I mean, this is all my fault anyway. Emy wanted to go to Khaz Mal, and it was my decision to join the amazons. We shouldn't be here. Abraham, I want you to know that I never intended to put you or your family in danger. This isn't your fight."

Abe and Nicholas shared a gaze but said nothing. They didn't appear happy at Cyrus' suggestion, either. Not that Cyrus needed their approval. He waited out of respect for his elders, as he'd always done, but as far as he was concerned, the decision was made.

"Actually, that's the best idea for everyone," Emy said, hesitating. "Not only will we remove the danger to all of you, but Aiguo will waste precious time trying to seek us out. If he tracks the amazons to here, he could make the incorrect assumption that we're hiding out and spend days watching the farm."

The silence continued, but now Abe appeared confused, and Adelpha cocked an eyebrow at Emy.

"You get used to it," Nicholas told them.

"What?" the rakshasa said.

"Why is it that whenever we agree, it's for different reasons?" Cyrus asked her.

"Are you implying that my reasons are wrong?" Emy bit back.

"Um, well, yeah. I suggested we leave to remove them from danger. You suggested we leave in the hopes that the danger will stay here."

"That's not what I said," Emy snarled, forgetting she was still in human form. "What I suggested made the most tactical sense."

"Stop," Abe shouted. "Just stop. No one is leaving until the morning. I need time to think this—"

Emy straightened so fast that it made Abe pause. Her eyes went wide, and her breath caught in her throat. Before anyone could say a word, she lashed out, grabbed Cyrus by the wrist and drug him up the porch steps and into the house. Once inside, she crouched down below the window and pulled Cyrus down, too. Her grip was like iron, and Cyrus was too shocked to resist.

"He's here," she whispered.

However, in the silence of her sudden departure, that whisper carried. Adelpha, Abe, and Nicholas, still standing in their spots, turned out towards the darkness as the sound of quiet feet pacing through tall grass grew loud enough to be heard by normal human ears.

Nicholas grabbed his hammer with both hands. Adelpha pulled her bow into position and grabbed an arrow. Abe cocked his elbow back, sweeping his long coat behind him to reveal the uniquely shaped holsters that held a small L-shaped tool of metal that Cyrus had never seen. It took a moment, but Cyrus soon realized these were the dangerous six-shooters the elves had once told him about. That meant Abe was a gunslinger. Cyrus could hardly believe it.

Momentarily, a lone figure emerged from the darkness. He was of average height and build with dark brown hair drawn up into a queue. He had a firm jaw and small ears but was otherwise neither ugly nor handsome. The wall Cyrus and Emy hid behind was made of wooden planks that had cracked and shrunk with age, and Cyrus sneaked a look through the narrow gaps. As he gazed upon this man, he could have sworn he'd never seen him before, yet his gut said there was something familiar in the way the man smiled. The way Cyrus felt, it was like he should know this man, yet his mind strangely claimed he'd never set eyes on him before. Then suddenly everything came flooding back to him.

"Good to see you, Nicholas," Aiguo said.

Chapter 13

"What a surprise," Nicholas responded. "The first thing you said to me was a lie."

Aiguo chuckled warmly. He folded his arms behind his back and straightened up, the smile on his face never flinching. That said, he kept his distance on the outskirts of the light's reach, no more than a pace away from shadowy concealment. Neither of the trio made to approach him, but as Aiguo's hands disappeared from sight, Abe drew an hand close to his guns.

"Relax, Abraham. I only came to talk," Aiguo said, bringing his hands back into view and holding them out. "And yes, I know your name. We've never met, but my lord was sure to tell me in great detail about you and your family. Judging by your stance, I believe you've heard of me, too."

"Nothing flattering, that's for sure," Abe muttered back, the wind carrying his words.

"Oh, on the contrary. You three seem ready to run for the hills just at the sight of me. That's very flattering. Or perhaps I'm missing something? Perhaps you know I'm not alone tonight. Perhaps you've been expecting me. And let's face it, how could you possibly know to expect me unless you know why I'm here?"

Aiguo paused and, when no reply was offered, his smile faded.

"Let's drop the pleasantries, then," he said. "Where is she?"

"Just missed her, I'm afraid," Nicholas answered. "My brother here is quite rude and inhospitable, as you've seen. He sent her and the werewolf boy on their merry way the second he realized you were following. Nothing we could do to convince him otherwise."

Aiguo scoffed and shook his head.

"Please give me more credit than that," he said. "Regardless of our shared hatred for each other, Nicholas, the least we can do is extend a bit of professional courtesy. I have among my crew a tracker from Savara who specialized in hunting down runaway slaves. Do you have any idea how hard it is to track someone in a desert, through ever shifting sands? To her, the Great Plains is child's play. I know the rakshasa is here, so when I asked where she was, what I meant was, is she in the barn or the house?"

Abe and Adelpha shared a glance, then looked to Nicholas. The big man raised his head and scratched at his beard, sighing. Cyrus couldn't tell if he was trying to buy time or just thinking of what to say. Cyrus wanted to do something. Anger boiled within him, and he hated sitting still while others suffered on his account. However, Emy's grip on him was like iron.

Nicholas sighed and finally replied.

"Aiguo, I'm going to put this as simply as I possibly can: Piss off."

Another chuckle was the reply, and the smile returned.

"Come on now, Nicholas," Aiguo replied. "Be rational. You don't owe that creature anything. You did your duty to Krunk and shipped her out of Juatwa. It was her stupid decision to come running to here of all places. Don't let her bad choices put you and your family in harm's way."

Until this point, Nicholas had kept one foot on the ground and one foot raised up on the porch, leaning casually over his bent knee. Now he put both feet on the ground and faced Aiguo. It gave Cyrus some slight pleasure to see Aiguo flinch, even with so much distance between them.

"Is that a threat?" Nicholas asked.

"Now, now," Aiguo replied. "Don't do anything you're going to regret. I've already warned you that I'm not alone tonight, and we both know that I'm not alone ever, if you know what I mean. Lord Takeo Karaoshi's shadow falls upon the world. There is no hiding from him, and soon, there will be no running either. Please, Nicholas, you know that I have no interest in you or your family, and the Dark Lord shares this view. However, he wants that creature, and if you stand between him and what he wants . . . well, you've already crossed that bridge, haven't you?"

Nicholas had his back turned to Cyrus, so the only thing Cyrus could see was the way Nicholas' shoulders tensed at that comment. Cyrus pulled against Emy's grip, wanting to act on the anger that welled within him, but she didn't budge.

"Let go," he growled. "He knows we're here."

"Do you want a knife in your skull, you idiot?" she bit back. "Keep down."

"He wants you dead, not me."

"You want to take that risk? What are you going to do anyway?"

Cyrus paused, clenching his teeth to the point where they hurt. He did so without thinking. Whenever he looked upon Aiguo, all he could see was his mother's burnt flesh and dead lips. All his pain and agony came rushing back, how everything had been ripped away from him. His whole werewolf clan was dead and for what? Pointless, stupid, senseless. Even beyond his personal feelings, the sheer cruelty in Aiguo's act chilled him to his bones. All he could think about was how Ralph had described Belen's death. How Aiguo had given the order without pause, without thought, so easily and mercilessly massacring people who had never done him any wrong.

"I don't know," Cyrus admitted.

"Then at bare minimum, wait until you do," she advised.

He stopped fighting her.

"Listen," Aiguo spoke up, breaking the silence. "Abraham, Adelpha, come now. I know you two surely don't want to rouse Takeo's wrath by harboring this fugitive. Talk some sense into your younger brother, or don't—just hand her over and ignore his dim-witted views. Either way, the result is the same. Once I have her, I'll disappear, and you'll never see me again. Everyone wins this way."

Abraham kept his hand close to his hip and raised his chin. Defiance stained his stance, but before he spoke, he looked to Adelpha. She gave him a nod, and then he spoke confidently.

"Maybe I want Takeo to show his face," Abe said, none too kindly.

Aiguo laughed loudly. Abe swallowed hard.

"I thought we were done lying," Aiguo said, pausing to laugh again. "Abe, please. No one wants that. I was with the Dark Lord when he landed in Lucifan. We were greeted by a vampire and a small army, and I saw the fear Takeo's mere presence generated in them. That bespoke intelligence on their part, not cowardice. When I say that you should hand over the rakshasa, I'm not issuing a threat, but a warning.

"I'll tell you what, I'll make this easy. Don't hand her over. Simply turn her out. Let her run. You're probably realizing by now that you can't shelter her forever, and if she's listening to me, then she knows that, too. Let her make a break for it, and who knows? Maybe she'll get away. You can sleep soundly knowing you did all that you could to help, because if you keep her here, Takeo will come, and he will not be as kind as me."

Abe swallowed again and looked to Adelpha. The defiance in his stance had melted away, as had Nicholas' shoulders dropped. Adelpha reached out and pressed a hand to Abe's back, seemingly taking away the burden of responding.

"He's right," Abe whispered, helplessly.

"We can't," Nicholas said through clenched teeth.

"I didn't say—"

"I'll handle this," Adelpha whispered, cutting them off.

She stepped forward and raised her voice.

"What about Cyrus?" she said.

Aiguo frowned and shrugged.

"As I said," he replied, "my lord has no interest in him. A few of my men aren't too happy with the stunts he pulled back in Angor, but if you hand over the rakshasa, all can be forgiven."

"Give us the night to think about it," Adelpha said.

"I want an answer now."

Adelpha had started to turn away, but when he said that, she froze. She turned back to Aiguo and drew to full height.

"Excuse me," she said. "Let's get one thing straight, you wretched little blight of a man. You haven't just trespassed and threatened Nicholas' family, but mine, too. His nephews are my sons, whom I carried for nine months and birthed, and then carried again back to their father. In that barn are two dozen amazons who have no doubt been listening to this conversation and armed themselves for a fight. Next to me is a gunslinger who can put a bullet through your head before you can blink, and let's not even get into what will happen when Emy decides she's going to fight instead of die. Oh, and I'm sure Nicholas and Cyrus will want some revenge, too.

"If we're going to be honest with each other, then you ought to realize that you have no power tonight. If violence breaks out, unless you're hiding forty heavily armored soldiers out there, you will be slaughtered. Our losses will be so minimal that we won't even break a sweat digging a mass grave to bury all your corpses in before the banshees arrive. Plus, we could still hand Emy over to your master with no consequences, because if I know anything about Takeo, it's that he doesn't give a damn what happens to you.

"So, I'm going to say this one last time. You will give us the night to think about it, and in exchange, I will let you live. Is that clear?"

Aiguo stood still. He didn't break eye contact with her, but he did hesitate. Abe and Nicholas shared a glance and smirked. Aiguo swallowed hard enough to make his throat bounce.

"Fine," he replied. "One night."

Then he faded into the darkness.

* * *

Not much sleep was had that night. Somewhere in a fit of suppressed rage and anxiety, Cyrus drifted off, but he woke early before the sun rose. He left the dark, concealed basement where he and Emy had been instructed to hide for the night and ventured onto the back porch, taking a seat on the last wooden step. He stared up at the sky and contemplated what he had gotten himself into.

"A leaf in a storm," he muttered.

That's how he felt, directionless and frail, caught in a world of chaos that was not of his making.

It baffled him how much his life had been upended in such a short time, and losing his mother was only part of it. He was also in a new place, with new people, but more than that had changed, too. He tried to put a finger on it and stumbled across the realization of how sheltered he'd been. In Angor, traveling between a broken home and a foreign conclave, his world had been small and his problems well defined. He hadn't grasped it then, of course. He'd known there was a grander scale beyond the forest, but he could never have predicted the effect its presence would have on him.

Here he was, caught in a battle that not only involved the entire world, but had been going on for a generation, and he felt like he barely understood the half of it. In truth, he wondered if the people he was fighting with even knew the full truth—or if anyone did.

Yet he was trapped. Like a leaf, he was lost to forces beyond his control. He felt locked into traveling with Emy, seeking out this

124

angel, and trying desperately to survive being hunted for it. Could he even walk away at this point if he wanted to? Hadn't Aiguo said that Cyrus had made himself an enemy?

"Damn this," Cyrus whispered. "I didn't want this. I didn't want any of this."

But what excuse was that? He didn't consider himself a philosopher or a poet, but wasn't all of life this way? He hadn't wanted a lot of the things that had been forced on him. He hadn't wanted to be a strange type of werewolf. He hadn't wanted an abusive stepfather. He hadn't wanted to be bullied as a child. Come to think of it, as far as he could tell, his entire life had been one constant stream of him reacting to things that had been forced upon him.

And when that struck him, it hit hard.

"Oh good, you're awake," a deep voice said from behind him, followed by the heavy creak of wood.

Cyrus turned to see the towering figure of Nicholas standing in the doorway of the house. The man was shirtless and didn't flinch in the cool morning wind or under the surprised gaze of Cyrus at seeing such a hairy chest. Nicholas could have doubled as a werewolf.

"Stay there," Nicholas said.

He closed the porch door. Cyrus heard some old wood creaking, then saw the man emerge once more. He'd thrown a loose shirt on and had strapped his large hammer to his back. Cyrus leaned back, wary.

"You got a weapon?" Nicholas grumbled.

"Do I need one?"

"Depends. Are you blind or stupid? Last night a man showed up looking to kill you, now here you sit on the back porch, alone and exposed. From now on, you better sleep with a weapon, you understand? Now go get that sword I saw you carrying earlier and come with me."

Cyrus sat still, defiantly, resenting that feeling of being a leaf again. Yet, like the wind, Nicholas seemed unperturbed at the resistance of one so insignificant. He towered over Cyrus, unyielding. Cyrus sighed, stood up, and went inside. He returned with his sword.

"Are we going to fight or something?" Cyrus asked.

"Shut up and follow me."

Nicholas trudged off away from the house and the barn, not bothering to check that Cyrus was in tow. The sheer arrogance of it irked Cyrus, but he followed anyway, realizing he couldn't fight the wind just yet. He needed to know where he was going first.

They traveled a short way down the hill from the house to a small bluff, and there Nicholas stopped before a dead patch of dirt. Cyrus didn't pay much attention to the anomaly at first, but then its uniqueness jumped out at him.

In his short time in the Great Plains, Cyrus had quickly come to realize just how homogenous the landscape was. Low hills and yellow grass as far as the eye could see. Green was not seen but rarely on the tips of small leaves that hung on the scattered, thin trees that dotted the land, and rare also, was bare dirt, because the stiff, tall grass out here grew well in this place of infinite sun and finite rain. Yet here, right before him, was a perfect oval of barren soil. The grass grew hardy and strong on all sides and then stopped in a clearly defined line. It wasn't a large oval, though, only about the size of a person. Nicholas' gaze rested on that dirt, hard and thoughtful.

Cyrus blinked at it. He waited for Nicholas to say something. The silence drew out.

"Um—"

"I said shut up, boy," Nicholas interrupted. "I'm trying to think."

Cyrus suppressed the urge to point out how rude that was, and that the elves would never tolerate that sort of thing. It seemed that living in a society with manners was yet another privilege he'd taken for granted. Silence drew out, then Nicholas took a deep breath.

"You've noticed the dirt here, right?" the man said.

Cyrus looked at him sullenly.

"You can talk now," Nicholas said.

"Yes," Cyrus replied. "Obviously."

"Well, what you don't know is that this here is a grave. My sister is buried here. Next to her, right there on the opposite side of us, is where they buried my mother."

Cyrus went still and all his anger melted away. Embarrassment fell over him.

"Oh," he mumbled. "I'm sorry. I didn't—"

Nicholas cut him off with a raised hand.

"Save the apology. I'm still trying to think," he said. "I've never been the best with words, but I've got something important to tell you. If I don't get this right, you could die."

Cyrus balked, his hands coming away from his side. He couldn't help but reach for his sword. Nicholas saw the movement and shook his head.

"Not right now, you dolt," he said.

Nicholas groaned, reached up, and pulled his long hair back in a way that stretched the skin on his face.

"You know whom my sister was by now, right?"

Cyrus nodded, then answered, "She saved Lucifan from an invading rakshasa, and she was close with Takeo. He, um, took a turn for the worst after she died."

"Something like that," Nicholas said. "Many years ago, he and I stood right here. My sister hadn't been buried for long, and we were all still coming to terms with it. I thought of him as a brother back then—maybe in some ways I still do. My mother was alive but struggling like the rest of us. I wanted to go out and see the world, again, become a legend, a hero, escape the pit of misery this grave brought me, all that youthful nonsense. I didn't give a damn about what I'd been given, only about what I could get. Instead of realizing that the pain I was going through was ten times worse for my mother, I only focused on myself, and I left with Takeo and two others to change the course of history.

"I wish I could say for the better, but that would be a lie.

"I'll not make excuses. I didn't do my part to change Takeo before he turned down the wrong path. I thought Gavin would take care of that, and, in the meantime, I fed off Takeo's glory. I should have realized what my goals were costing me. Instead, I lost my best friends, and when I came home a failure, I found I'd lost my mother, too."

His eyes flickered to a spot beside the barren soil, where he'd said his mother was buried. Cyrus let his gaze fall.

"What I'm trying to say here, Cyrus," Nicholas continued, "is that I was headstrong and selfish in my youth. I wanted what I wanted, and I never considered the cost of those things until it was too late. I didn't listen to anybody but myself, and I was the biggest damned idiot that was ever born. Now here I am, begging for scraps at the table of a brother who does his best to hide his resentment and trying to play uncle to a group of kids who treat me like an outsider."

Nicholas stopped and shook his head. He closed his eyes and buried his face in an open palm.

"What am I saying?" he mumbled. "Listen, all I want is for you not to end up like me. You got that?"

Cyrus didn't say it, but he understood only one thing so far: this man was bad with words.

"I feel like you're trying to help me," Cyrus broached.

"Exactly!" Nicholas said. "Yes, exactly, thank you. You're listening. Alright, let me explain the plan today, okay? Last night, while you and Emy stayed in the basement, I hatched a plan with my brother and Adelpha. We're all going to Lucifan."

"Wait, what?"

"All of us, even little John. Well, not the old man. My father's not doing too well; he hardly remembers who he is these days. He'll have to stay behind, but it's what he would want anyway. Thankfully, when we all leave, Aiguo will follow. He won't waste his time with Father, though a part of me wishes he would. Poor old man ain't really there anymore, as much as it pains me to say it. However, the rest of us are going to Lucifan, today."

"No, that's not what I meant," Cyrus said. "You hatched a plan without me? Without Emy? You didn't think to get our input? With all due respect, you do realize that we're the ones being hunted, right?"

"You can stick your 'due respect' where the sun don't shine, boy," Nicholas bit back. "As you've seen, Aiguo will kill anyone to succeed. If you and the amazons left for Lucifan, Aiguo might try to capture one of my nephews to get Emy to come back, then kill him whether she returns or not. So, we're all going to Lucifan, and my brother won't return home with his family until he can travel with the amazons safely. By then, you and Emy will be long gone, and

Aiguo will have no choice but to follow you. That's how we keep the children safe. Got it?"

They locked gazes for a moment. Being tall, Cyrus wasn't used to looking up at people, but Nicholas' height was on a whole different level. Cyrus stared up, knowing he'd lost this argument, yet also understanding that he wasn't completely wrong. He was determined to carve out at least some measurement of respect.

"I didn't say it was a bad plan," Cyrus said. "I just wished that decisions affecting my life had included my opinion. Maybe I could have helped."

"You're that easily swayed, huh? You're worried about the children, too?"

"What kind of question is that? Of course, I am."

Nicholas sighed and shook his head, dropping eye contact in clear disappointment. Cyrus' anger dispersed into a cloud of confusion.

"Is," he started, stumbling. "Is there something wrong with that?"

"Listen, Cyrus," Nicholas said. "This is the reason I brought you out here. I could have told you the plan at the house, but I wanted to say this in private. A man's pride, especially a young man's pride, has a well-deserved reputation of getting in the way of his sense. I want you to think for a moment, think very hard about this situation, and about Takeo. You've witnessed first-hand Aiguo's cunning and cruelty, so it should speak volumes to you that I am more terrified of Takeo Karaoshi than I am of Aiguo Mein.

"You see, I bowed out of the fight against Takeo because I understood his inevitability. I did my best to dissuade Emy from her goals but, well, Takeo is out for her blood, so she has little choice. Also, she's well equipped to handle this. The rakshasa race is something else, boy. Her body is so efficient, she could drink seawater in the desert and stay hydrated. Her fur coat will keep her warm in the snows of the north. She can change her appearance, she'll never bleed to death, and even if she's caught off guard, she won't be helpless, not with her strength and speed. Best of all, she'll live for hundreds of years, so all she has to do is avoid Takeo, and he will die of old age before she's lived beyond her prime. Her greatest strength, though, is that she understands Takeo, what he will do, and what it will take to survive against him.

"You do not.

"I realized this when you suggested running off by yourself to save us. Stupid idea, boy. Takeo would pounce on that a mistake like a dragon hunting a goblin. I mean, it's noble to be concerned about a child's safety, but you'll find reality far less kind. Takeo once leveraged a whole city of children to take one person's head. Could you match that, boy? No, so I want you to listen and understand when I say this. Cyrus, you do not have the stomach for this fight.

"After you help Emy find this angel, do yourself and your dead mother a favor and go back to Angor. If you don't, you will run up against Takeo, and that only ends one way."

Nicholas dropped a hand to the barren soil before them and said no more.

Cyrus gazed at it. His stomach churned slowly, but he couldn't put what he was feeling into words for a few moments. When they finally came to him, he shook his head.

"I can't believe it," Cyrus said. "I offer to risk my life to save someone else's, and I'm considered the weak one. What sort of world do you live in where that makes sense? Perhaps Takeo has already won.

"Thanks for the advice."

Cyrus turned and left before Nicholas could say any more. There wasn't anything left to discuss.

Chapter 14

Cyrus spent the first part of the trip to Lucifan in silence. Nicholas' speech had bothered him more than he cared to admit, and it took some time to figure out why. It reminded him of his stepfather.

Ralph hadn't just been cruel. He'd justified his cruelty as a necessary evil for some greater good. It went beyond hypocrisy to a sort of intentional destruction of morality. Over and over and over Cyrus had watched Ralph use his power to plague the lives of those in his care, and to what end? With every act of violence, Ralph would say it was for the best, yet year after year went by, and things only got worse. It was a stark contrast to the elves, who actively worked with each other every day to build a better place. People were happy there, and Cyrus wanted that. The evidence was just so clear, so astoundingly clear.

When Cyrus had acted in violence once towards the elves, to hit back at his bullies, he'd watched as that one act had taken his situation from bad to worse. Things hadn't improved until he had done the hard job of putting the lives of others before himself. He saved his mother, and his former bullies became his friends. A person didn't achieve anything of worth through cruelty and violence, and anyone with half a brain and a semblance of humanity ought to recognize that.

But no. It seemed like the world around him had been sucked into a battle to destroy itself, and Cyrus just couldn't believe it—didn't want to believe it.

He didn't get long to stew the thought over, though. With their already large party grown larger thanks to the Stout family, conversation was inevitable. Or rather, Adelpha was inevitable.

"I swear, that Aiguo has no idea how lucky he is," she vented, striding alongside Cyrus. "I'll have you know that in my younger days, I wouldn't have given him the chance to walk away. We'd have buried his generic face and slave-hunting goons before sun-up. I'm not blowing smoke here, either, let me tell you. When I was a little older than you and I'd just met Emily, we were set upon in Lucifan by some ogres. We all survived, but my sisters and I took our revenge to the fullest by slaughtering those behind it: a foreign ambassador and his whole crew docked in the Lucifan harbor. I'm telling you; I was not a person to piss off back then.

"But, well, times change. I lost sisters then, and I've lost sisters since. Every rash decision I made put those I loved at risk. It was different when I was younger; life was a battle, and fighting was worth dying for. Now though? Now I have children, and my friends have children, and I just don't know. It's not the same. I think about things now. For example, I wanted to put an arrow in Aiguo's head that night, but I stopped because I had to think, was it worth it? At the end of that fight, if I lay dead in Abe's arms, or he in mine, or our children were left without parents, would it be worth it? No. Aiguo is only a symptom. Takeo is the disease. If we'd put Aiguo down, it would only be a matter of time before Takeo came, and there'd be nothing to do at that point. This is the better option. In Lucifan, you two can sneak off in a hundred different ways in a hundred different directions, and Aiguo can be left stranded in pursuit of nothing but wind.

"You know, you're a good listener, Cyrus. Has anyone ever told you that?"

"Huh?" Cyrus said. "Oh, oh yeah. Thank you."

"You're not angry with me?"

"For what?"

"For not killing Aiguo. I know you want him dead; anyone would after what he did to your mother. You're not angry at me for letting him walk away?"

Cyrus thought about that. He'd never considered that he had justification to be angry with Adelpha. Should he be angry? The answer bounced back soon enough.

"No," Cyrus replied. "I don't expect others to fight my battles. What Aiguo did is between him and me, and that's the way it should be settled. Not that I can expect him to face me one on one in a circle."

"Hm?"

"It's a werewolf thing. The ultimate form of law is a trial by combat. A challenge is issued, two enter, one walks away. That's how I got my mother home."

Adelpha raised an eyebrow.

"Efficient," she said. "We amazons don't have that, but it sounds like something we should. There is some poetic beauty there."

A memory flashed through Cyrus' head: blood flowing from his chest, burnt flesh, and his jaws locked around Ralph's throat, tasting fur. He remembered the adrenaline, he remembered the elation of victory afterwards, but he remembered that moment the most. The moment when he could have crushed Ralph's throat but didn't. He remembered proving right there, to himself as much as everyone else, that he wasn't just the better fighter, but the better man.

The honorable man.

"I'm not sure," Cyrus said. "I wish it didn't have to come to that."

"Don't we all. It would be nice if everything could be solved with a handshake and an exchange of words. If only people like Takeo and Aiguo didn't exist, right?"

Cyrus huffed.

"Right," he replied.

Someone whistled, and Cyrus perked up to see whom. At the front of the pack, he spied Octavia and Emy waving at him. Cyrus gave Adelpha a respectful nod and dashed to meet up with them.

"You looked like you needed rescuing," Octavia called out, smiling as Cyrus joined them.

"This time wasn't so bad," he said. "She means well."

"It's clear she cares about you," Emy said. "If I didn't know any better, I'd say she was trying to be your surrogate mother."

"Oh, that's just an amazon thing," Octavia replied. "We like to think of ourselves as one big family, so anyone older than you can be thought of as your mother."

Cyrus warmed and smiled.

"Well, that sounds awesome," he said. "Everyone should be so lucky."

"It has its drawbacks," Octavia replied, shrugging. "In a world like that, no one minds their own business. If you and your friends get in trouble, it's the whole village's problem. I'm sure you didn't have to deal with that."

Cyrus cut himself off before he could reply with, 'I didn't have any friends.'

"Nope," he said. "I was on my own for months at a time growing up. That and, well, both of my villages kind of expected trouble from me. That made it pretty easy to get in and out of."

"Oh, did you do anything crazy?" Octavia asked, grinning. "What's the craziest thing you did?"

Cyrus made a show of thinking it over, but the answer was easy.

"I charged a bugbear once and attacked it," he said.

"No!" Octavia gasped.

Emy's ears perked, and she cocked her head at Cyrus.

"I swear," he said, glowing a little from the attention. "I was following two elves on a full moon night, and they made the mistake of stumbling into one. I dove out to save one of the elves from getting crushed, and then the three of us got locked into a fight with it. I would have died if one of them hadn't put an arrow through the beast's eye. That elf actually became my best friend."

Cyrus stopped there as he remembered Katar. It dawned on him that they might never see each other again, and that made him sad. Cyrus swore under his breath. Why did he keep doing this to himself?

"The perfect trifecta," Emy noted. "Crazy, stupid, and brave."

"Gosh, I want to have a story like that," Octavia said, then her face lit up with another smile. "Oh, oh, we're getting close!"

"Close?" Cyrus said.

"To Lucifan. We have to be. The others told me it's only a day's walk from the Stout farm, and also, you can smell the salt in the air. They told me to watch for that. We've got to be getting close."

Cyrus breathed deep and noted the change. The air had cooled, too, and it reminded Cyrus of the ocean waves he would visit on Angor's western end. He seemed to recall being told that Lucifan lay along the coast, but all he could remember was how grand Lucifan was supposed to be. The elves had explained to him that Lucifan was the largest city in the world, but Cyrus wasn't too keen on picturing what a city was supposed to look like. Angor contained nothing but trees, mountains, and tents, which hadn't given him much to conjure up a 'land of stone.'

Reaching the top of the next hill fixed that.

Lucifan sat at the bottom of a slowly descending hill all along its western half, as if the city's sheer weight had pressed it into the ground. The city molded against the shore in a giant, dense half circle, presenting a vast swath of civilization at the point where yellow plains met ocean blue. Countless square stone buildings, tall as Angor trees, filled Cyrus' vision in loosely defined rows, pressed tighter together than he thought possible. The smallest buildings formed the outskirts, and they rose in height towards the center where a massive spire shot up from the ground in what could only be a monument to man's defiance of gravity. Even at this distance, Cyrus could see the crowds of people filling the streets, flooding into and out of the city, while a fleet of wooden ships with white sails clogged the harbor. In short, it took Cyrus' breath away.

"Wow," he said.

"Amazing, isn't it?" Emy said with a smirk, watching Cyrus carefully. "Humans can do quite a bit if they cooperate."

"I'll admit it," Octavia said. "It looks better in person. We have a number of artists back in Themiscyra, and Lucifan is a common thing to paint. I've seen lots of portraits of this place, but wow. It's amazing to think that so many people and creatures live here in harmony."

"Oh, I wouldn't say harmony," Emy said. "The knights exist for a reason."

"Don't tell me anymore," Octavia demanded. "I want to see the rest of it for myself."

They pushed on down the hill, descending towards a well-trodden path leading into what was clearly a main thoroughfare through the city, judging by the width of the road. Cyrus caught a glimpse of his next major shock: Lucifan's streets were paved with stone.

"Well, I'll be damned," he whispered. "They even put stone on the ground."

"The founders of this city spared no expense," Emy said. "And this is only one of the many projects the Angels did for the good of the people."

"That's just," Cyrus paused, but couldn't find the words to continue.

"Equal parts selfless and selfish? On one hand, to do something so grand to advance people's lives by only a small amount seems amazing, yet the sheer defiance of the natural world seems pompous?"

Cyrus shook his head and looked at Emy.

"Yes," he said. "That's exactly it."

"It gets better," she replied.

And it did. Cyrus had been too distracted to notice at first, but as his eyes scanned building after building, his attention eventually fell upon a gargantuan statue in the city's harbor. Just at the shore's edge, overlooking the ocean, a massive work of stone towered over all. The statue had been shaped to look like a human male in exceptional physical condition, wearing nothing but a short skirt of some sort and a helmet that revealed its face in a 'T' shape.

Cyrus cocked his head at it.

"That's the colossus," Emy whispered, noting Cyrus' gaze. "It can move."

He jumped.

"Wait, that thing moves?" he stammered.

"It did, once upon a time," she replied. "Apparently there were three of them, and they roamed Lucifan as its eternal defenders. However, when Emily died, the last one stopped moving. All our hopes rest on this hunk of stone still being able to take orders."

Cyrus gazed at it appreciatively. He tried to imagine it moving, walking about, and he thought about the treants back home. Those creatures were made of wood, and yet they moved. Was it really so crazy that in other parts of the world stone could do the same?

As they approached the city, and the crowds grew in detail, Cyrus' wonder never waned. The sheer number of people baffled him, as did the towering buildings and the constant noise. People shouting, carts turning, feet shuffling, and not to mention the sights to see. No two people seemed to dress alike here. He saw people in colorful robes, layered vests, white shirts, or next to nothing at all. Some wore sandals or boots or something as simple as cloth wrapped around their feet. Women, and a few men, wore bits of metal hanging from their ears, neck, and fingers—a few even had metal in their noses, lips, and eyebrows. Cyrus was so caught up in the otherworldly experience of it all that it didn't dawn on him until far later that he should be downright terrified.

Cyrus was a werewolf, and tonight he was going to change in this city full of people.

Although Cyrus had never left Angor, he'd known, like any good werewolf, to fear normal humans. His kind was banished for a reason. Seeing all these people with swords and daggers hanging from their sides, Cyrus scooted up to Octavia and whispered to her.

"Where are we going?"

"The best place outside of Themiscyra, or so I'm told. One of the newer taverns built after the Battle of Lucifan. You'll see."

Cyrus gazed up at the late afternoon sun.

"And how long will that be? It's kind of important for me to know."

Octavia cocked an eyebrow at him and frowned. He couldn't blame her for forgetting he was a werewolf and tonight was a full moon. Tracking the cycles of the moon wasn't necessary for those who lived outside of Angor.

"We're close, boy," Nicholas said, coming up from behind. "Don't worry. Tavern's got rooms with locks and we can cover the windows."

Nicholas set a heavy hand on Cyrus' shoulder, and a bit of relief poured over the young man. Some streets later, they arrived at their destination: a sturdy, unmarked door with a wooden sign hanging over the top of it. On the sign was carved a large, unblinking eye with an hourglass shaped pupil. Cyrus frowned at it as Nicholas pushed him inside.

The amazons poured in like weary travelers returned home. They threw their gear on the floor, sighed, smiled, and greeted the tavern's only inhabitant with a chorus of cheers and gratuitous hugs. That inhabitant was an older lady with a brown apron and a limp, but she seemed not to notice her sharp contrast with those that had just arrived, and she greeted them with equal yet measured happiness. Cyrus learned her name was Margret, because he would have to be deaf not to hear all the amazons shouting her name. Margret paused when she saw the amazons had company, but one look at Adelpha and no questions were raised. Drinks were poured, food was served, and Nicholas took Cyrus upstairs. They selected a room, went inside, and Nicholas showed Cyrus how to lock it.

"Simple latch, you see?" he said. "You'll be fine."

"I can't believe I didn't think of this," Cyrus replied. "I mean, a city full of people? It should have occurred to me. But then again, I didn't know what 'full' meant. I mean, I could hardly walk! How does this place have enough food to feed so many people?"

"Well, sometimes it doesn't," Nicholas mumbled. "Listen, I wouldn't worry about tonight. Most people have only heard of werewolves in stories. They wouldn't know one if it licked them in the face. If we threw a long cloak over you, not a soul would bother you in the dead of night unless they intended to rob you, in which case you'd make them regret that decision."

Nicholas fastened and covered the windows, glanced around the room, and nodded in satisfaction.

"Gotta say, they did a nice job rebuilding this place after the old one burned down. And don't you worry about this city or its problems, Cyrus. We won't be here long. Early next morning, I'm taking you and Emy down to the docks and putting you on the first viking longship bound for The North. Emy will know how to keep your true selves hidden, even in a place as cramped as a ship, and I'll be sure to pick out a crew that knows you're friends of mine."

"Thank you," Cyrus said, honestly. "Really, thank you for all of this. And I'll take that advice you gave me to heart, though I think we'd be better off if you came with us."

Cyrus said that last part as an afterthought, a means to compliment what he perceived to be a man doing his level best to help a complete stranger. However, Nicholas stiffened, and his reply came out measured.

"Don't mention it," he said and left.

The noise from the street had dimmed as the sun set, but neither was quite finished yet. Cyrus took one last peek out the window and then laid himself out on one of the beds, stared at the ceiling, and waited for the change.

"What am I even doing?" he whispered.

He'd already established he was lost, cast adrift, aimless in a world driven hard by purpose. He sensed it in everyone around him. Emy could hardly have a normal conversation without her personal vendetta bubbling to the surface. Adelpha's love of family directed her every move. Nicholas, too, stewed upon something buried deep within him. Even that sick Aiguo man bled a lust for power that tainted the ground he walked on.

And that grave, that perfect oval of dead grass, hung over Cyrus like a dark cloud. There was something in it, a sacrifice, a love, a soul, that had struck a match. The world was on fire, and Cyrus was but a leaf drifting among the waves of heat, dodging the tendrils of flame.

"Perhaps he's right," Cyrus said, thinking of Nicholas. "Perhaps this isn't for me. Perhaps I should just go home."

Yet, when he said that, it didn't feel right. Home was supposed to be Angor, yet the word didn't bring back feelings of want like it used to. Without his mother, with all that death hanging in the air, not even the glory and respect of the elves could bring back what he had lost.

As he dwelled upon the moment, when the last embers of his innocence had been doused in blood, a memory surfaced.

"I don't know what kind of man I want to be, Ralph, but above all, I never want to be like you."

Cyrus was going to have to make a choice, and he needed to do it soon. If not, the winds were going to drive him right into the flames. He already knew he wanted to be the better man, someone his mother would be proud of, someone Vin had tried to mold him into; he just had to figure out whom that person was.

Chapter 15

Cyrus didn't sleep, not in the normal sense. He stared at the ceiling in his werewolf form and took in the stench of the city through his long and sensitive nostrils. The salt gave the human scent of the place a musky quality, and it did little to mask the horrid smell of the sewers. While Cyrus had seen the density of the city during the daylight, it was during the night that he truly took in how packed this place was. He'd never considered until now just how unclean a place like this could be, but his nose did not lie. Lucifan's impressive existence lost its charm of novelty. This was not a place for him.

Someone tried his door late at night, a drunken amazon trying to get into the wrong room. One of her sisters pulled her away. Beyond that, he did not hear much else once the party downstairs ended in the late hours of the early morning. When the sun finally came up, Cyrus felt his body shrink down to a human size, and he rose feeling restless and itchy. He unlatched his door but didn't leave quite yet. He stopped, took a seat on the floor, crossed his legs, and closed his eyes.

"Today will be a new day," he whispered, taking deep breaths. "Today, I will try again."

He purged his mind of thought, of worry, of pain, of confusion, of indecision, of pleasure, of surety. He lived only in that moment, in the present that existed into infinity. From here, anything was possible.

It was a simple routine, but it helped. This was something Vin had taught him long ago to help Cyrus move past his many, many failures. He hadn't done it since he'd rescued his mother, but he hadn't forgotten how. Cyrus' memories were full of countless times when he was proven to be less than his peers. He was slower and dumber than the elves, weaker than his elders in the werewolf clan, emotionally sensitive and unworthy of love everywhere he turned. He wasn't a hero. He was hardly an afterthought.

"You think too much about everyone else," Vin would say. "That is how an elf thinks about their village, but you are not an elf. You must learn to stand on your own, Cyrus. There is only one person in this entire world you should compare yourself to, and only one person I want you to be better than: the person you were yesterday."

That had been Cyrus' first true lesson in self-confidence. In a storm of withering feelings of inadequacy, Vin had tossed him a frame of reference, a starting point. He did not, could not, imagine being better than all the superior people around him. However, he could imagine being better than himself. From that perspective, his perspective, he had nowhere to go but up.

Just like now.

Cyrus took a deep breath and stood up. His mind was clear. He opened the door and left for the stairs.

He knew it was early morning and that many of the amazons had been up late. However, he didn't bother to mask his heavy footsteps. He figured the doors were solid enough and the amazons were still drunk. As Cyrus descended the stairs, he quickly found he'd made the wrong choice, though for different reasons.

"It's not your choice; it's his," someone argued.

"Choice? What choice? Aiguo moved faster than any of us thought, so now we're out of choices."

"You can't just bring him to his—"

The voices cut short as Cyrus reached the bottom of the stairs, and Cyrus knew he'd been heard. The only logical conclusion was that they'd been talking about him. He paused, anger whipping through him at being talked about in secret, but he let it go soon enough. He was used to that sort of thing. Of course, that didn't mean he wanted to tolerate it.

He strode down the last steps and burst into view.

The tavern's ground floor was sparsely occupied this morning. Only one table remained filled by the familiar faces of Adelpha, Nicholas, and Emy.

They all stared at Cyrus.

"Well, I guess we can dispense with the pleasantries and lies," Cyrus said. "Emy heard me coming and cut you short, Adelpha, am I right? What don't I have a choice about, Nicholas?"

Nicholas looked to Emy, but the rakshasa let her eyes fly to the ceiling, communicating total neutrality. Then Nicholas passed his gaze to Adelpha and met nothing but cold, unrelenting expectations. Nicholas sighed and gestured to an empty chair beside him.

Cyrus took a seat.

"Sleep well, boy?" Nicholas asked.

"Never," Cyrus replied. "Not during a full moon. So, I guess we will be doing pleasantries?"

"Humor me. I wasn't feeling festive last night, so I hit the sack early. Didn't do me much good. I've been up for a bit, running about, and this morning has already gone to shit."

Cyrus folded his arms across his chest and looked to Emy and Adelpha accusingly.

"I don't need as much sleep as a human to function," Emy said. "You know that."

"And I had children to tuck in and a toddler kicking me all night," Adelpha replied. "That's why I'm up."

Cyrus nodded, accepting the responses and deciding this wasn't a conspiracy to keep him in the dark. It was just an impromptu discussion that should have waited for his arrival.

"Well, if we're going to be pleasant about this, has everyone eaten?" Cyrus asked. "I'll bet this conversation will go better with a full stomach."

Adelpha stood up.

"Excellent idea. I'll be right back," she said, then to Nicholas, "But don't wait for me."

"I'll fetch water," Emy pitched in, vaulting up, as well.

They left, and Nicholas watched them go like an ally left to rot on the battlefield.

"You know, I can't make up my mind about you," Cyrus said.

Nicholas scoffed and said, "As if that's of any importance."

"See, right there. You're going through this immense effort to help Emy and me, yet you act like we outright begged, borrowed, and stole to get you to do it. You appear bitterly reluctant at every turn, almost spiteful, which doesn't make a drop of sense to me. I've already offered to free you of this burden, and I was insulted for it. What gives? If I didn't know any better, I'd say you're jealous."

Nicholas' eyes popped, if only for a second, and Cyrus dropped his look of scrutiny for one of surprise.

"So that's it, is it?" Cyrus said. "Then why don't you just come with us? You're not scared—"

Before he could continue, Nicholas' eyes snapped towards Cyrus and darkness filled them. Cyrus paused as he was overtaken by the urgent desire to back away.

"Listen, boy," Nicholas said. "There are many things you can accuse me of, and 'scared' is one of them. However, don't ever accuse me of fearing something you don't, because that just makes you look stupid. Got me?"

Cyrus swallowed, feeling suddenly very warm despite how cool the morning air was. He nodded. Nicholas relaxed.

"You're not the first one to make that call, though," the viking continued. "Emy asked me the same thing, if I'd join you two. No surprise, really. You will be headed up to Khaz Mal in the winter. That's a risky venture even for someone who knows the landscape, like myself. It only makes sense she'd ask me to come along. But I got my own reasons for staying behind, understand? And what they are, they have nothing to do with what we were talking about before you came down."

Cyrus nodded, respectfully this time. He felt himself being drawn in by this man. There was something intense about him, raw and savage, lurking beneath a thinly veiled restraint. His size and strength cast off the misleading guise of a dumb brute, but the more Cyrus talked with him, the more he realized that a sort of primal wisdom lurked within him. Like the oldest werewolf in the pack, Nicholas had seen things that others only dreamed of—or had nightmares about. It was visible in the shine of his eyes, in the gnarled look of his hands, and in the hunched back of a man carrying something that grew in size and weight every night.

"I'm listening," Cyrus said.

They met each other's gaze. In a moment of silence, something akin to respect passed between them, and Nicholas nodded.

"I meant what I said about getting you two out of here as soon as possible," Nicholas said. "I figured it was for the best, for your safety, and for the safety of others. This is the part I want you to think about.

"When I woke up this morning, before the sun came up, I was determined to fulfill my promise of getting you two out of this city. I marched down to the docks and started looking for a ship headed north, piloted by someone I could trust to keep their wits about them. Turns out that one night's rest was all the time Aiguo needed to get ahead of us. Not a single ship is leaving the port. They're all being paid by the leprechauns to stay put.

"My best guess is that we walked right into a trap. Takeo knew that if Emy ever wanted off this side of the world in a hurry, she'd make her way back to Lucifan and take a ship. So, he tempted the leprechauns with power or threats or whatever cockamamie scheme he pulls out of his arse every day and planned for this exact scenario. All Aiguo had to do was follow us to Lucifan, get to the leprechauns, and say the magic words. Poof! You're stuck here, and that's only part of the bad news.

"If Takeo can ground an entire fleet of ships, you can bet your life he can conscript a group of thugs to track us down. Our need to get you two out of Lucifan just got worse—if you can believe that.

"However, not all hope is lost. The leprechauns got money, sure, damn near all of it in this city, but that don't mean they have the power. Don't matter how civilized a place pretends to be, power always falls first and foremost to those most capable of violence, and that'd be the knights. They don't have a monopoly on violence, but they have the dragon's share, and the knights listen to one man and one man only. He rules this city like an indefinite steward waiting for its true king to come along.

"If we appeal to this man, he can get us the strong arm we need to break the leprechaun's hand of gold."

Nicholas paused, and Cyrus incorrectly took that as a sign to respond.

"Okay," he said, "but how do we get this man to care about us?"

Nicholas swallowed, hard. His throat bounced as the viking's gaze drifted to the center of the table. Cyrus became aware that neither Adelpha nor Emy had returned.

"Well, first off, I shouldn't have said he was a man," Nicholas forced out. "He's a vampire."

He paused. Cyrus shook his head. He'd heard of vampires from the elves. They were supposed to be some sort of nocturnal humanoid, like werewolves, but immortal. Cyrus didn't see anything to be alarmed about just yet.

"And?"

"And he's not just any vampire," Nicholas pressed on. "His name is Mark O'Conner. And he's your father."

Cyrus blinked. The words passed by him like a breeze so unfamiliar and unexpected that his mind didn't absorb them. He had to repeat Nicholas' statement in his head, twice, before any sort of shock began to dawn on him.

"My," Cyrus said, stuttering. "My father? Like, my real father?"

"No, your fake father. Yes, of course your real father. Though he wasn't a vampire or a ruler when he was with your mother."

Cyrus blinked again, and his lips parted. He tried to process what had just been told to him, but his mind couldn't get past just taking it in. Cyrus hadn't thought about the fact that he had a father in years, let alone whom or where he was. Just to accept that fact was like breaking through a stone wall with a dull knife.

Cyrus had only asked Belen about his father once that he could remember, when he was old enough to comprehend that Ralph wasn't his 'real' father, as the other children said. And that meant Cyrus had a 'real' father somewhere else in the world, and that his mother would know whom that was. Cyrus had only asked her once because, well, the answer had left a bitter taste in his mouth.

Belen hadn't said much, not even his name, but she had used a plethora of colorful words. She'd said things like coward and idiot, feckless and scum. The bile that poured from her so quickly had burned the idea of a 'real' father from Cyrus' mind for two reasons. First, the fact that Belen had said these things about this man while she found ways to compliment and love a man like Ralph could only mean that Cyrus' father was an absolutely horrible person. Secondly, like any young man, Cyrus assumed that no apple fell far from the tree. If Cyrus' real father was that terrible, it meant Cyrus had the potential to be that terrible, too. All of Belen's insults might have been aimed at an invisible person to her, but their shadows fell upon Cyrus' already-depreciated view of himself.

It hurt to hear her speak about his bloodline so vehemently. It hurt enough that he never asked her about the man again and his mind forgot his existence in the name of self-defense.

Now Cyrus was in a tavern with a dry mouth, an empty stomach, and no ability to cope with such shocking news.

"I," Cyrus mumbled. "I don't understand. You knew all this time?"

Nicholas met the young man's gaze for a few moments, then dropped his head in shame.

"Not just me," he said. "Adelpha and Emy, too."

Cyrus' first emotions beyond shock took hold of him: anger and betrayal. He latched onto them, not only because it was justified, but because it also helped distract him from facing the fact that he had a father and he was in this city.

"You all knew, and you didn't tell me?" Cyrus demanded. "Why? How? Were you going to let me walk out of here without knowing? Without ever knowing?"

"Look, you can't be angry with us," he said, throwing his hands up. "Well, I guess you can, but hear us out. Adelpha said it best. If your mother never told you about your father, then she must have had a reason. We weren't about to override her careful, obvious choice, especially just after she was killed. You see? Right? Not evil. Just trying to be respectful. On top of that, it's not like a good opportunity came up, you know? I mean, you didn't ask any of us about your father. Perhaps you didn't want to know, we figured."

"Ask?" Cyrus said, his anger rising to a boiling point. "Why would I ask any of you? Why would I think, even for a moment, that any of you knew my father? What is this . . . why would . . . ah!"

Cyrus let his head fall on the table and covered the back of his head with his hands.

He couldn't fathom anything. His anger was lost in a sea of confusion as he tried and failed to process the renewed concept of a father. Nothing had prepared him for this. He'd been taught how to hunt, to fight, to stand up for what was right, but never this. Honestly, in some regards, he'd always assumed that his real father was dead. Might as well be, anyway, considering how he had abandoned Belen and his child in a loosely defined penal society under the abusive power of a man like Ralph.

Now it turned out this man was alive. He was a vampire and the ruler of the greatest city in the world. He was a man of not only physical power but great authority. However, worst of all, the hardest fact to absorb was that he had a name: Mark O'Conner.

Cyrus pushed his head down into the table and groaned.

"So, this is your plan?" Cyrus said. "Take the long-lost son to the King of Lucifan and what? Tug at his heartstrings? Need I remind you that this is the man who left my mother and I to rot in Angor, while apparently, he had the power to rescue us all along? I don't mean to be rude, Nicholas, but, well, your plan is horrible."

Nicholas didn't so much as blink at first, but he did nod after a moment.

"Yes, it does," he answered. "Unfortunately, it's the best plan we have."

Chapter 16

Cyrus would be lying if he said he had no interest in meeting his father; however, he also couldn't get over the fact that it seemed like a bad idea. But what could he say? No? Nicholas had a point. If Aiguo was already in Lucifan, then they needed to take to the seas as soon as possible. Taking off on foot would be a nightmare, especially if Aiguo had resources like this and could purchase mounts and additional supplies. Cyrus couldn't well say to Emy, who was literally running for her life, that meeting his father sounded too traumatizing to help her out. What sort of person would that make him?

But even beyond the logic, the more Cyrus thought about it, the more he realized he couldn't leave Lucifan without doing this. As much time as he'd spent trying to purge the concept of a father from his mind, his heart never forgot. From the moment Nicholas had said the words, Cyrus began to wonder what sort of man his mother had decided to have a child with. Curiosity, and hope, quickly planted itself within him. Belen had more than hinted that this man was nothing to look up to, yet even then, Cyrus wanted to see. He had to see. Like it or not, with his mother gone, that meant his father was the only family he had left.

Mark O'Conner. What a strange name.

When they left the tavern, they planned to leave for good. With their intentions discovered by Aiguo, Cyrus and Emy couldn't afford to spend any more time in this city than necessary. They packed up and said their goodbyes, which were brief and passed out to relatively few. Adelpha was the most emotional, wishing Cyrus enough good luck to keep him safe the rest of his life and pouring more motherly love upon him than he knew how to handle. Octavia was the next most generous, and she gave Cyrus and Emy equal shares of well wishes, then winked and whispered that she hoped to see them soon. Throughout it all, Cyrus couldn't help but overhear the conversation between Nicholas and his brother as the two shook hands.

"Are you sure you don't need an escort?" Abe asked.

"Three will travel faster and quieter than a dozen in this city," Nicholas said. "Also, no offense, but you'll stick out like a sore thumb as a gunslinger. This is for the best."

"Well, stay safe out there, and come back right after you drop them off at the docks. I can meet you there, at least?"

"No, no," Nicholas replied, shaking his head.

They paused, each taking turns searching the ground and ceiling for something to look at.

"It was a pleasure to have you back," Abe finally offered.

Nicholas chuckled.

"Let's not start lying to each other now," he replied. "It was awkward for me, too. If I don't come back, give the old man my regards. Tell him even though he was wrong about me, I was wrong about him, too. I don't care if he hears you or not."

Abe's face turned wary.

"Hey, don't say that. You're coming back. You said you were going to be careful."

"And I will," Nicholas said, shrugging.

They shared a hug more awkward than the one Cyrus and Adelpha had shared. Then they left, taking their morning breakfast of bread smeared with butter with them.

As the tavern faded out of sight, the trio slunk their way through the city's darkened streets, where the morning light had yet to touch. Emy changed her appearance to match somewhat with Nicholas, making her large, muscular, and bearded. They now looked like a small group of hardened warriors, which made most people look the other way.

However, it also made Emy's expressions harder to read. Cyrus was looking for a different sort of change in her, like regret or guilt at having kept the knowledge of his father hidden. Although they hadn't been traveling together for long and Emy had already established a reputation as a bit of a trickster, Cyrus had wanted to believe that the two of them were beginning to break through that. He had hoped that Emy saw him as a potential friend, or at least a confidant, which only made sense considering how long they'd have to spend traveling together. And such a person would certainly feel some sort of shame at hiding something like this.

However, if Emy felt such things, she did not show them. Either that or Cyrus could not read them. The tragic conclusion led Cyrus back to a feeling of loneliness, which wasn't so foreign to him, unfortunately.

He wasn't about to dive back into the well of pity, though. Such emotions did him no good, and he'd crossed that bridge this morning when he claimed that today would be a new day and he would try again.

Cyrus set his concerns about Emy, Nicholas, and his father aside and took in the city. He wasn't going to be in Lucifan much longer, one way or another, so he might as well take it all in. That wasn't easy, though, because Lucifan was still waking with the rising sun and Nicholas was doing his level best to avoid any and all attention. He took sharp corners and kept a snarl on his face while Emy watched their back. Cyrus didn't know if she was trying to use her sense of smell, too, but if so, he hoped she was having better luck than him. Lucifan's stench hadn't lessened this morning, and Cyrus couldn't pick out a unique scent if someone wafted it in front of his nose.

Yet Cyrus wasn't completely lost. Between gaps in the buildings, he realized their destination was the large, tall tower in the city's center. As they approached, it flashed brightly on one side where the sun struck it full on and cast a dark shadow that fell over the city on the other. Narrow, empty alleyways became harder to find the closer they got to the tower. The metaphorical heart of the city teemed with life, even at this early hour, and the number of people Nicholas had to snarl at increased. Cyrus kept his head down and hunched forward, trying to make himself appear smaller. It didn't seem to work, especially once shops began to open and merchants began shouting for attention.

Thankfully, Nicholas' glare kept most of them from directing any attention at the trio.

Some were still brave enough, though. One shopkeeper shouted at Cyrus, saying a new weapon would surely suit a young man such as himself. Another boasted of having the best brew in the world and stood flabbergasted as Nicholas led on. A beggar was brave enough to reach out as Cyrus passed, her dirty and thin hand outstretched with a slight shake.

Cyrus only paused for a moment. He'd seen these wretched poor yesterday, and they'd struck him as a clear impossibility. It didn't make any sense, he thought, that a city capable of building such immense structures and wealth could somehow struggle to feed the people that lived there. When he'd asked Nicholas and Emy about them, however, the two had said these people were called beggars, and they lived off of handouts from the city's wealthier classes. When Cyrus asked why, they only answered that it was complicated.

Now there was this old woman before him, wearing dirty, ragged clothing, asking Cyrus for money he did not have. But Cyrus did have something, though, and he only stopped for a moment, because there was no hesitation in his decision.

Cyrus pulled out a good amount of the food from his pack and handed it to the beggar. The old woman's eyes went wide as an armful of bread, some dried nuts and fruit, and a cured bit of meat fell into her possession.

"Tha-thank you," she stuttered. "Thank you, kind sir."

"Please, share with others," Cyrus whispered.

As they left, Cyrus noted that this act had drawn the attention of more than a few street goers. It had only taken a moment, and Nicholas hadn't stopped, but Emy had given him a disapproving stare. As they dashed to catch up with Nicholas, she hissed at him.

"That was stupid," she said. "We're going to need that food."

"I don't know about that," Cyrus replied. "Did you see her?"

"She's not going to Khaz Mal. This city has so much food that it throws it away. How do you think these people are still alive? You don't think she really relies on random people walking by to feed her, do you?"

Cyrus sighed and shook his head.

"Whatever, call me stupid, then," he muttered. "As if doing the right thing has an intelligence level."

"She's right, boy," Nicholas said as they caught up with him and disappeared down another alley. "That was stupid, right or wrong. I knew a man once who enjoyed being stupid, so long as it made him right. His name was Gavin, and he's dead now."

Rage welled up in Cyrus, but he fought it down. He didn't understand why he should be berated over what was clearly the right thing to do, over and over again. Or at least he thought so. It's what he would have done back in Angor, anyway. Food was shared among the clan. That was a rule because the clan was only as strong as its weakest member, and one never knew if this would be the winter that they went hungry. When times were good, one shared the wealth, because when times were bad, it would take everyone working together to make it through.

"Gavin couldn't have been all good," Cyrus bit back. "He helped a man like Takeo, so he must have been just stupid."

Nicholas stopped dead in his tracks. Cyrus nearly ran into him.

The big man turned slowly, shoulders tensed, the snarl on his face never leaving. They had stopped short of the busy street up ahead that would finally take them to the large wall surrounding the tower.

"Don't you talk about Gavin that way," Nicholas warned. "You don't know him. He spent his best years trying to keep Takeo from going down the wrong path, and in the end, he gave his life so that his child could survive."

Cyrus blinked but refused to back down.

"So, what are you saying? That good deeds are their own reward, worthy of respect?"

Cyrus smiled, feeling he'd won a mark, but Nicholas stayed rooted.

"I never knocked the deed, boy. I said it was stupid, and that being stupid gets you killed. You're damn straight that Gavin was a good person, worthy of respect. He was the best, finest gentleman I knew, mostly. He had his flaws, I'll admit, but that's the difference between him and me. I was selfish, and I survived."

"Must be a shame, then," Cyrus replied, "because you look miserable for it."

Nicholas froze, stunned. For a moment, Cyrus thought Nicholas was going to hit him, but the big man slowly regained his composure.

"You," he replied, pausing to turn away. "You don't know me, boy. You don't know the whole story."

Nicholas walked off, continuing their path forward. His shoulders hung heavier than before, and his gait was shorter, but these were minor adjustments that held little interest for Cyrus. He instead looked at Emy to gauge her reaction.

She frowned and sighed, like a parent before arguing children.

"He's right, you know," she said. "You don't know the whole story."

"But did I say anything wrong?"

She pursed her lips and didn't answer. Cyrus smirked, glad to give as good as he got for once. Emy shook her head and followed Nicholas into the void. Before Cyrus went with them, he looked back the way they'd come. The old woman was barely visible, but Cyrus could see she'd been joined by a couple other such beggars, and they were sharing the food he'd given them.

"Worth it," Cyrus whispered.

Then he followed, too.

Nicholas made the last dash across a busy street towards an arched, double entryway into a courtyard before the great tower. The entrance was vast to Cyrus's eyes, capable of letting two bugbears walk through astride without trouble. The way was open to all, barred only by a set of guards that flanked the place and appeared fresh-eyed. Cyrus took them in with curiosity.

They were both clad in metal armor from head to toe. Their helmets and shields sat on the ground, though, leaning against the doorway. Cyrus had seen people like this sporadically in his short time in Lucifan, but they had been one of countless strange things clouding his vision at the time. Cyrus deduced from his talks with the amazons and others that these were the famous Knights of Lucifan because it was hard to imagine them being anything else. He'd never seen such armored suits before, and he imagined it must be unbearably hot inside them with the sun pouring down. Good thing there was a nice coastal breeze.

Nicholas approached with confidence.

"I'm looking for Doles," he said.

The two knights, both not much older than Cyrus, shared a glance. They hesitated to answer, invisibly arguing over who was going to address this hulking mass of flesh and his two companions. One conceded and turned back to Nicholas.

"Well, I think you're at the wrong place, uh, sir?" he said. "If you head down that way, you'll find the main administration building, where you can file a formal inquiry or whatever you need. I'm sure they can help you."

"I'm short on time, boy," Nicholas barked. "I know he's in there somewhere. I need one of you to go and fetch him, quickly."

Again, the knights shared a look, then shifted in a way that put their shields closer. Again, the same one took the duty of replying.

"I'm really sorry, but that won't be possible. Doles isn't someone you can just summon, and we aren't to leave our post. Really, if you'll just head down that way and—"

"What's your name, boy?" Nicholas demanded.

The young man paused. Annoyance slipped into his features. Whether it was at the age-related remark or at Nicholas' refusal to take 'no' for an answer, Cyrus couldn't be sure. It was probably both.

"Sir Clyde," he said, with emphasis on the 'Sir.'

"Well look, Clyde," Nicholas went on. "You got a commander, right? Someone you answer to, and that you could fetch at a moment's notice? You'd have to so that you could get reinforcements, if needed. He or she got a name?"

"Yes," Clyde replied, flatly, yet showing remarkable patience as far as Cyrus was concerned. "His name is Sir Mathew."

Nicholas balked, faltering for the first time.

"Well, I'll be damned. What luck! Fetch him, Clyde. Quickly now."

"He's going to tell you the exact—"

"Nevermind that, just tell him Nicholas Stout is at the gates and wants to speak with him. And tell him I'm looking for Doles, too. And Sir Mark O'Conner while you're at it. Might as well just run straight up the ladder if I can."

Sir Clyde balked this time.

"Did you say Stout?" Clyde asked. "As in, Emily Stout?"

"I didn't stutter now, did I, boy? Hurry it up."

Clyde only hesitated a moment before running off, leaving his partner alone and equally baffled. Nicholas didn't pay her any mind, but Cyrus did. She had a rigidity about her that implied she liked routine or it was otherwise forced upon her.

Like the young man, her demeanor had changed at the Stout name, and it wasn't difficult to deduce why. Any doubts Cyrus had about the fame of this young girl, Emily Stout, evaporated.

They didn't wait for long, but it sure felt like it, standing in silence under the sun's gaze. Cyrus heard Clyde's approach before he saw him, which owed little to Cyrus' sensitive ears. If there was one thing about wearing a suit of metal armor, it's that it was noisy to move in.

And Clyde brought company.

Striding ahead were two men, one closer to Nicholas' age and one who could have been their father. The younger, middle-aged man was tall and had his head shaved bald, while the older one was a short, portly fellow with bushy eyebrows and a hurried pace. Clyde and the bald man had to rush to keep up with the old man.

Nicholas grinned triumphantly at their approach.

"Doles, my good man," Nicholas called out. "And Sir Mathew! It's been too long."

They did not reply, but instead closed the gap. Cyrus tried to decipher which name fell to which man, but he picked up that Doles wasn't given the 'Sir' designation, and as far as Cyrus could tell, a knight ought to receive it. However, the old man didn't look like the others. He didn't dress in armor, or carry a weapon, or even look like he knew how to use one. He hunched where the others stood up straight and scowled while the others held a reserved look. Cyrus guessed the older one probably wasn't a knight, and therefore, that he was Doles. What he couldn't figure out, though, was how a non-knight clearly had authority over a knight. Cyrus had thought knights were the supreme authority in this city, under his father.

Then Cyrus got nervous, as he suddenly remembered why they were here.

"You've got a lot of nerve showing up here," the oldest one, Doles, responded. "And it seems you've brought some mercenaries. I expect no better of someone who traveled with the Dark Lord."

Nicholas cocked his head and frowned.

"Alright, I'll say I expected some hostility, but you do know that I don't travel with Takeo anymore. We parted ways. I didn't share his view."

"But you helped his rise to power," the middle-aged one, Mathew, said. "I don't care if you are Emily's brother. You should bear some responsibility for that."

"Firstly, how do you know I don't?" Nicholas countered. "And secondly, would you be telling Gavin this same thing?"

Mathew faltered. Nicholas shook his head.

"I thought not," he continued. "But look, I'm here for a different reason. I need to see Mark."

"That's what Sir Clyde tells me," Doles answered, "which is the only reason I'm here. I figured if you were making that sort of request, you probably have something really stupid on your mind, so I might as well come and deal with it. You're lucky you came so early. The day's only just beginning, otherwise I wouldn't have time for this sort of shenanigans."

Nicholas waved, brushing Doles' comments aside like dust in the air. He turned to Cyrus, and the nervousness that was building in Cyrus rose to a whole new level. Nicholas gestured to him, and there all eyes fell. Beads of sweat began to collect on Cyrus' forehead.

"I'm trying to be discreet," Nicholas said. "You might want to banish the knights for this spectacle, Doles. However, if you must know, all I have to ask is, does this lad look familiar?"

Doles' gaze fell on Cyrus like a hammer to an anvil, then flipped back to Nicholas with annoyance.

"No," he said, firmly. "I've never seen this boy in my life."

"Not him, idiot," Nicholas spat. "I know you don't know him. I said does he look familiar, as in, similar to anyone you know?"

The old man eyed Nicholas hard, but Nicholas was a mountain of stone, unyielding in his defiance. Doles sighed and shifted his gaze back to Cyrus, slowly this time. He looked over the young man, still just as lost as before, yet Cyrus could tell the old man was thinking now. It didn't take a genius to start putting this puzzle together.

According to Nicholas, it was known that Mark had a lost son somewhere in the world. Nicholas was now in Lucifan, demanding to see Mark. At Nicholas' side was a young man who Nicholas claimed bore resemblance to someone Doles would know well. Intuition told Cyrus he must look a lot like his father, but he didn't know. He'd never met the man. However, he'd known since he was a child that he didn't look much like his mother.

Slowly but surely, that hard look of annoyance slipped from Doles' face into one of apprehension and disbelief.

"Are you saying—" Doles whispered.

"I'm not saying a damned thing," Nicholas cut in, "and neither are you. I just want to see Mark. You hear me?"

Doles continued to eye Cyrus. He licked his teeth, then made a clicking noise.

"Fine," he said. "Follow me."

Chapter 17

They were led across a courtyard and into a tall, wide structure
that Cyrus discovered to be barracks for the knights. What caught
Cyrus' attention, however, were the windows. Each bay had metal
shutters, as opposed to normal wooden ones. They were
systematically being shut, one by one as the sun rose, using a
padlock for each. The halls echoed with the squeal of iron hinges
and the slam of metal on stone. Slowly but surely, the sun's light
was being purged from the barracks, replaced by candlelight that
glowed from sconces on the walls. Inevitably, some light still
peeked through the cracks, but it was like a shadow of its source.

Doles stopped outside a seemingly random door that must have
had a horrible draft, because the air temperature plunged. A chill ran
up Cyrus' spine.

"Huh," Nicholas said, as Doles went to rap his knuckles against
the door. "Still in his old office, eh? I thought he'd be in the tower
by now."

"Those thrones are reserved for the angels, Lucifan's true
rulers," Doles answered. "Sir Mark is merely a steward until Ephron
returns."

"Yeah, like that's going to happen," Nicholas muttered.

Doles gave the door a knock, his old bones ringing sharply
against the weathered iron. Inexplicably, the air grew colder until
Cyrus felt the need to rub his forearms and mist formed at his
breath. He blinked in shock, for he couldn't detect the slightest
breeze.

The door groaned as a metal bolt slid back, and the door
cracked open. Cyrus' stomach flipped, even though he couldn't see
inside. Only Doles and Mathew were visible to the opener, and
behind them was Nicholas. Emy and Clyde took up the rear, with
Clyde giving Emy odd glances. Not that he could be blamed. Emy's
chosen form made her look like a deranged henchman. It was a form
that made people want to keep quiet.

"What is it?" came a voice from inside. "I'm about to turn in for
the day."

Cyrus paid close attention to the voice. It was deep, aged, and
tired. One could hear the burden of responsibility in it.

"Sir," Doles replied, his breath drifting into steam. "Nicholas Stout is here to see you. He's brought someone with him, and he claims it's urgent."

"Does it concern Takeo?" the voice spoke with interest now. "The fugitive he's after, perhaps?"

"I don't think so," Doles went on. "However, you know I wouldn't disturb you if I didn't think it was worth your time."

A pause followed, long enough to make everyone uncomfortable. Well, everyone except Nicholas. He seemed oblivious to social cues, or at least unconcerned with them.

"Well, I hope it will be quick," the voice sighed. "Let them in."

"Do you need a guard, Sir?" Mathew offered.

"Please, Matt, I'm a vampire. If anyone needs a guard, it will be them. And besides, if they did bring methods to kill me, well, one can only hope."

"Sir," Mathew said, shaking his head. "You know I hate it when you talk like that."

A melancholy chuckle was the only reply. The door swung fully open, and what was left of Cyrus' stomach dropped away from him.

The first thing Cyrus noticed was that Sir Mark O'Conner was older than he had expected. He hadn't expected anyone young, but Mark bore many years of service in the aged lines that ran down his face and fingers. The second thing Cyrus noticed was that Mark had thick cheeks. They weren't noticeably different, per se, but Cyrus had always felt his face was a bit thicker than his mother's, and he now knew why. Mark was also tall with a shaved head and eyes of a sharp, unnatural blue, which contrasted brightly against his dark skin.

For all the attention Cyrus bore into Mark, none of it was returned. Mark only spared him a glance before focusing on Nicholas, with a scowl.

"Well," he said. "Are you coming in?"

"Gladly," Nicholas replied.

"Ah," Doles protested. "Just you and the boy. Your slab of muscle can stay outside."

Emy snarled but stayed put. Nicholas shouldered his way past Doles and Mathew, and Cyrus followed in a daze. His ability to speak had been sapped.

Mark's room was modest: a desk, a bed, a chair, and a nightstand. Candles provided the only light, and they were weak, casting shadows along the stone walls. The room was ice cold. Frost collected on a few surfaces, noticeably the wooden frame of the bed. Cyrus shivered and wrapped his arms around himself, even as he closed the door. He stared at the latch, wondering if it would be polite or impolite to lock it, then decided he'd rather not trap himself in here. He left it unlocked.

Mark went to the desk and took a seat.

"Well," he began, leaning back and placing his hands on his chest, fingers interlocked. "I take it you're not here on Takeo's behalf."

"You know I cut ties with that man," Nicholas said.

"So you say," Mark replied.

A curiosity dawned on Cyrus. Steam wafted from Nicholas' every word, whereas when Mark spoke, not an ounce of steam came out. Cyrus realized that his father was the source of all this unnatural cold, and he could only assume it had to do with his vampirism.

The world grew stranger every day.

"Alright, you want to cut to the point, that's fine by me," Nicholas said. "We're short on time anyway. I need to set sail, along with these two, but your damned leprechaun buddies are paying the entire dock to keep in harbor. I need you to fix it."

Cyrus paused. This was the first time he'd heard Nicholas say that he planned to go with them. Before he could point it out, though, Mark laughed. Just once, but it was equal parts carefree and exhausted. Cyrus let the moment pass, figuring he could talk to Nicholas about it later.

"I had heard that the leprechauns were being awfully generous as of late," Mark said. "Ships staying in harbor generate a lot of gossip in the city. I assumed they were trying to play some sort of bidding war with the merchant guild, so I dispatched a few knights to investigate. Let me tell you, Nicholas, what the leprechauns are doing is an expensive venture, and they don't typically do expensive. Whatever game they are playing will end in a couple of days at most. As for me, my relationship with those little creatures is strained, at best, and I'd rather not get in the middle of it. Besides, even if I wanted to, I doubt I'd do it for someone like you. One of

Takeo's former lackeys come back from exile to hurl rude demands at my face? You've got some nerve showing up and acting like this."

"I've got some nerve being alive," Nicholas countered, then grinned. "But don't you worry, old man. You're not going to do this for me. You're going to do this for him."

He flipped a thumb over his shoulder at Cyrus, and Cyrus' stomach flipped once more. Mark followed the motion, as if only now realizing that Nicholas hadn't come in alone, but spared Cyrus nothing more than a glance. When his gaze fell on Nicholas again, he was beyond agitated.

"Really? For him? I don't recognize him. I keep thinking this is wrapped up with Takeo somehow. When he was here, he said something about finding an old friend. Yet, it can't be this man. He's young. Can't be the fugitive, either. Takeo made it clear that his fugitive is female."

"Nah, you've never seen him before," Nicholas continued, clearly enjoying Mark's ignorance. "However, that doesn't mean you don't know him. Look again. Anything unique?"

Mark sighed and gave a long blink. He flicked his gaze back to Cyrus, unperturbed at how Cyrus was watching Mark's every move with rapt attention. Cyrus couldn't shake the fact that his father was standing right before his eyes. Every moment that passed and every word that slipped from his lips served to increase Mark's presence in Cyrus' mind. Meanwhile, Mark gazed with the least possible interest upon Cyrus. He completed his second pass and shook his head.

"I don't understand this game, Nicholas," he said. "I don't know whom this is. Someone Emily knew?"

Nicholas frowned.

"Really? Nothing unique about him?"

Mark looked once more. Cyrus' stomach did another flip.

"His eyes are grey," Mark said. "That's uniq—"

Mark's eyes flashed wide, and his body went completely still. His gaze changed, passing from disinterested boredom into riveted investment. Nicholas grinned again. Mark's mouth fell open.

"You should see him during a full moon," Nicholas went on. "His eyes get stranger. One turns brown, the other blue."

Mark didn't hear him, or at least didn't appear to. He turned his whole body toward Cyrus and stared unblinking with a shocked realization, mixed with disbelief. Cyrus stared back, equally attentive, and for once, Mark recognized that. Their gazes met for the first time in joint understanding. Nicholas, for all his size, could have been invisible.

"I, uh," Cyrus said, struggling for words, "I didn't know you knew my eyes were grey."

"It's one of the only things I was ever told about you," Mark replied, still awestruck. "You, um, you are, eh—"

"Cyrus. Just Cyrus."

"No, that I know, too," Mark went on. "I was going to say, 'my son,' but I guess we're past that now."

Despite himself, Cyrus chuckled with nervous energy. Blessedly, some tension fell away.

"And you're my father, it seems," Cyrus broached.

Mark blinked a few times and shook his head.

"Well, this is a shock," he said. "Now, don't take this the wrong way, but, well, um, what are you doing here?"

Cyrus tensed up again.

"Huh? What do you mean?"

"As I said, I was only ever told a few things about you. I knew your name, your eye color, and that you were with your mother. I knew you were both werewolves, but that you had special control over that form."

"From whom did you hear this?" Cyrus said.

"Takeo," Nicholas popped in, "like you've been told. It was him and Gavin who took you to the last angel. On their way to Juatwa, they passed through Lucifan, picked up an ogre and me, and told Mark about you."

"Yes," Mark said. "He made it sound like you were safe and sound with Belen. I thought you'd stay with her forever. Where is she?"

Cyrus swallowed hard.

"She's dead," he whispered.

Mark balked, but nothing more. He flicked a look of disbelief at Nicholas, who nodded in grave confirmation.

"Dead," Mark repeated. "Dead how?"

There was something in that comment, the tone, perhaps, that set off a spark. Anger welled up in Cyrus, and for fully justified reasons. How dare he ask how she died? She'd died because she and her son were abandoned by the very man asking that question. They were taken in by a cruel, merciless stepfather who did the bare minimum to shelter them from a harsh, unforgiving landscape. All the while, they could have been plucked from such a world by a man with power, living in a place that had such treasures as individual wealth and boring bureaucracy.

Cyrus snapped his response.

"Murder," he said through clenched teeth. "She had her throat cut."

Mark blinked and raised a hand as if to put his fingers over his mouth but stopped shy. He again looked to Nicholas for confirmation.

"One of Takeo's lackeys," Nicholas added. "A shifty, pitiless creature who should have been strangled at birth. Instead, he lived and now sows sorrow in his wake. He wasn't after her; she just happened to be in his way as they were passing through Angor."

"What is he after?" Mark asked, still nothing more than mildly stunned.

Cyrus' anger boiled.

"That fugitive you were talking about, I assume," Nicholas said, and it was clear to Cyrus that Nicholas was selectively lying to steer Mark down a more productive path. "I had hoped you would have more answers, but apparently not. Cyrus, here, is on the run now. As you know, he and Takeo have a past, and I'm doing what I can to keep your son from falling into this lackey's hands. He's in the city somewhere, and we need to leave immediately."

Mark blinked multiple times, taken aback by the flood of information. He stuttered, stumbling over a series of questions, but he never got to them.

"How could you leave us, huh?" Cyrus burst out in the brief silence.

Mark swiveled from Nicholas.

"Excuse me?" he said.

"You left us," Cyrus said, hands balling into fists. "I didn't even know your name. You could have come for us at any time, and you didn't. Now she's dead."

"My son—"

"Don't call me that."

"Cyrus, then. Belen was a werewolf. She was safest among her people. Besides, with her condition, bringing her here would have been a nightmare."

"A nightmare for whom? You? I dealt with her condition using nothing but wood and rope. You live in a city of stone and iron. Do you have any more excuses for abandoning us?"

"Actually, I do. This situation is far more complicated than you can imagine. Not only did I think you and your mother were safer and better off among your own people, but perhaps you haven't noticed that I have a condition of my own, vampirism, which means that I will die in sunlight. It's a remarkably debilitating disease that prevents me from doing what you said."

"And you couldn't send anyone? You don't have an army at your command?"

"At my command?" Mark scoffed. "Typical youth. I, and the knights for that matter, serve at Lucifan's bidding. The Order isn't my personal army, as if I were some tyrannical king. I've learned my lesson, and paid the price, for daring to think that once before. I live my life in repentance for that. You couldn't possibly understand."

"Oh, I think I understand enough. You claim you thought we were safe? All my life, my only source of knowledge about you came from my mother, and let me tell you, she never had a kind word to say. However, among all the insults of cowardice and inconsideration she leveled at you, I asked her if you were really that bad. She replied that when she was at her lowest, abandoned by her sisters, turned into a werewolf, and pregnant with me, she wrote you a letter asking for help. You knew then, yet you never showed."

Mark went still. A moment passed and he drew in a long breath. When he let it out, his shoulders fell ever so slightly.

"I'll admit to that," he said. "That was the 'old' me, if you will. I was selfish, power-hungry, and in the midst of making a terrible decision that would have repercussions far beyond my understanding. The relationship I had with your mother wasn't so much one of love, but one of passion. I saw her once a year, and although we enjoyed each other's company, that was enough for the both of us. We were both extremely independent, and I figured she'd make it out just fine. I certainly couldn't, and didn't want to, take on a child at that moment and deal with the problems only a werewolf can bring.

"By the time I realized the error of my ways, things had changed. I'd become a vampire and the ruler of a city that had nearly been reduced to rubble. That's when Takeo, and Nicholas, here, came to me after seeing Belen and you. They told me everything I would knew about you. Your eyes, your condition, but most importantly, Takeo told me that you were safe in the loving arms of your mother.

"Should I have helped her when she asked? Yes. However, I am not lying when I say that I thought you were safe and better off without me."

This time it was Cyrus who looked to Nicholas, questioning, and Nicholas once again nodded in confirmation. Cyrus shook his head.

"Well, it wouldn't have killed you to check in on us once in a while," Cyrus replied. "Perhaps things would have been different. Perhaps she would still be alive."

Cyrus regretted those words the moment he said them. He blamed this man for a lot of things, but he had just implied that he blamed Mark for Belen's death, which wasn't true. He blamed himself for that.

Yet that didn't stop Mark from dropping his head.

The conversation between them died out, silence filling the cold air. Nicholas watched nervously, looking between Mark and Cyrus, who were no longer looking at each other. He shifted and cleared his throat.

"Alright, well, listen," he spoke up. "I suppose that could have gone better, but we need to go. Like I was saying, Mark, the docks are locked up tighter than an old man's pride, and I need to get your son to safety. What do you say? Could you spare us some coin and metal-clad muscle to convince one of these ships to set sail? I know at least one of these ships is dying to leave, they just need an excuse."

Mark ignored him and raised his head. He sighed at Cyrus.

"Well, like it or not, earned or not, and regardless of past decisions, you are still my son," Mark said. "If it's protection you need, there's no need to run away. That is the one thing I can provide, and plenty of."

"I'm not running away from anything," Cyrus replied. "I'm running towards something."

"Oh? And what's that?"

Cyrus risked a glance at Nicholas, unsure if he was about to reveal something he shouldn't. Nicholas didn't speak or move, so Cyrus decided that was enough of an affirmation to proceed.

"I'm seeking the angel," Cyrus said. "The one who, well, made me like I am."

Mark raised an eyebrow. Then he drew in a deep breath and nodded.

"And here I thought you'd have been too young to remember Ephron," Mark said.

"I was. I had to be told about him. However, it makes sense."

"So, advice then," Mark went on. "That's what you're after. Your mother died, your world is broken, and now you're looking for guidance. And such as the world is, you'll find no better guide than that of an angel."

Mark continued to nod, but then shook his head.

"However, as understandable as that is," he continued, "I have to ask you to wait. If you're being hunted, and your hunter is here in Lucifan, then we have a chance at catching him. By then, this silly leprechaun scheme will have broken, and you can take any ship you desire. I knew Ephron, and I miss his guidance dearly. If there's anyone in this world I'd want him to help, it'd be you. And perhaps Takeo if they ever meet again."

"Eh, let me cut in here, if you don't mind," Nicholas spoke up. "Admirable as that offer is, Mark, it can't happen."

"Excuse me?"

"Catching the hunter. Takeo's sent a right bastard after your son, and you won't catch him. His name is Aiguo Mein. Ring any bells?"

Mark blinked, and said, "No."

"I can almost guarantee he would have been at Takeo's side when they landed. Do you remember anyone standing next to him? Do you remember Takeo being alone? What did the man look like?"

"No, Takeo was never alone. There was a man next to him. I remember," Mark paused. "Strange. Actually, I don't seem to. This is odd. I remember thinking to myself that I would scan over every individual in Takeo's presence so that I would know his underlings. I committed them to memory. It was an old trick I used when I was just a regular knight. I distinctly remember committing to memory a man standing beside Takeo, yet I can't recall a thing."

"Yeah, that's him alright."

"No, you don't understand," Mark continued. "It's like there's a blank space in my mind. I can see Takeo perfectly, and a few others, yet where that man stood is a white shadow of nothingness. I wrote down their descriptions, I know I did. Hold on."

Mark dug through his drawers until he found what he was looking for, a single piece of parchment. He rolled it out.

"Smooth face, average build and height, black hair, brown eyes, ears appear slightly smaller than one would expect. By the angels, I even wrote down the name 'Lord Aiguo Mein'. I don't recall hearing it. What happened to my memory of him? What sorcery is this? Is he even human?"

"Yes, though you'd be forgiven for thinking otherwise," Nicholas said. "He made a deal with a jinni to make him forgettable in people's minds, or something along those lines. The jinni cheated him, though. You can still remember him by being more, eh, abstract in your approach. If the man makes your blood boil and your skin crawl, for example, you can retain your memories by focusing on those feelings. Look, Mark, all you need to know is that your knights stand no chance of finding this man before he finds us. Even if they had a drawing of his face, exactly as it is, they wouldn't remember to look for him."

Mark gaped at Nicholas in clear disbelief, yet the overwhelming evidence could not be denied.

"How can such a man lead anyone, or give out orders for that matter?"

"He has his ways," Nicholas said and shrugged. "Being in his presence frequently helps, he has others repeat his orders on the spot, things like that. Like any living creature, he's learned to get by. Just trust me when I say that your son is not safe in any heavily populated city."

Mark blinked again and dropped his head. He looked over his paper, his note on Aiguo, and tried to grasp at his world that had been flipped over on its head in the past few minutes.

"I'm sorry, it's just, this is a lot to take in," he said. "I've only just met my son, and now you're telling me I have to send him off?"

"It's not just him saying that," Cyrus cut in.

Mark looked up. He and Cyrus shared a gaze not as menacing as before, yet not as warm as when they began.

"Yes, I see," the old vampire said. "You're determined on this part?"

Cyrus nodded.

"I would warn you that Takeo is not a man to tangle with," Mark pressed, "but it seems we're already beyond that part. Do you have any idea why he's after you, at least? Why would his underling go through all the trouble of tracking you down and killing your mother?"

Cyrus shrugged. He knew he had to make something up.

"Maybe he's after the angel," Cyrus said.

Mark and Nicholas froze.

"Hold on," Nicholas spoke up first. "Mark, didn't you say that Takeo said he was visiting an old friend?"

"Yes, and I assumed that was you."

"Well, it wasn't. How many other 'old friends' does Takeo have? Couldn't be the amazons, and he's not in the city anymore, right?"

Mark shook his head and replied, "No. He left quickly, on foot, which means he wasn't going to visit any vikings either."

"Damn," Nicholas swore. "It all makes sense. Takeo can't complete his world conquest without Lucifan, and everyone assumes that colossus is guarding the city. If there's anyone who can change that, it's Ephron."

"And I let him live," Mark muttered. "By the angels, I let him live. I thought there was no way he'd come for Lucifan, not after

Emily gave her life for it. What was I thinking? Nicholas, you knew Takeo best. If he finds Ephron, would he—?"

He couldn't finish. He stared hard at Nicholas, but the viking didn't shrink from that gaze. Nicholas sighed and nodded.

"Looks like we have another reason to get going," Nicholas said, then glanced at Cyrus. "We need to find Ephron before Takeo kills him."

Chapter 18

The goodbye was awkward, to say the least. How could it be anything else? Cyrus had barged into Mark's life just as suddenly as Nicholas had barged Mark into Cyrus' life, in a situation where only a brief encounter was possible. And with the sun steadily rising, Mark couldn't escort them to the docks himself. They had to part ways right there in that room, and it only then dawned on Cyrus how stupid this entire plan had been. Wouldn't it have been better for both of them to go on living as they had, completely unaware of the other's existence, in total ignorance of the peril each of them was placed in?

And yet, Cyrus couldn't say he would take it back. Not even as Mark forced out parting words.

"I, uh, I know you won't listen to me," he said, drawing close. "I mean, why would you? You've gone your whole life without my advice, so why would that change now? However, I'm not asking you to listen to me as your father, but as an experienced old man. If I could convince you to stay, I would. I wouldn't send anyone against Takeo that I wanted to survive. You seem set on this, but please, promise me this. If you see Takeo, do not fight him. Run."

Cyrus paused for a moment, then nodded.

"Well, it sounds like I won't have a choice," Cyrus said. "He won't be alone."

"Even if he is," Mark pressed. "Especially if he is."

Another pause, another nod. Cyrus looked deep into that sharp, unnatural blue gaze and saw the fear there. He could smell it, even, as only a werewolf can. It did not bode well that an immortally strong creature, leading an army of warriors, would speak this way about someone else.

"I will," Cyrus said.

"And I'll make sure he does," Nicholas added.

Mark ignored the big man and reached out to touch Cyrus' shoulder. He did it slowly, as if Cyrus might withdraw if he went too quickly. However, he let it happen, and Mark's ice-cold hand fell on his shoulder in what they both knew might be their one and only moment together.

Mark made a hasty note and handed it to Nicholas. Some words were exchanged with Doles and Sir Mathew at the door, and Cyrus and Nicholas left, taking Emy with them. They waited in the courtyard with Sir Mathew and soon a handful of knights filtered out to join them. The knights mounted up on some of the most unique creatures Cyrus had ever seen: these large, four-legged beasts with long snouts and great feathery wings. Something called a pegasus, apparently, which reminded Cyrus of the elven hippogriffs back home. Then they made for the docks in the widest, most populated street in Lucifan, parting the crowd with ease.

As their procession drew a wave of onlookers, it seemed an oddity to Cyrus that their trio should spend so much time and effort traveling stealthily into Lucifan only to turn around and attract everyone's gaze on the way out. He scanned all sides, worried that Aiguo's expert knife thrower might be so brave as to risk an assassination in broad daylight. He watched Emy, too, expecting that if anyone could sense impending doom, it would be her. She appeared just as watchful as him, but otherwise unconcerned.

At some point, she scooted closer to Cyrus and whispered over the hum of the crowds.

"I overheard everything," she said. "Is Nicholas really joining us? Did he wink at you when he said that?"

"I don't think so."

The circle of mounted knights forced the three of them to walk in a triangle, with Nicholas taking the lead. Judging by the tension in his shoulders, he was just as wary about this short trip as Emy and Cyrus were. He kept scratching his shoulders, beard, and neck, keeping one hand close to his maul at all times.

"I thought he was lying to my father," Cyrus said, then paused, realizing he'd meant to say Mark, but hadn't. "You know, to get him to agree to let us take a ship."

"Yes, I thought so, too, but that doesn't make Mark wrong. He said we'd be better off with Nicholas, and he's right. It's winter in the Khaz Mal Mountains, and that means the going will be tough. And trust me, if I think it's tough, it's going to be very tough. Nicholas knows that place well. Plus, if Takeo is going to be there, we could use his help. He'll know how to handle Takeo."

Cyrus dissected Emy's words. He'd come to realize that Emy had a way of speaking that skipped specific steps, things she thought were obvious.

"You're saying that if Takeo catches us, Nicholas will be able to talk to him," Cyrus said.

"Yes, he's done it before," she answered. "Nicholas ferried me away from Takeo the first time, and Takeo let him go despite it."

"But you won't get away this time. If Takeo catches us, he'll kill you."

"Me, yes."

Cyrus paused, then drew in a breath.

"You're saying that if Nicholas is there, Takeo might spare me," he said, then added, "for the crime of helping you."

Emy blinked, seemingly confused why Cyrus was repeating what she had clearly indicated.

"Yes, exactly," she said. "With the possibility of running into Takeo, everything has changed. We need to get Nicholas onboard, literally."

"Why do I get the feeling that when you say we, you're talking about me."

"Because that's exactly what I'm saying, and you're not an idiot. At least, not a total idiot. Average for a human, I'd say."

"Uh, thanks?"

Emy brushed the comment off with a wave.

"Nicholas won't go on my behalf," she said. "He knows he won't be able to save me if Takeo shows up. However, it could be different for you. I've seen him risk his life for a near stranger before, another younger man who had spirit. You could make that happen."

Cyrus thought for a moment. It didn't take long to see the wisdom in her words, but there was one key point she was missing.

"But," he said, hesitating, "wouldn't that just risk his life for the benefit of mine?"

Emy paused. Cyrus could almost hear her brain click with a combination of realization and disappointment.

"You're not going to do it, are you?" she said. "I take that back. You are an idiot, even for a human."

"And you play games with people's lives, trading one for the other as if they were currency. I'm not going to help you rope Nicholas into this to assuage your feelings of guilt over ruining my life."

Emy flinched as if struck. In some ways, perhaps she was.

"You know, this is exactly why I enjoyed traveling alone," she said.

"Better to be alone than in bad company."

"Forget Takeo. You'd better convince Nicholas to join us to protect yourself from me."

"Please," Cyrus scoffed. "If I recall, last time we had a go, it didn't work out for you."

"And that's about to change—"

"Will you two keep it down, huh?" Nicholas barked. "I'll clock you both if I have to hear any more of that squabble. We're here."

Embarrassment forced a reluctant truce. Emy and Cyrus turned away, and Cyrus saw what 'here' was.

The wide Lucifan street spilled out before an even wider dock, which was a magnificent wooden platform that sprawled out over the water. Cyrus marveled at the simple invention, not having seen such an obviously useful structure in his life. Oh, and then there were ships.

Huge, massive boats with sails and masts and people everywhere, climbing, moving, hauling, singing, yelling in a chaotic yet coordinated display that took Cyrus' breath away. He'd only seen ships from a distance, when they'd come to Lucifan at first, and only then as distant blurs on the water. Seeing these behemoths of lumber, floating on water with ease, took away what little breath he had left.

And to think he was going to travel on one of these.

Nicholas turned to Sir Mathew and gestured to the ships.

"So, what's the deal, eh?" he said. "I pick out a vessel, and you tell 'em to get out of town?"

"Something like that," Mathew replied. "O'Conner is a bit more tactful than that. We'll promise to double the leprechauns' offer, in exchange for giving you three safe passage and a hasty departure."

Nicholas grinned and winked. Sir Mathew remained unmoved. Undeterrable as ever, Nicholas ignored him and turned to Cyrus, clapping the youth roughly on the shoulder.

"Follow me, lad," he said. "We've got something to talk about."

"Not me?" Emy cut in.

"You can overhear just fine," Nicholas replied, already wheeling Cyrus off some paces away from the group.

It wasn't easy to find a private spot on that crowded dock—impossible is the correct word. In the end, Nicholas found a place nearby a group of pirates who were consumed by a game of dice. That seemed good enough to him. He clapped Cyrus on the shoulder again, hard, and grimaced. Cyrus wasn't sure why. If anyone should grimace, it should be himself, because he was the one getting hit.

"Well, we've been over this before," Nicholas started. "I'm not the best with words, so I'll just get out with it. I overheard your conversation with Emy back there, and you two got one thing right. If Takeo's here, that changes everything."

Cyrus took a deep breath as hope filled him.

"You're going?" he asked.

"No. And neither are you."

For a moment, Cyrus didn't react. The rebuttal struck so swiftly that Cyrus had to blink and think before it registered.

"I'm sorry," he said, shaking his head. "Come again?"

"If you're thinking back to that conversation with your father, you should have known I was lying out my arse the whole time. I never had any intent to follow you two. You don't need my help to travel across some mountains. However, if Takeo's up there, then—"

"Stop right there," Cyrus cut in. "I'm not talking about you at this point. You said that I'm not going, as if you get to dictate what happens to me. We've had this conversation already, haven't we? As I recall, the only person who gets to decide where I'm going is me."

"Yeah, well, I was getting to that if you hadn't interrupted me. Did you not hear the part about the Dark Lord scouring Khaz Mal for the angel? At this point, we can damn well scrap this entire plan. We're not going to Khaz Mal, and neither is Emy. I'm sending her to who-knows-where faraway, and you and I are heading back to the farm to bunker down. Aiguo doesn't want us, so once Emy's gone, we're free and clear, and alive, which is more than I can say for Ephron."

Cyrus balked.

"You'd let the angel die? You're not going to warn him?"

"Let him die? By Valhalla, boy, that angel's probably already dead. I'm not about to let you and Emy go tromping off to join him."

"No, no, that can't be."

"Oh? And why not? You think Takeo will find it in his non-existent heart to spare a creature he already helped try to kill once before?"

"No. I'm saying that if Takeo had found and killed the angel already, he'd be back in Lucifan by now."

This time Nicholas balked. It took him a few blinks to recover his power of speech. Cyrus couldn't resist a triumphant smile.

"Alright, I'll give you that," Nicholas said. "Still doesn't change the fact that we're not going. Even with Ephron alive, we won't find him any sooner than Takeo. Rather, we're more likely to find Takeo first, since he'll be hunting the same prey."

"Unless Ephron is avoiding him," Cyrus pressed, feeling momentum. "Like he dodged Emy, perhaps the angel is dodging Takeo, too. Perhaps Ephron will be looking for us. It actually makes sense, as it's the only reason to explain why Takeo hasn't found what he's looking for."

"Shut your damn mouth, boy! The Dark Lord isn't someone you can reason with, and you can't leave without my help. What I say goes, and I say neither you nor Emy are taking a ship to your death."

"And I'm saying I don't care what you say! We'll leave on foot, then."

"Not gonna happen," Nicholas said and loomed closer.

"And why's that?"

Nicholas put his massive hands together and popped his knuckles. Then he grinned. Cyrus stared at those hands, then into the eyes of the lumbering wall of muscle in his path. At that moment, Cyrus knew he was making the right choice. If there was one thing he'd learned, it was that if people had to resort to violence to stop him, then he was going the right way.

"It's going to take more than that to stop me," Cyrus said. "I've taken more than one beating in my life."

Nicholas cocked an eyebrow.

"That determined, are you?" he said. "Even against the likes of me? You know you don't stand a chance."

"Doesn't matter. How would you feel, huh, if you quit without trying? Without knowing?"

"Oh, I know," he said, grinding his teeth. "Against this opponent, I know you'll lose."

"You don't know anything. You're just a bully, a shadow of a man living in fear, and that's what you'll be remembered for."

Cyrus had meant for the words to sting, but the stunned look that came over Nicholas went further than he expected. Nicholas' jaw dropped, and a touch of color faded from him. His eyes hollowed out for a moment, lost in a thought that Cyrus had no ability to discern. He tensed, waiting for the strike. He waited several heartbeats.

However, Nicholas didn't swing. He lowered his hands, slowly, and went limp in quiet thought. He shook his head.

"Nah," Nicholas said. "You ain't worth it."

Cyrus relaxed.

Nicholas swung.

The strike was unbelievably fast, like an arrow released from a bow. Nothing that big should be able to move that fast, yet Nicholas' fist darted out with enough power to smash a log. If it had not been for years and years of training against rapidly striking elves, Cyrus would never have been able to get his hands up in time.

Yet he did.

Nicholas' destructive blow planted directly into both of Cyrus' open palms with not a breadth of space to spare before it would have struck the boy's face. Cyrus tumbled back, nearly tripping, but caught himself after a few steps. He planted his feet and took a sharp breath. He must have looked stunned, almost as stunned as Nicholas looked.

The viking stood there, fist outstretched, jaw once again hanging loose. The two stared at each other in mutual disbelief.

Cyrus blurted out the first words that came to his lips.

"Did you just try to hit me?" he asked.

Nicholas blinked.

"After you got me to let my guard down?" Cyrus added, trying to explain himself. "That's low."

At that moment, Emy came up to them. A smile slipped across her face as she stared at Cyrus, proudly if he could judge.

Nicholas hardly noticed her. His attention fell to his fist, where he stared at it like he'd never seen such a thing.

"Oh yes, it was a surprise for me, too," she said. "You think I'd be that cruel, to bring someone who stood no chance on his own into Khaz Mal?"

"Where did you learn to fight, boy?" Nicholas demanded.

He hadn't lowered his fist. Cyrus hadn't lowered his hands.

"From an elf," he replied. "A one-armed elf, by the way. Maybe you should have learned from her, too."

"She also trained a human," Emy cut in. "Isn't that right? You said some foreigner took lessons from her, say about fifty, sixty years ago? And that person left a katana as a parting gift."

"Yes, I said that. And why is that so important? It was ages ago."

Nicholas turned to Emy and blinked his disbelief. A single, knowing nod was her only reply.

"What?" Cyrus demanded. "Why is this so important?"

Nicholas didn't answer, not at first. He stared at his fist again, then his feet. His eyes were wide, and beads of sweat formed along his hairline. He shook his head, clearly arguing with himself—no, steeling himself. He swallowed hard and looked up at the colossus that towered over them all.

"This is it," he whispered.

If it hadn't been for his enhanced hearing, Cyrus would have missed it. Then Nicholas turned to him.

"I'll tell you on the ship," he said.

Chapter 19

Nicholas didn't take long to select a ship. He found a viking vessel moored alongside the docks, singled out the captain, and engaged in a shouting match that drew enough attention to make Cyrus nervous. He was glad the knights were nearby.

It turned out Nicholas and the captain knew each other, or rather knew of each other. The captain introduced himself as Jarl Kvar Erikson, and he was a bald, heavyset man. Cyrus learned from Emy that a jarl was a type of king among the vikings, as well as typically the captain of a ship. Kvar then followed up Nicholas' announcement with, "You're the Immortal Slayer?"

For the first time, Cyrus got a glimpse that perhaps Nicholas was more than hot air. Meanwhile, Emy whispered to Cyrus.

"Well, it didn't go like I thought, but it worked," she said. "Nicholas is coming. I can't believe this big oaf thought he could stop us."

"I can't believe he changed his mind so quickly," Cyrus replied. "He seemed rather against the whole thing to begin with."

"I think he's been fighting the urge to go ever since we met. You don't know Nicholas like I do. He's wilder than most animals. Staying cooped up on that farm was killing him inside. He was just looking for an excuse to go somewhere, a purpose to fulfill. He'll be happier than ever, watch."

Once pleasantries—for lack of a better word—were exchanged, payment was then promised by the knights, and Kvar had everything he needed to take them aboard and cast off. Cyrus learned a lot of things in that short time, like that viking ships' sails could only be used in certain weather, under certain wind conditions, and that otherwise the ship had to be physically rowed by the crew, using massive oars that required two people to maneuver. Cyrus also learned that part of their payment included participating in said rowing.

It was hard labor.

The viking ship steered and rowed out of the harbor, then twisted until the wind caught the sails just right, pushing them north along the coast. Only then did Cyrus get a break. Strong as he was, he'd never applied his strength in such consistent, unyielding rhythm. He could tell his arms and shoulders would be sore in the morning. His rowing partner, a massive woman missing three teeth, gave his back a hearty slap of a job well done. Then she laughed when he winced in pain.

The crew broke away and gathered around for food and water. Some went below, others pulled out dice and played games. Kvar stayed in the back, leaning on a massive rudder to steer the ship, keeping the winds moving it along while fighting the waves that tried to push them into the rocky shoreline.

Nicholas made his way to the bow, which was currently vacant. Cyrus and Emy joined him.

Cyrus couldn't say that Nicholas looked happier, but he certainly wasn't as dour. Nicholas gazed headlong into the open ocean, hair flying about him, and took in every breath of salty air that battered against him. He didn't even flinch as the water struck the ship and splashed him. If Cyrus could describe it, he thought Nicholas appeared at peace.

"Two things always struck me about Takeo," Nicholas began. "Firstly, he's a damned good fighter. Impossibly good, some might say. Sure, he spent his whole life fighting, and clearly, he'd been born with natural talent, but the way he fought was unnerving. He dodged like no one I'd seen before, and no one I've seen since. Most warriors either carry a shield or wear armor to block blows, or they keep their distance and wait for an opening. Takeo though, I swear he can see an attack coming before his opponent thinks to swing. He dodges on a razor's edge, with hardly a hair's breadth to spare. His body is covered in scars from slight miscalculations, but flesh wounds don't drop a foe in a fight. They can get infected, sure, but Takeo's body puts up a wicked fight. I've seen him recover from countless things that would have killed a lesser man.

"Takeo learned these techniques from his brother, who supposedly learned them from their father, who supposedly learned them while traveling abroad. Takeo never put much thought into it, but I did. See, I've traveled the world, fought a lot of people and a lot of creatures—ain't nothing out there that moves like that son of a bitch. At least, let me rephrase, nothing I've ever met.

"Secondly, Takeo has something else unique to him. While every samurai has a family sword, only the Karaoshi blade comes in a treantwood sheath. I'll cut to the point. You know who deals in woodworking with treantwood? Elves and amazons. You know which of those two I've never fought? Elves. Takeo Karaoshi fights with elven techniques. Someone taught his father some fifty or sixty years ago techniques that can only be formed over hundreds of years of practice, who then passed those skills onto his sons who were unnaturally talented as it was. Like giving a kanabo to an oni, as they say in Juatwa.

"I never shared these thoughts, but I can't be the only one who came to this conclusion. It only makes sense the more you think about it. Elves live for hundreds of years and hone their skills to unprecedented levels. They taught my sister bow techniques that made her utterly unmatched on the battlefield, and that was with minimal training. And it would be just like an elf to rely on speed and dodging, as opposed to brute strength or heavy armor.

"You see, Takeo taught me some of his techniques, but it's not the same. Quite frankly, he's not that good of a teacher, and quite frankly, I've already had my own fighting styles engraved into me. To fight like Takeo—truly like him—you have to be untainted. You have to be fast, fearless, and intelligent to a degree that's difficult to reach by anyone who has been taught to avoid stepping in front of an oncoming blade."

"And you think I have those qualities?" Cyrus asked, elation filling him.

"No."

Cyrus' smile fell.

"Emy has those qualities," Nicholas continued without missing a beat. "But you know what she doesn't have? A teacher."

Cyrus paused, his defeated attitude stalled by a bout of surprise. Well, first it was confusion. Any halfwit could see at this point what Nicholas was getting at, but the thought was still too shocking for Cyrus to grasp.

"Me?" he stuttered out.

"Yes," Emy explained, an excited smile spreading across her face. "It took him a while, but Nicholas has finally caught on. Remember how I told you that Takeo never trained me to fight? He knew, he always knew, just what I would be capable of if given proper guidance."

"I tried to teach her, honestly I did," Nicholas went on. "But I'm trying to pass on skills that have been handed down and changed through four different teachers, each one muddying the techniques along the way—worst of all, myself. But you, Cyrus, you've been taught by the very elf who gave Takeo the edge he has over all others. This will sound crazy, but I think you possess our only chance at taking that bastard down."

"And, and," Emy jumped in, cutting Cyrus off before he could stammer out another line of disbelief. "On top of that, you are completely right about the angel. It's what I've been thinking, too. If Takeo had found Ephron, he'd be back in Lucifan by now. Between the knowledge you possess about Takeo's fighting style and the potential power this angel could give, it might just be enough."

Nicholas took a deep breath, but Cyrus stopped him before either could launch into another explanation.

"Stop, stop," he begged, holding up a hand. "One thing at a time. This is unbelievable."

"Knew you'd say that," Nicholas said.

"I'm not a teacher," Cyrus replied.

"And why not?" Emy said. "Have you ever tried to teach anyone?"

"No, but, well, I was considered a bit of a failure among the elves, and among the werewolves, I guess. How can I be a success to you?"

"Was it your sword technique that was a failure?" Nicholas asked.

"Well, no, but—"

"Cause that's all I'm asking of you," Emy cut him off again. "Just show me what Ven showed you. I'm not asking you to make me a master, or to be perfect. I just need to know what you know."

"And find that angel for you," Cyrus added.

"Yes, and find the angel," she said.

Cyrus shook his head. He thought back to that conversation the two of them had in the forest, when Emy had figured all of this out. Cyrus had been too dense to pry, but Emy had formulated a plan right then and there and shared it with no one.

"No wonder you came back for me," he said. "You didn't feel guilty about the danger you put my clan in. You realized you couldn't leave the forest without me."

"I felt a little guilty," Emy replied.

"What were you going to do? Strongarm my stepfather into helping you recruit me?"

"It doesn't matter what I had planned, or my reasons behind it," Emy pressed. "That's all in the past. Maybe I came back for you for selfish reasons, but what does that matter? I still came back because you are important, and you need to understand that this isn't a responsibility you can shirk. You've heard now, from many people, what we—no, the world—is up against. Worse, in the form of Aiguo, you've only glimpsed the surface of the lengths Takeo will go to see his vision completed. Not a single one of us has the luxury to be stubborn or noble."

"She's right, lad," Nicholas spoke up. "This is bigger than any of us. I wasn't willing to stand up so long as I thought we stood no chance, but between the angel, you, and Emy, I realized it was time to go all in. It's now or never. What kind of man do you want to be?"

Cyrus fell into silence. He'd been thinking about that a lot lately. He wondered if Nicholas knew about it, too. Cyrus knew he wanted to be a 'good' man, whatever that was. The elves had sworn to teach him right from wrong, but the only thing he'd learned from them was that good could be evil, too. The elves protected themselves and the treants, but they could be cruel and cold to those on the outside. His stepfather had shown him true cruelty, of course, but still that only showed Cyrus what not to be. Now here was another offer, from two still mostly strangers, asking him to go on a crusade against a man he'd only met as a child.

Yet weren't they right? Hadn't Cyrus seen and heard all he needed to know? From Angor to Lucifan, the only thing people seemed to agree on was that Takeo was a nightmare coming for them all. They had tales to back it up. On top of that, there was Aiguo, and Cyrus stopped thinking there.

He remembered his mother, dead in his arms, and he nodded.

"Okay, I'm in," he said.

"Yes!" Nicholas and Emy cheered in unison.

"But!" Cyrus pressed. "No more lies. Both of you have been keeping things from me in one way or another, and that's not going to work. You want my help, you want to go all in, then let's start now. If you're keeping anything else from me, let's hear it."

Nicholas and Emy paused in their exuberance to share a glance. In that instant, Cyrus realized he was about to be lied to again, yet he had the profound suspicion that these two were lying to each other, as well.

"Nope," Nicholas said, looking back to Cyrus.

"That's the important stuff," Emy followed up.

Cyrus sighed.

* * *

Their trip to the Khaz Mal Mountains would take a good two weeks, Nicholas said. That would put them at the southern edge of the mountain range, where they could begin traveling north and west as the terrain allowed. It sure beat traveling by foot, which could take months.

In the meantime, Cyrus filled his days by beginning Emy's training, only to find she wasn't completely inept to start. True to his word, Nicholas had tried to teach Emy some things, but the viking style of combat seemed to rely much more on brute strength than cunning speed. It was strange to think of his own training as a fighting style, Cyrus thought. He'd only been taught one way to fight, and also had only seen that one way throughout his life. No creature of Angor fought with a sword. What Ven had shown Cyrus had been treated as fancy art among the elves, about as useful as an interpretative dance. Not only did the forest have a lack of metal for proper swords, but in a place where stealth was key and engagements were small, striking from a distance gave intelligent beings the advantage over dangerous foes like bugbears, treants, and werewolves. Only an idiot would try to fight a bugbear with a sword.

Yet here Cyrus was, on a ship, traveling to a place he couldn't remember, teaching a rakshasa a skill he'd been led to believe was mostly useless.

183

"There is no trick to a near dodge other than practice," Cyrus explained. "Ven used to tie my hands behind my back and swing at me with various lengths of sticks. I got hit, a lot, but overtime I began to judge distance and timing by eyesight alone. The trick is that you can't just run away. You can't walk backwards faster than your opponent can walk forwards, so you have to keep close enough to make them think they can hit you. Ven might have only had one arm, but I swear that made no difference. My only reprieve was when she was swinging, so I learned to bait her with just enough space. She started with that, so I think we should, too."

Cyrus felt like a fraud as he spoke, but Emy listened with rapt attention. She watched Cyrus' every move, nodded at his words, and flexed her muscles as if trying to engrain his speech into her very fiber.

"Okay, let's get started," he said, clapping his hands together.

The best the viking ship had for sticks were the personal fishing rods of the crew, who were rather reluctant to give up their prized, food-finding possessions. They demanded to know the reason, and once Cyrus explained in his most mumbled, embarrassed fashion, they howled and gladly handed their poles over.

Then they all gathered around to watch Emy get beat with a stick.

Nicholas tied Emy's hands while Cyrus shifted awkwardly under the eager grins of the crew. Now he really felt like an idiot. Had Ven really taught him anything by doing this? Was he doing it right? What if this entire exercise had served no other purpose than to get Cyrus off his lazy, childhood feet? The more he thought about it, the more idiotic this seemed. All he had to do was look around at the hardened warriors grinning in anticipation.

"Cyrus!" Emy shouted, perhaps for the third time.

"Huh, what? Sorry," he said, breaking out of his trance.

"Remember, don't hold back," she commanded. "It's fine if you hit me. I don't break easily."

Cyrus wondered who was actually in charge here.

He swallowed his pride and put his faith in Ven. If Emy could stomach the eager grins of onlookers, then he could, too—especially since he wasn't the one being hit this time around.

He swung fast and hard. Emy leaned back. The pole struck her square in the jaw with a sickening crack, and the entire viking crew winced and then laughed so hard they fell over. Cyrus balked.

"Oh, sorry! I'm so sorry," he said.

Emy snarled and whipped her head back to face him. A huge red and purple welt was already forming on her face. She glared at him, and Cyrus thought she was going to attack him.

"Don't apologize," she snapped. "Hit me again!"

The viking crew stopped laughing. But then Cyrus swung and hit her again, and the crew fell apart once more.

Chapter 20

They practiced for hours, it felt like. Cyrus had to hand it to Emy. She was right; she didn't break easily. With his extra reach, the lack of space on the boat, her tied hands, and the rocking from the waves, Cyrus hit her dozens of times. It wasn't like she gave him a choice either. Anytime he felt bad and tried to pull a punch, she noticed, and she warned him sternly.

"Let me be clear," she'd said. "When Nicholas unties me, I'm going to beat you with every bit of energy I have left, so you had better strike me until I can't move anymore. Are we clear?"

Nope. Cyrus did not hold back.

To the viking crew, this must have been the strangest spectacle. Although Cyrus was both tall and muscular, he easily looked the shortest and skinniest between Nicholas and Emy's chosen form. So here was this young lad, beating an ugly behemoth of a man with a stick, seemingly without pity, remorse, or end, and what proved even more shocking was how the one being beaten kept getting back up. First the vikings laughed, then they howled, and then they started betting. After the first dozen solid blows, they assumed whatever was going on was about to end. After all, how much punishment could any one person take? They could be forgiven for not knowing Emy was a rakshasa.

It was also understandable that afterwards the crew began to notice certain oddities.

They made comments about how strong this person was. When one viking tried to play a trick on Emy by sticking out his foot to trip her, she noticed and kept on walking, practically breaking the man's leg with the force of her kick. The crew also began to whisper in corners how strange it was that Cyrus slept under such a large pile of blankets and panted all night long. And why did he piss in a bucket rather than go outside and relieve himself over the side of the ship like a normal person? It got bad enough soon enough that Nicholas and Kvar had to have words.

"Now look," Kvar whispered in a conversation Cyrus was clearly not supposed to be able to overhear. "I've got nothing but respect for you and your legend; and we both know I was paid well to take you where you want to go, but, by Valhalla, Nicholas, what did you bring aboard my ship?"

"Ain't none of your concern, that's what," Nicholas replied.

"Hey, don't take that tone with me. You know as well as any viking that everything that takes place on a jarl's ship is his or her concern. My men are setting watches and sleeping with weapons in hand, you know that?"

"Look, I ain't asking for much. It's a short trip. Another week and we'll be out of your hands. You and your crew ain't got nothing to worry about."

"I heard some nasty in rumors in Lucifan, you know. Word is you left the Dark Lord's service. Some say you're on the run from him. I'll bet he'd pay big to know where you were last seen."

A moment's silence passed as the temperature dropped across the ship. Cyrus couldn't see what was happening because he was below deck, but a faint scent of fear slipped by his nostrils, and it didn't smell like it was coming from Nicholas.

"Careful," Nicholas whispered. "You're talking about the Dark Lord now, see? That's not good for one's health, you've probably heard. You were in the taverns, eh? Anyone tell you that although this might be your ship, these waters you're sailing on might not be free one day? Yeah, I see it in your eye, you've heard. But if you want to send word to the Dark Lord, you go right ahead. However, when you do, you better be prepared to answer his question."

"His question?"

"Why'd you let us leave alive?"

Another bout of silence followed, broken by Nicholas scoffing.

"That's what I thought," he said. "And you best remember this, if you don't keep your crew in line, I'll be the least of your problems."

Cyrus had trouble falling asleep after that. There was only one place to sleep, in the cramped hull of the ship, and as he looked around at the swarm of bodies lying down, all he could picture was a swarm of knives. He was glad the trip would be over soon, and for the first time in perhaps forever, he wished the full moon would last a little bit longer.

He envied Emy's ability to change at will. He'd never thought such a thing was possible. He wondered on some level if her kind and werewolves had some sort of relation, but that didn't seem likely. Werewolves were just infected humans, while a rakshasa was something else entirely. However, despite that, he couldn't help but feel like they were two sides of the same coin. Both could shift into strong, fast creatures, covered in fur and armed with claws and enhanced senses. So maybe Cyrus' version was tied to the moon's cycle, and most werewolves were deranged creatures when changed, but the similarities had to count for something. He began to feel a kinship towards her, especially when surrounded by normal humans terrified that such creatures existed.

Weren't they both being hunted? On the run from the same thing and running towards the same thing? Shouldn't that matter?

Cyrus decided it did. At least, it mattered to him.

However, for all the hostility he felt, it turned out Kvar had a change of heart somewhere in those last few days.

Kvar took them ashore personally, a gesture that, in itself, seemed respectful to Cyrus. Kvar could have sent anyone to do this task, or no one at all, really. Once on the rocky shores, on the other side of crashing waves that masked their conversation from the ship, Kvar rubbed his bald head nervously before looking Nicholas in the eye.

"I wanted to apologize for my words earlier this week," the jarl said.

"Away from your crew?" Nicholas pointed out.

"Yeah, well, you know how it is. Image is everything for a jarl, or any viking, ain't it? I'll be honest, these are some strange times. The world is teeming with rumors about this Dark Lord, and I knew you and he were close once. Well, that's what I heard, anyway."

"You heard right, though we aren't anymore."

"I couldn't be sure of that. I took you aboard partly because I wanted to hear the truth of things. You know, he's making war all over the world, they say. This Lord Takeo Karaoshi, he's even fighting with the dwarves, can you believe that? Wants their mines to build weapons for his growing army, I hear, and they told him no. Can't blame them. Ain't no one fights the dwarves, but this man is doing it. I can admire that kind of tenacity, but I'm not so stupid as to admit that don't scare me some, too, especially when I hear he ain't lost yet. What you said to me, how these waters might not be so free one day, struck to the core of what's been keeping me awake at night.

"So, you called my bluff. I ain't going to tell the Dark Lord about you. It's clear you mean to oppose him, which is enough for me, though I have no idea how you three are going to do that. However, I can do better than wish you luck."

Kvar had come to shore with a pack. He reached into it now and pulled out dried and salted meat by the handfuls and shoved it toward them.

"Food for the journey. The going gets tough in Khaz Mal in the winter, as you know. Food can be hard to come by; this should help. I noticed the younger one here looked like he wasn't quite ready for this trip. His pack looked a bit light. We got food enough for our trip, though, and I'll not have any effort that opposes the Dark Lord going unassisted. Here, take it all."

Cyrus balked just long enough to show his appreciation, then eagerly began shoving his pack full of food. Emy and Nicholas, too, filled in what little space remained, and then all three took fistfuls for an early snack. Jark Kvar Erikson grinned and nodded, and Nicholas nodded back. They paused, then clasped arms.

"Best of luck," Kvar said.

"We won't forget this," Nicholas said. "I pray you see your home safe and sound, soon."

"And unburned by a samurai army," Kvar laughed nervously.

Then he left them, taking back to his ship and commanding his men to row them back out to sea. Their rhythmic chanting and grunting faded rapidly in the strong ocean breeze and crashing waves, but the ship stayed in sight for quite some time.

Meanwhile, the trio turned to look at each other, or more specifically, at Cyrus. He smiled wide and held up his handfuls of food triumphantly.

"Ha!" he said. "See? And you thought I was an idiot."

"I still do," Emy retorted. "Except now you're a lucky idiot."

"Eh," Cyrus said. "It's just the world giving back. It's like Ven always said. The future isn't a guarantee, so always do the right thing now."

"Your Ven sounds like she never had to fight for her life," Nicholas mumbled.

"She had her arm torn off by a bugbear," Cyrus replied.

Nicholas blinked.

"Alright, well, let's just hope you keep getting lucky, then," he said. "We're going to need it."

* * *

Once seeing it as a novelty, Cyrus was fast becoming used to encountering new things. Within moments of piercing the Khaz Mal Mountains, Cyrus discovered snow and companions: biting cold and sound absorption. He also found out that he had never truly seen a mountain before.

Cyrus had thought he had seen mountains in Angor. There, the ground rose and fell, sometimes to grand heights that took hours to climb. He had thought most of them rather steep, too, requiring a route that switched back and forth to surmount. A small handful were even sheer to certain height. Now, standing here, Cyrus realized that what he had seen all his life were impressive hills, for Khaz Mal was made up of nothing but true mountains.

Huge, massive columns of rock jutted up into the clouds, sheer for as far as the eye could see. As they began to climb, Cyrus realized that trying to reach the top of any of them would take days. They didn't just climb back and forth, but up and down, too. The vaulted terrain presented countless insurmountable obstacles that towered all around them. Between the elevation, the cold, and the relentless climbing, Cyrus found himself breathing hard in no time at all, his breath materializing as steam even in the light of the sun.

And the silence. Deafening, that was the only word. Cyrus had always thought of Angor as quiet, but he'd been wrong. In Angor, one could at least hear the water rushing from nearby streams, the leaves twitching in the breeze, and the occasional harpy song in the distance. In Khaz Mal, there was nothing. The snow that fell from the sky landed on the ground without a whisper. The rocks stayed perfectly still. Even the water was frozen and unmoving. The only time Khaz Mal made noise was when Cyrus didn't want it to, like with the wind.

There was no breeze in these mountains. It was wind—howling, bitter, biting wind—and it sank its teeth into any exposed piece of flesh. Cyrus' eyes stung, his teeth chattered, and the tips of his fingers and toes beneath his layered clothing went numb. They were better off than his nose and ears, at least.

At the end of the first day, Nicholas found a shallow crack between a massive boulder and a mountainside. He asked Emy to poke her head in and have a sniff.

"There won't be a troll in there," Nicholas said. "We'd smell it from here, but there could be orcs or wargs. Too small for a cyclops."

When Emy checked, shook her head, and went inside, Nicholas commanded they sleep close together for warmth. Whatever nervousness Cyrus felt about that suggestion evaporated as soon as the heat from two nearby bodies pushed back the bitter cold and seeped into his bones. Then the sun went away, and it grew colder.

The wind howled all night, waking Cyrus up multiple times. It was so loud that Nicholas' snoring was blocked out. Cyrus could hardly believe it, that anyone could sleep soundly in weather like this, but then exhaustion took hold and he was knocked out by the lulling warmth of Emy's closely pressed body.

Emy had shifted back into her rakshasa form. It didn't take a genius to realize this was for the fur, as Cyrus remembered how much warmer he felt when he shifted into a fur-covered werewolf. Cyrus leeched that heat from Emy at night and, for the first time in his life, wished with all his heart that the moon's cycle would come again soon. He wanted to be covered in fur, just like her. Even Nicholas had a healthier dose of body hair than Cyrus.

And perhaps that was why, in the morning, when Cyrus finally awoke, he looked up to see Nicholas was already awake. The man stood at the shallow cave opening, shirtless, chest hair swaying in the morning wind. He scratched absentmindedly.

"Hey," Cyrus croaked. "Aren't you cold?"

"Of course, I'm cold," Nicholas replied. "It's colder than a dwarf's arse this morning."

"Then why are you just standing there?"

Nicholas didn't reply, at first. He gazed back out and drew in a breath.

"It's been a long time," he finally said.

Cyrus felt there was more to it than that, but he didn't press. After a lifetime among the elves, he had learned not to press.

"What are we looking for again?" Cyrus asked as they got on the go. "The angel? Ephron? How will we find him?"

"There's no 'we' for this one," Emy answered.

"This one's on you, Cyrus," Nicholas said. "Those who have seen angels, felt their aura, can sense it in a way others will never know. At least, that's what Gavin told us."

"Wait, I'm just supposed to feel this out?" Cyrus said, having to shout over the wind as they turned a corner along a narrow ridge.

"Rough, isn't it?" Emy replied. "Think about it as I had to. I climbed all over these mountains and found nothing. There are countless places to hide, and no tracks to be made for an angel. They fly over the snow, don't need to eat, or sleep, and don't defecate either, apparently, because I never found a damned thing. So, yes, this is what we're forced to resort to."

"Okay, so, I may be a little late on thinking about this, but, uh," Cyrus said, "I don't even remember meeting this angel. I was too young. How am I supposed to remember how it makes me feel?"

"I'm trusting in Gavin on this one," Nicholas said. "Trust in him, too. You'll know."

"But how? When?"

"I don't know, Cyrus," Nicholas said. "Could be some weeks from now, could be tomorrow. Like we said, this one's on you."

Once again Cyrus found himself exerting great effort not to beleaguer this insanity. Yet, he'd decided to come here willingly, so to protest at this point would only make him look like an idiot. As unhelpful as their advice was, that didn't change the fact that Cyrus couldn't blame anyone but himself. He might be able to blame others for the indirect decisions that led him to this point, but how he reacted to those situations had been entirely his choice. That's what Ven always taught him. Actions were beyond his control. Reactions, though, were all his own.

"Think, Cyrus, when the sword comes for you," she would say. "It's your decision to move. It may not seem like much of a choice, but it's still your choice. That distinction, that thin line, must forever stay in your mind. It's as important to morality as it is in combat."

He'd asked her to explain further, but she'd said the truth of it would come when he was older.

Traveling through the frigid mountains of snow and rocks wasn't all aggravation, though. There were glimpses of true beauty now and again, including when Cyrus would stop to marvel at the sheer expanse of the terrain before him. They crossed naturally arch bridges of pure ice, skirted the edges of valleys of colossal size, and even saw an avalanche from a distance, perhaps the most terrifying act of nature Cyrus had ever seen. Sometimes, when they reached the top of a peak, Cyrus would gaze out at the endless landscape of mountains and simply stare in awe. It was quite unlike anything he'd ever seen or imagined. On top of that, as sparsely populated as Khaz Mal was, what life did exist was fascinating. They had a close encounter with a cyclops once—close as in the cyclops was far away on another mountain peak. Nicholas explained that the only reason Cyrus could see the creature at all was because a cyclops was massive, like a treant, only of flesh and blood. Also, they only had one eye and had a knack for throwing boulders at their prey. Cyrus wondered how that could be, as having one eye surely presented a depth perception problem. How did a cyclops know how far to throw its boulder? Nicholas had shrugged as if such questions were futile.

"You don't need to know the distance if you throw hard enough," he'd said.

Yet those creatures paled in comparison to dragons. In fact, everything Cyrus had seen in his life up until this point paled in comparison to dragons. Massive, scaly creatures of solid color, they soared over the peaks on great, outstretched wings. They were majestic, powerful, and terrifying all at the same time. Only once had Cyrus seen one breathe fire on some poor prey at a great distance, and yet the sight alone had nearly knocked him off his feet.

Then one morning, Cyrus saw orcs, and that was memorable for an entirely different reason.

He woke up first thanks to rolling onto a protruding rock, so he decided to get up, stretch, and see where they'd ended up. They'd had trouble finding shelter the previous night and had to make do with a shallow overhang. Their surroundings were otherwise unknown, as the darkness had been too thorough to see much else.

Cyrus scrambled up the closest ledge, dimly aware of Nicholas and Emy rousing as he left.

The ledge he found was narrow and covered in ice, but Cyrus risked standing on it simply for the view, which was marvelous. He looked out over a vast, snowy valley that gleamed in the morning light, sucking in his lips to keep the bitter wind from drying them out. Cyrus began to scan the landscape as he always did, looking for a path forward, and searching himself for any feelings or signs that an angel could be nearby.

He felt nothing and tried not to be discouraged again.

However, his eyes picked up on something. On the other side of the wide valley, on an equally precarious ridge, Cyrus spied another humanoid figure pop into view. It was oddly shaped, though, in that it seemed bulky. He couldn't tell much else from this distance. He squinted as Nicholas scrambled up from below to join him.

"What do you see, boy?" he asked, nearing the top.

"A person, maybe?" Cyrus replied. "Seems big, but not big enough to be a cyclops."

Cyrus, not really thinking things through, went to wave out of habit. When seeing a stranger in Angor, it was best to start out on friendly footing. His hand went up just as Nicholas popped his head over the ridge.

"Get down!" he yelled, grabbing Cyrus by the ankle and yanking hard.

Standing on ice, Cyrus had no chance of staying upright. His leg was ripped out from under him, and he hit the ridge on his chest, knocking the wind from his lungs. He almost fell off altogether if not for Nicholas' grip. The viking yanked him again, back onto the safer side, and Cyrus caught the ledge with his hands.

"Ow! Why'd you do that?" Cyrus shouted as air refilled his lungs.

"Shut up, boy," Nicholas replied. "Not so loud. Your voice could echo across this whole valley. Can't you see that's an orc?"

"No," Cyrus said, gritting his teeth against the pain in his chest. "I've never seen an orc before. And what am I getting down for. It's all the way over there. We didn't duck down when we saw that cyclops."

"That's because the cyclops was too far away, and slow. Orcs are fast, Cyrus—very fast. Their arms are so long they can use them to help themselves run, and they climb like you wouldn't believe. If it saw you, it might well go get the rest of its clan and come after us. Then we'd really be in trouble."

Cyrus nursed his pained chest and said no more. He wanted to argue that he would have gotten down just as quickly on his own, but Nicholas wasn't one for apologizing no matter the circumstance. The two squinted against the sun as Emy joined them.

"I don't think he saw you," she said, squinting, too. "Looks like its head is swiveling about, I think, like it's looking for something. I think we're in the clear."

"Yeah, we must be," Nicholas said. "If he'd seen Cyrus, he'd be gone by now to fetch the others. Always in packs, those ones. Let's go. We'll give that location a wide berth just in case."

Yes, it was memorable, especially the bruise across Cyrus' chest. That took forever to heal.

Chapter 21

Cyrus felt it first thing in the morning. He awoke in a way that he had not done in a very long time: rested and warm. There was nothing different about the air. It was still frigid to the bone. There was nothing different about where he'd slept. It was still unforgiving rock. The warm and rested feeling that came to Cyrus originated seemingly from within him, and it gave him pause.

He dared to hope it was a sign of the angel, but that didn't sound right. When he'd fallen asleep, he hadn't felt any different. He'd been just as cold, hungry, and tired as he'd always been throughout their several weeks long journey through Khaz Mal.

Cyrus went to shake Nicholas awake but stopped. He turned and shook Emy awake instead.

"Hmm, what?" she grumbled, cracking one eye open.

"I feel something," he said.

She paused, taking in the urgency in his voice. Then she popped up to a seated position.

"You do?" she said. "What do you feel?"

"Warm, sort of," Cyrus replied, matching her eagerness. "And, well, comfortable. Safe, maybe is the better word. Safer?"

"You sure you're not slowly freezing to death? I think that's what happens when you get close to dying of cold."

Cyrus frowned and waited for her to chuckle. She didn't.

"Alright, well I don't think that's the case," he said. "I hope."

"Let's assume you're going to survive. The angel, then? It must be."

"Once again, that's what I hope."

They both scanned their surroundings. Nothing seemed different by sight, smell, or sound.

"So, where is it?" she asked.

"I don't know," Cyrus replied. "You two just told me that I would know somehow, and I haven't noticed anything since we got here. However, what I'm feeling right now, it's different. But you don't feel anything?"

"Nope. Maybe we should go back to the idea that you're dying."

Cyrus cocked his head at her, then kicked Nicholas. Nothing happened. He kicked Nicholas again, hard.

"Urm, I'm up, I'm up," Nicholas mumbled. "One of you better be dead, waking me up while I'm sleeping well."

"That's actually the debate," Emy replied.

Nicholas' eyes flew open. His hand was already around the handle of his maul, which had been lying half under him as he slept. However, when he saw that neither Cyrus nor Emy were bleeding or otherwise in pain, he scowled.

"What is it?" he asked, annoyed.

"Cyrus says he feels warm," Emy said. "He thinks it could be the angel, but it's also possible he's dying from exposure to the cold."

Nicholas' hand flew to Cyrus' forehead. The hand was ice-cold.

"Nah, he ain't dying yet," Nicholas said.

"Thank you," Cyrus replied, pushing the hand away. "I also feel rested."

"So?"

"I haven't felt rested in weeks. We've been sleeping on rocks."

Nicholas glanced down to the rock he'd been sleeping so comfortably upon. Then he glanced back at Cyrus.

"Could be you're finally toughening up," the viking said. "Not being so wimpy anymore."

"Are either of you going to take me seriously? I'm telling you, this is a sudden and obvious change, and if it isn't exactly what we've all been waiting for, then I have no idea what to do. Are you going to help me or not?"

Nicholas and Emy shared a glance and a hint of embarrassment passed between them. Nicholas rubbed his eyes.

"Alright, okay, sorry, just trying not to get my hopes up," the big man said. "Let's see. Gavin told me about the angels more than once. He told me being near them always made him feel safe and warm."

"Safe," Cyrus repeated. "That's exactly how I feel."

Now even Emy perked up.

"So, what do I do?" Cyrus asked.

"I don't know," Nicholas shrugged. "The way Gavin explained it, it seemed like a proximity thing, like fire. The closer you were, the stronger you felt."

"Let's get moving, then," Emy said.

Cyrus nodded. They all got up and packed what little supplies they had gotten out the night before. They emerged from their shelter, and all eyes fell on Cyrus.

"Well?" Nicholas said after a long pause.

Cyrus wasn't sure what to do. Nothing had changed in the half dozen steps he had taken out into the snow, except that now he felt colder as the merciless mountain wind beat against him. Cyrus swallowed and deflected his gaze, keeping the icy air from pushing into his nostrils. He also kept quiet as he'd realized that answering Nicholas' question would do him no good. He'd have to go this alone.

"This way," he said, hoping he hid the uncertainty in his voice.

Cyrus climbed one low ridge and then another, trying to find the path of least resistance, or at least one that wouldn't require him to dig his hands into the snow and latch onto ice-covered rocks. However, after no more than a few minutes' travel, he paused.

"Wait," Cyrus said, curiously. "I think I'm going the wrong way."

"Hm?" Nicholas replied. "You feeling okay, lad?"

"Maybe? Hang on."

Cyrus ventured off to the left. He couldn't say what struck him at first, but he'd lost confidence on the path they were originally following. He couldn't say what was going through his mind now, but this new direction felt right.

"This way," Cyrus said.

Emy smiled.

"He's got it," she whispered.

Nicholas didn't look too sure, but he followed all the same, even as Cyrus chose a particularly harrowing path straight up a large, sheer boulder. They had to go up, taking turns, with Nicholas lifting each of them up to the top, and then the two reaching back to haul the massive human over the side. From their new vantage point, they found themselves on the false summit of an even larger peak.

Cyrus gazed at it, for the first time feeling the overwhelming desire to climb.

"How far?" Emy asked, following Cyrus' gaze.

"To the top," he said. "We have to reach the peak."

Nicholas whistled as he took in the mountain.

"You won't be able to do it alone," he said.

"Maybe that's the point," Cyrus replied.

Up and up and up they climbed. It was a brutal ascent between the biting cold, the ice-covered rocks, and the relentless wind. Cyrus almost tumbled over the side once, but Emy caught him. Nicholas outdid them both. Practiced and sturdy, his long arms reached and found holds with a surety Cyrus envied, and Nicholas would then pull or twist his body with ease until he found similarly hidden pockets of purchase. On more than one occasion, Cyrus stared dumbfounded as Nicholas turned and climbed sideways up a chute or over a boulder in ways that would never have even occurred to him. Emy seemed no less awed, but she tempered her stares with scholarly interest, attempting to take the same path Nicholas did, although she often had to cheat by sticking her claws out for extra purchase. For everything else, there was rope and extra hands, and level by level they climbed.

As they neared the top, all three were out of breath thanks to exertion and thin air. However, the closer they came, the better Cyrus felt and the harder he pushed. As they rolled over the ledge of another ice shelf, gasping for air and avoiding the vertigo that came when one peered back over the side, Cyrus paused to glance around.

They weren't quite at the top, yet, but something caught his eye. At the far end of their narrow ledge, he saw what appeared to be a human-sized crack in the rock, lit by the sun. He couldn't say what caught his attention at first, but it dawned on him that the sun was off to his right somewhere. It shouldn't have been able to light up anything over there.

Yet, just as he was thinking this, the light went out. Not slowly or gradually, but all at once like a candle being blown out. And just as Cyrus was considering this oddity, it was back.

He stood up and inched his way along the ledge towards it. Even as one of his feet slipped along the ice, he felt nothing but confidence.

"Woah, easy there," Nicholas called after him between gasps for air. "Maybe there's an easier way up."

"Nicholas, look," Emy said, standing.

She'd noticed the light, too, and began to follow Cyrus. Nicholas went quiet. He paused for a moment, clearly unsure of the ice and narrowness of the ledge, but conceded to follow.

Cyrus came to the large crack and reached his hand out, touching the light with his fingers carefully as if it might burn him. Warmth spread into the numbness that permeated his hand, and he smiled.

"Well? Are you going to come in?" a voice echoed out from the crack.

Cyrus slipped again on the ice and dropped low to keep himself from falling. Emy, who'd reached him by now, grabbed his shoulder to steady him. The voice had also caught her off guard, but her claws kept purchase on the rock. Nicholas stared speechless from the back.

"It's been some time," the voice continued. "I've been searching for you ever since I felt your presence. I knew the danger, but, well, a shepherd worries for his flock, as they say. I can only imagine how much you've grown. Step into my light, Cyrus, and bring your friends with you."

The voice echoed, yet it shouldn't have. It wasn't loud enough for that. Cyrus' confidence seeped away from him in the shadows of uncertainty, the innate fear of the unknown, before he swallowed down his hesitation and braced himself. He took a deep breath and slipped into view.

Cyrus could not have been less prepared.

The crack in the rock grew wide, then narrowed to a point beneath an overhead slab, creating a small cave barely large enough for its one occupant, especially with its great, feathered wings filling the void. Yet, Cyrus had been prepared for the wings. He had been told angels could fly, so he could only assume they had wings, though he hadn't thought to imagine them as covered in spotless, snow-white feathers, which contrasted starkly with the angel's humanlike skin and black, curly hair. It even took Cyrus a moment to notice how tall the angel was, and that the angel was wearing nothing but a thin, modest, white linen cloth. He was too distracted by two things: firstly, that the angel was impractically beautiful, and secondly, that the light that shined out of the cave came not from a fire or a lamp, but from the angel's eyes.

Or rather, to be more specific, the angel's eye sockets glowed. Where eyeballs and irises should have been was a hollow space that poured out the light of the sun, as incandescent and warm as the real thing, and so intense that it hurt Cyrus' eyes to gaze upon the source directly. Yet gaze he did because it also hurt to look away. Framed in that golden light, previously unimaginable beauty filled Cyrus' vision. The angel had a face and a body of such chiseled perfection that it would take a sculptor a lifetime of experience to imitate.

And that was just how things appeared. As those rays of holy light fell over Cyrus, what he felt was indescribable. All the cold about him was banished in an instant, replaced by warmth and safety and love. Cyrus fell to his knees, overwhelmed with disbelief and unable to comprehend the sudden change in his heart. He felt like a child again, wrapped in his mother's arms, protected and valued and understood in a way that was innate and pure. Tears formed in his eyes, and he made no move to brush them away.

Emy rounded the corner next, and if she felt anything that Cyrus did, she betrayed no signs. That wasn't to say she was emotionless, however, as her mouth fell open and her eyes went wide, clearly taken by the majesty of this creature. How could she not? Eyes of sunlight? The magnificence was overwhelming. Nicholas, however, appeared just as dumbstruck as Cyrus. He mumbled some swear words and stumbled against the closest rock wall, catching himself as if physically struck.

"Ephron?" Nicholas mumbled.

"Yes, you've found me, but before we go any further, I must first apologize," the angel said. "To you, my dear."

Cyrus and Nicholas gaped at Emy. Neither could imagine Ephron capable of any wrongdoing.

"Me?" Emy replied, equally surprised.

"Yes, for avoiding you all those months ago," Ephron said. "I sense living things in the same way they sense me. I see not people, but their souls, and in you I sensed an old acquaintance I'd rather not see again."

"Takeo," Emy whispered. "You know he hunts you. And you thought I was him?"

"No, but I cannot read your kind as easily as I read humans, and I did not know your intent. I kept my distance, although I must commend your tenacious efforts to track me down."

Emy pursed her lips, suppressing a smile. Although she wasn't as humbled as the humans, it was comforting to Cyrus to see her enjoying the angel's company.

"When I sensed you traveling with these two," Ephron continued, "I realized I had misjudged you. I took the risk to hide here. I felt it was necessary. Not only to see the brother of Emily Stout, but to see a past soul I had tried to help. I had to know, Cyrus, if I had helped you as I had hoped."

Ephron's light fell directly onto Cyrus now, piercing in its intensity. Cyrus could have sworn the rays went through him, like a fire's warmth on a cold night, heating him from within. He mumbled a cry of surprise and closed his eyes, squeezing tears down his cheeks.

"Pain," Ephron said, speaking with the sorrow Cyrus felt. "Suffering. I fear to ask. Cyrus, have I wronged you?"

"No, never," Cyrus answered without thinking. "My mother, she died."

Ephron put a hand to his lips, and Cyrus felt guilty for causing this creature any moment of suffering. He never should have said anything.

"That is terrible," the angel said. "I can only imagine your pain. Have you come seeking answers, my child, or solace?"

Cyrus was about to say no, but stopped. That seemed a lie at this moment. Sure, Emy's request had provided him the opportunity to come here, but had that really been the reason? Were answers, and solace, really what he had been seeking this whole time?

"I asked him to come," Emy jumped in. "To find you. We all came, actually, to find you."

Ephron frowned.

"All this trouble for me?" he said. "My, my, you are persistent, aren't you? To be so focused at your age. What is your name?"

"Emy," she answered. "Just Emy. I was named after, well, her."

"Emily Stout. The one who named you must have known her well."

She nodded but offered no more. Emy shifted her weight and leaned forward, staring intently at Ephron and not at all disturbed by his gaze.

"This is about Takeo?" Ephron said.

"This is about Takeo," Emy confirmed. "He hunts you. Do you know why?"

The angel smiled.

"Takeo does not hunt me. He is trapped. He seeks me, yet I hesitate. I do not think I can free him."

"I knew it," Nicholas blurted out, snot running into his beard as he blew out tears. "I knew it! You can help him, can't you? It's that sword of his, ain't it? I watched as it changed him, cultivated that dark side in him, and shut out the light my sister saw. I always knew it."

"He's not a lost child, Nicholas," Emy retorted. "Takeo is beyond saving."

"Stop, please," Ephron spoke up, raising hands that were spotlessly clean. "There is no need to argue. You are both right in your own ways. However, to answer your question, Nicholas, no. You speak of my saving Takeo as a certainty when it is anything but. The only certainty is that I cannot run from him forever. We must meet, and soon, though I have hesitated for quite some time. Now I know why."

He spread his hands, gesturing to all of them, and smiled once more. It made Cyrus smile in return.

"Please," he said. "Ask whatever you need of me. I am here to help."

"The colossus," Emy spoke up immediately. "I need it to stop Takeo. Can you give me control of it, as Emily once had?"

"No," Ephron replied just as quickly. "It was never mine to give."

Emy froze. All her momentum, all her hope, all the light in her eyes went cold. She didn't even breathe.

"But," she mumbled.

Ephron shook his head, regretfully but firmly.

"I came all this way," she continued. "Surely?"

The angel's face never changed. He turned slowly from her to Cyrus.

"I'm sure you have questions, child," Ephron said. "And I hope you'll find the answers satisfying."

Cyrus did have questions. So, so many questions. What should he do? Where should he go? Did Ephron know his mother? What did he think of her? Would he get better? Would the world get better? Was it wrong to want revenge for his mother's death? Was it wrong not to want revenge? Did it make him less human? Was he a bad person? Could he be a good person? Was that even a worthy goal?

Life. All of life was a question, too many to ask, and none of them seemed likely to produce a satisfying answer. Would an angel even know what to say?

Yet then Cyrus glanced at Emy and saw her distraught expression. Unlike Cyrus, here was someone who was focused and determined with the will to succeed. She'd put all her effort into this worthy goal, stopping the Dark Lord, who sowed terror and death in his wake. Now here she was, blunted and left hanging, all her hopes and dreams smashed against cold, unyielding rocks. Did Cyrus not owe her for saving his life in a way? Had not everything that had happened to them since they'd met seemed like destiny?

Cyrus paused at that. He didn't want to think of destiny in terms of revenge, but he could think of it as helping. Perhaps it was his destiny to help Emy fulfill hers. And if not, well, he would find his purpose eventually, maybe even one as worthwhile and driving as her own.

"The Dark Lord," Cyrus said. "Takeo, I mean. As Nicholas said, whatever potential he once had has rotted away. His underlings kill indiscriminately to serve his will. The mere mention of his name frightens all. He's attacking peaceful civilizations that haven't caused anyone harm in living memory. These things cannot be ignored. If the colossus cannot be commanded and you cannot save him from himself, then you must give us something else. Tell us, how can we stop him?"

Cyrus glanced at Emy and nodded. She smiled back, grateful. Ephron, though, only turned his head and grimaced. As he lowered his eyes, the cave darkened.

"Of course," he whispered. "I should have known it would come to this. My brother, Quartus, may his soul rest in peace, saw this coming. When Takeo last came to me, I saw the darkness within him and did what I could to seal it up. Somehow, my seal did not hold, or it was broken. I still wanted to believe that Quartus had not died in vain, that he had given his life to prevent this moment, but now I cannot ignore the truth. His plan merely gave the world a chance. He died not as payment, but as a gamble."

Ephron shuddered and closed his eyes, shutting out the last bit of light and hiding himself in shadow. When he opened them again, new resolve washed over his beautiful figure. It swelled Cyrus' heart just to gaze upon it.

"So be it," the angel said. "What you seek is nothing short of greatness. You are but frail individuals set against an overwhelming tide of power. It will take more than skill, or luck, or wit to take up this challenge. What you need is a miracle."

"Are you saying it's impossible?" Emy asked.

"Shh," Cyrus cut her off. "Listen."

"Improbable," Ephron pressed. "That is the difference. It pains me to send you down this path, as it will cause nothing but suffering, but so you asked, and so shall I obey. You need a miracle, but it must be of your own making. Head north, to the land of ice and warriors. At the very edge of these mountains, you will find a village. Small but hearty, there exists in those mountains an ancient dragon, red as fire and a thousand times as fierce."

He paused. Cyrus thought the angel would continue, but he didn't. Cyrus and Emy shared a glance.

"You want them to slay a dragon?" Nicholas practically shouted. "You can't be serious. Improbable, my arse. Impossible is the only word for that task."

"As I said, it will take a miracle."

"And how's that going to change anything?" Nicholas demanded, which Cyrus thought was quite bold and a touch rude. "Are they going to inherit fire-breathing capabilities or something?"

"Perhaps if we slay this dragon, people will listen to us," Emy offered.

"Oh yeah, that'll be the day," Nicholas scoffed. "You slay a dragon, you're going to get a handshake from the jarl, an offer of marriage from the innkeeper's daughter, and a dandy song in your honor. You know what you won't get? Any closer to impressing Takeo or keeping his armies from devouring all the land."

"Nicholas, please," Cyrus begged. "He's just trying to help."

"Help? No, he's going to get you both killed, that's what."

"You care for them," Ephron interrupted.

Nicholas froze a moment before shaking it off.

"Of course, I care for them," he said. "I promised her father I'd look after her."

"Not just her," Ephron continued, peering deeply into Nicholas. "For Cyrus, too. Wait, yes, you see yourself in him, don't you?"

"Alright, enough of this. We're done."

"You see in him all the potential you once had. That he could overcome where you fell short."

Nicholas' stare could have killed, and Cyrus wondered how anyone could look at an angel that way.

"You know, I ain't above punching you," Nicholas said.

"No," Ephron replied, seeing the truth and finally relenting. "No, I suppose not. You must forgive me if I went too far. I was just intrigued is all. The affection you show reminds me of another. A bittersweet memory—I did not mean to relive it at your expense."

"Well, if you're done filling these two with nonsense, I think we all have the answers we came for. You're still alive, Takeo is looking for you, and you can't help us. Problems solved. Let's go."

"Nicholas, we can't just leave," Cyrus said.

"And why not?"

Cyrus paused. Nicholas' sudden turn to rage was unexpected, to say the least. Wasn't he also in awe of this creature's mere existence? Didn't it fill him with warmth and love, passion and comfort? From Cyrus' perspective, he didn't need a reason to stay here—Ephron was reason enough. Yet, he had to admit that it was exhausting staying alive on this peak. He was having trouble breathing, and it was only partly due to the lack of oxygen.

"I'm afraid he's right," Ephron said. "It is not safe to be around me. I am sought by the man you've set yourself against. The longer I linger here, the more I put you in danger. I will help however I can, but we have spent too much time here already. If you have any final questions, ask them."

Nicholas folded his arms over his chest, while Emy shook her head. Cyrus hesitated, not because he had to think up a question, but because he was afraid to ask it. It took a moment for him to swallow his pride and force the question out. He had to know.

"Ephron," he said. "Do you, would you know, what kind of man I should be?"

A silence fell over the group far heavier than Cyrus expected. He felt his cheeks glow red and he lowered his head so as not to see how Emy or Nicholas were looking at him. All the embarrassment he'd hoped to avoid fell over him, even as Ephron hummed his surprise.

"Cyrus, my child," the angel said. "Is that what's been bothering you?"

He came forward, and Cyrus took a half-step back. Not in fear, of course, but in shock. He felt that his own presence would somehow taint this beautiful, perfect creature, and he feared for its purity as it approached him. Yet, the cliff edge left him nowhere to go, and he remained motionless and helpless as Ephron bent down to eye level.

Ephron reached out and touched Cyrus' cheek, lifting his face up to gaze into his eyes. Ephron's fingers were softer than he could have imagined.

"Cyrus, you should know that no one can answer that question but you," Ephron said. "However, I can give you advice, and this is advice I follow, as well. I find creatures of all kinds try to make decisions they think are 'best' or 'right' in the moment, but they only realize the consequences afterwards. Remember, whatever choice you make, it is you who must live with it. Make choices that you are proud of, that you will not regret, and in doing so, you will eventually become the man you didn't know you wanted to be."

Out of the corner of his eyes, Cyrus saw Emy swallow hard and Nicholas shift uncomfortably. It seemed he wasn't the only one that needed to hear that.

"Thank you," Cyrus whispered. "And I will."

Chapter 22

Ephron was kind enough to fly them one at a time off the top of the peak. For the second time, Cyrus got to experience the thrill of flight, and this time under happier conditions. It pained him to see the angel fly away and to feel the cold slip back into him. Ephron took flight in the opposite direction, due west, deeper into Khaz Mal. The trio watched him go and then set off back across the mountain range they'd traversed to get here. Back across narrow ledges, under immense boulders, over thin ice bridges, and through piles of wind-blown snow. Cyrus tried not to hate every minute of it.

They took a short rest on the side of a steep mountain ledge that protected them from the wind. As usual, they were taking the longer, arduous path around yet another valley. Nicholas always insisted on this, as he said traveling through a valley was a quick way to die. Not only would one be easy to spot by dragons, orcs, and every other meat-hungry creature in the mountains, but it also put one in danger of avalanches. Worse, the 'valley' could be a frozen lake that had thawed just enough to break under foot. All were valid points, of course, but it didn't make the going any easier.

"So, what's our plan?" Cyrus asked as they plopped down and took sips of water.

"Our?" Emy replied. "And here I thought you'd want to head back to the forest."

"I still can," Cyrus admitted. "I've been thinking. The forest, the elves, they'll both outlive me. I can always come back to them, and maybe I will sooner rather than later. But for now, I was talking more about our immediate plan of getting out of these mountains."

"The North is the closest region with access to ports," Emy said, carefully.

Nicholas didn't buy it.

"Hey now, nothing's changed," he said. "Neither of you better be thinking about slaying that dragon. Stupidity outright, that's all that is. I ain't even got to convince you. Just think about it. Supposedly there's this big, red dragon flying around, terrorizing villages filled with warriors just waiting for the chance to die an epic death. You don't think they haven't tried to bring this dragon down, huh? Whole villages of the toughest men and women you've ever seen have been burnt to ash by those creatures. There's no argument to be had here. It'd be easier to slay a hydra."

"That's been done before," Emy muttered.

"Okay, bad choice of words," Nicholas replied, scowling. "That's just an old sailor's saying. And Takeo didn't slay that hydra, he just made it retreat. On the other hand, it nearly killed him, would have killed him, had I not fished his sorry arse out of the ocean. You hear me? I don't care what you two do, but do anything else except fight a dragon."

Cyrus heard, but he didn't listen. He and Emy caught each other's eye, and he could tell she was thinking the same thing. A miracle, Ephron had called it. That's what they needed. So improbable it should be impossible. The idea was just too intriguing.

The conversation was far from over.

"Well, we still ought to head to The North," Emy said.

Nicholas sighed, defeated.

"Yeah, I know," he mumbled. "We should try and find a dwarven kingdom along the way. I could do with a warm meal for once, and some fresh supplies. You two done catching your breath? Yeah? Alright then, let's get moving. We need to find shelter before it gets dark."

Nicholas stood tall and stretched, curling his arms up and making his clothes bulge with the tension of his muscles. Cyrus and Emy went to stand, too, when Nicholas turned west where his height gave him a lookout across the valley.

"Get down!" he said.

Nicholas dropped and grabbed Emy and Cyrus along the way. They all hit the rocky ground with dense thuds. Cyrus grumbled but was glad a meatier part of him took the blow this time, rather than his ribs.

"Orcs," Nicholas said. "I think I saw an orc. Emy?"

"On it," she replied.

She tossed her pack off and went down on all fours. As she crept up the ledge to get a careful look, Nicholas called after her.

"Almost directly across," he said. "A little to the left. I think I saw more than one."

Emy peered over slowly, the fur on her head whipping wildly in the wind. She searched for a few moments, then turned back to them, smiling.

"Three of them, but they're no orcs," she said. "Come and have a look. You're not going to believe this."

Cyrus and Nicholas hunkered down and made their way up the narrow ledge. As Cyrus peered over, he searched through narrowed eyes into the fierce wind. He blinked until water formed, but then that began to freeze, and he had to wipe his eyes. His nose ran.

However, he was able to see what Emy saw after a moment. The three figures in the distance were clearly too small to be orcs.

"Humans?" Cyrus asked.

"Not just any humans," she said, still smiling. "They've been hunting me so long that I can recognize them even from this distance. It's part of Aiguo's crew."

Cyrus ducked lower, the memory of flying knives whizzing passed his head still too vivid to forget. Nicholas whistled.

"Wow," Nicholas said. "Are you sure? I'll admit it. I'm impressed. How'd he get here so fast?"

Emy shrugged.

"By boat? By unicorn?" she offered. "Whatever tracker he hired is worth her weight in gold, that's for sure. However, if you really want to find out, we can ask Aiguo just before I rip out his throat."

"Wait," Cyrus spoke up. "You want to go and fight him?"

"This is the perfect place," she countered. "Mountains like these provide ample places for ambushes and escapes. They're all Juatwa and Savara mercenaries anyways. None of them are familiar with this landscape, not like Nicholas is. This isn't just our best chance to pick them off, it may be our only one. Aren't you tired of being hunted, Cyrus? I say it's time we do some hunting of our own."

Cyrus wasn't too keen on this plan. He wasn't familiar with this landscape either, though if they attacked on a full moon night, he might stand a better chance.

"We might not have an option," he admitted. "If Aiguo was able to track us all the way out here, despite our head start, we may not be able to make it to The North."

"Exactly," Emy said, "and if confrontation is inevitable, then it should be on our terms."

"They haven't moved," Nicholas pointed out. "I think they saw us, or at least me. They don't have the wind or sun in their eyes."

They all paused and stared out across the valley. Cyrus couldn't make out distinctions, but the figures seemed to be directed right at them and none were moving.

"Well damn," Emy said, then swore. "There goes our element of surprise."

"Let's just be glad there's this valley between us," Nicholas said. "Even if they tried to cross it directly, we'll be long gone by the time they reach this spot. See, look. Others are joining them to have a look. Perhaps we'll see the bastard himself. Watch for a shorter one."

"Yes, this game we're about to play will take weeks to play out," Emy said. "It will be helpful to know what Aiguo is wearing."

They watched as three figures were joined by another two, and then a sixth. None were particularly tall, and between the wind and sun's glare, Cyrus wasn't sure even Emy could get a good look.

"They definitely see us," Emy said, holding a hand up to shadow her eyes. "One of them could be Aiguo, but I'm not certain. It's hard to tell with them all covered up. I'm not catching any scents either. Wherever the wind is coming from, it's not blowing from them to us."

Two more figures joined, and the ledge they stood upon grew crowded. One raised an arm, clearly pointing at the trio and shattering all hope Cyrus had that Emy was wrong. One of the newest figures to arrive dropped its hood. The wind caught loose hair and flung it about. Shoulder-length, black hair, if Cyrus had to guess.

Emy went completely still. Her whole body became ridged in a way Cyrus had never seen. Her ears flattened, the hair on the back of her neck stood straight up.

"It's him," she said.

"Who? Aiguo?" Cyrus asked.

"No," Emy replied. "Him."

She locked eyes with Nicholas, raw terror pouring out from her dilated pupils. The color drained from Nicholas' face as he gazed back across the valley in disbelief.

The unhooded, silhouetted figure reached down and grabbed what Cyrus could only assume was the handle of its sword. Then, against all rationality, it leapt from the cliff edge headed straight towards them.

"Run!" Nicholas yelled.

Emy bolted from the edge before the first syllable could leave Nicholas' lips. Cyrus stayed put for only a half second longer, stunned into inaction by the absurdity of what he saw. The lone figure was sailing through air, sliding down rocks, ice, and snow with such speed that surely it would die when it hit the ground. The figure slammed into the valley floor, rolled down the thick piles of snow, and then took off in a mad dash that was starkly inhuman.

Before he could take a breath, Cyrus' animal instincts calculated the time it would take him to reach their position. They didn't have long.

"Run, boy!" Nicholas roared at the end of the half second.

Cyrus went to stand, but Nicholas grabbed Cyrus by the back of his clothes and flung him away from the edge. Cyrus bounced off an ice-covered rock and sprawled across the snow. He staggered to a stand, but Nicholas was already on him, grabbing his clothes again and throwing him once more. Cyrus caught his footing this time only by turning himself into a dead sprint down the steep mountainside. He was running now to prevent gravity from making him tumble to his death. In the distance, Emy was on all fours, bolting with every ounce of energy she had.

"What is that?" Cyrus shouted. "What creature can possibly run like that?"

"Takeo, the Dark Lord, whatever you want to call him, just run!" Nicholas stammered, then screamed into the distance. "Emy!"

The lone figure of Emy, orange-black fur stark against white snow, stopped to turn back.

"The last ice bridge!" Nicholas yelled. "It's our only chance!"

Emy went hard right, hitting the ground on all fours again and dashing back up the mountainside north. Behind her trailed blood, showing she'd cut her paws on jagged rocks, but she didn't slow down.

Cyrus followed her direction, and Nicholas was hot on his heels, sucking wind with an effort that terrified Cyrus almost as much as what he had just seen. He lost sight of Emy as she disappeared behind a massive rocky spiral, and he doubled his efforts to get there before he lost her altogether.

He rounded the corner—legs and lungs burning between effort and drawing down icy air—and was shocked to see her waiting for him. She was at the bottom of a steep, yet low mountain. Cyrus remembered descending it, slowly, carefully, so as not to slip and break his neck at the bottom. Now Emy was crouched down with her hands interlocked and open, clearly ready to give Cyrus a lift up.

"Jump," she yelled.

He reached her, his foot hit her hands, and he jumped, preparing to catch whatever protruding rock he could and climb the rest of the way up.

Emy grunted and flung Cyrus into the air. He yelped as he soared up and up, over the whole cliff, and came crashing down on the very top. He almost had the wind knocked out of him when he hit the icy rocks, and as he struggled to stand, ignoring all the bruises, he heard a feral snarl as Emy jumped almost all the way up on her own. Her claws found purchase, and Cyrus had enough wit to drop back down, grab her arm, and pull her over the side. Nicholas was a heartbeat behind, jumping as high as he could but not nearly as high as Emy.

"Run!" Nicholas commanded as he climbed.

His movements were so frantic he nearly slipped twice, but his arms and legs were a blur, finding purchase as quickly as he lost it. Cyrus reached further down.

"I'm not leaving you," he called.

"Damn it, boy, run! Go, go now!"

Looking this way, Cyrus had a distant view of the spot the trio had just been at, overlooking the valley. He glanced that way just in time to see a dark figure appear.

Its entry was nearly as grand as its first leap. It vaulted over the ledge in clear disregard for whatever lay on the other side, sailing through the air as if it could fly—and at this point, Cyrus thought that perhaps it could. Dark, straight, shoulder-length hair snapped in the wind; it held a long, thin, curved sword in both hands. The thing soared with magnificent and terrifying grace before disappearing behind the rock spire. Cyrus could only assume that a drop from that height and at that speed should kill any mortal being, yet all he heard was a soft thump in the distance, and somehow that horrified him more than anything else.

Nicholas reached the ledge, and the next thing that came up was his fist. It connected with Cyrus' jaw and sent him sprawling back.

"Don't you wait for me," Nicholas roared as he rolled over the side. "Run with everything you have. Your life depends on it."

Cyrus got to his feet, his body alight with adrenaline between fear and pain. He tasted blood in his mouth and swallowed it down, then took off with all his might and speed.

He knew where the last ice bridge was, the one they'd crossed to reach this mountain shelf that bordered a valley. It was a long, narrow, thin bridge that spanned an impossibly deep ravine. They'd considered not crossing it at all, actually. When they did go across, they had gone one at a time, and with a rope tied around their waist. It was the best defensible position they could find. The three of them could hold off an army there. Cyrus just wasn't sure how they were going to get to it quickly enough, as it was down another sharp ledge that they'd had to carefully ascend just a short time ago.

Cyrus reached the ledge and paused. Emy was already scampering across the ice bridge, still on all fours and displaying none of the caution she'd used to cross it the first time. It was a dangerous thing, as the bridge was completely made of ice and snow, and one false move would send her tumbling to her death.

Cyrus peered over the edge at the long drop down to the ice bridge.

"What's the fastest way down?" he said.

He realized the answer before the words left his lips and turned around to see that Nicholas hadn't stopped running.

Cyrus got in one shallow breath before Nicholas slammed into him and sent them both sailing off the side. Cyrus howled on the way down, the seconds drawing out far longer than he thought possible, until they both hit the unforgiving rocks below. Air rushed out of Cyrus' lungs, and the back of his head slammed onto something hard. His whole world went white, then black, then sparkled as his eyes filled with tears and he gasped uselessly for air. Even his ears rang, but through the darkness, he could hear Nicholas telling him to get up and run.

Nicholas hauled the young man to his feet, Cyrus' head coming away from the rocks, sticky and wet, and flung him towards the ice bridge. Cyrus could hardly see it, but he knew better than to argue. Everything hurt, and he couldn't breathe. He became suddenly aware that he was limping, and then realized he'd sprained his ankle. He fell to his knees on the bridge and crawled, unable to trust that his blurry vision and hobbled foot would keep him from falling. He kept moving, unaware of anything around him. Then he must have reached the other side because Emy's clawed hands grabbed him by his shoulder and hauled him upright.

Cyrus' vision had cleared enough to see now. He turned back to find Nicholas wasn't right behind him. The viking had waited until Cyrus had fully crossed, not willing to trust the ice to hold them both. Nicholas took two steps onto the bridge before a dark figure vaulted overhead.

Just as before, the figure was unequivocally graceful and fearless. It soared rather than fell to the ground, heavy winter clothes billowing around it like wings. It struck the rocks with force and went to one knee, one hand on the ice and one hand clenched tightly about its sword. The figure's hair fell over its face like a curtain. Snow kicked loose from above drifted down and, where it touched the figure's pale skin, evaporated into mist.

Nicholas took one look at the figure, one look at Emy and Cyrus, and stepped back off the bridge. He drew his hammer and swung down with an almighty roar. His hammer hit the ice, and one long and deep crack ripped across nature's bridge. For a brief moment, it seemed like the bridge would hold, but then an ear-piercing crunch echoed out, and the bridge shattered into pieces. It fell in massive chunks into the abyss. Cyrus and Emy had to retreat to avoid falling in with the ice, and Emy dragged Cyrus to safety on his useless ankle. When everything came to rest, nothing lay between them and Nicholas but an insurmountable ravine.

Or rather, Nicholas and the Dark Lord.

Chapter 23

The one they called the Dark Lord stood slowly with head bowed. He raised his head at the last moment, hair parting around a face that Cyrus had seen before, thanks to Emy's disguise. He saw the same faint scar along his left cheek, thin lips, pale skin, and a calm disposition.

However, his eyes were a different story. Emy's disguise, as flawless as it had been, could never mimic what Cyrus saw there.

Blacker than a starless night, the pupils were unflinching and focused. Even from this distance, Cyrus was drawn in as if falling into the ravine between them. Takeo's eyes were like windows to his soul, and where Cyrus expected to see hate and malice, he instead found only sadness and resolve. Yet there were other noticeable aspects about this man that differed from Emy's disguise. Other things that Cyrus would never forget.

Takeo Karaoshi stood with absolute control, a tyrant over his own body and everything around it. He gazed with focus, breathed in a steady rhythm, and did not flinch a single muscle. Cyrus got the distinct feeling that Takeo's heart only beat with its master's permission and the snow that fell around them only did so upon his command. Despite the chaos of this entire scene, the Dark Lord somehow gave off the impression that he had always known this day would come and he had prepared for it in a thousand different ways.

Despite the fact that no one had moved, Cyrus already felt they had lost.

"Stand," Emy whispered to him, her voice strained to a breaking point. "Stand up straight. What's wrong with you?"

"My ankle," Cyrus replied. "It's twisted. I don't think—"

"Listen to me. Listen very carefully. It doesn't matter if your entire leg is shattered. You stand as if nothing is wrong. When you're a werewolf, you can sense weakness in other animals, right? You can smell it, and you know better than to show weakness before another predator. This is one of those moments, do you understand? Do not show weakness. Stand."

As Takeo's gaze drifted across the ravine, Cyrus understood instinctively before his mind could process Emy's words. He stood on his ankle and swallowed down the pain that shot up his leg in agonizing flashes.

However, Takeo spared Cyrus and Emy no more than a glance. He stared longest at the gap, judging it, and Cyrus did not breathe for fear that this creature of shadow and nightmare would clear the distance in one frightful bound.

Takeo dropped his gaze and sighed.

"Nicholas," he spoke.

His voice was softer than Cyrus had expected.

"Takeo," Nicholas replied.

A drifting snowflake touched upon Takeo's exposed blade, a flawless yet simple katana with a black handle. The snowflake disappeared into mist as if it had touched an open flame.

"Do you think you can walk?" Emy whispered. "We need to go. We'll need all the distance we can get."

"We can't leave him," Cyrus said.

"He'll be fine. These two have already been down this road. If Takeo was going to kill Nicholas, he'd have done it back in Juatwa. Nicholas will survive."

"I thought we had an agreement," Takeo said suddenly, breaking the silence between him and Nicholas. "You were to go home and stay there, and in exchange, I would let you live."

Emy, who had been trying to pull Cyrus away from the scene, froze.

"I don't know what you're talking about," Nicholas replied, then threw his arms wide. "This is my home."

"Please, Nicholas," Takeo went on. "This is no time for your infamous humor. I told you, never again. I told you that if we met one more time, it would be as enemies, and yet here you are, helping that damned creature. I thought you were smarter than this."

"That creature has a name," Nicholas said. "Krunk gave her one."

"And do you think the dead you hold allegiance to will be proud of your decision?"

"I could ask the same of you."

Their conversation went cold. Meanwhile, Emy had turned fully back. Her ears were straight up, and her whiskers were fanned out.

"Nicholas," she whispered, then called out, "Nicholas! You, you said. . ."

"I know what I said," he barked back, though he didn't turn from Takeo. "What are you two still doing here, huh? Run, damn it."

Emy shook her head. Her hand, still wrapped around Cyrus' arm, extended claws until the sharp points punched through his clothes and pressed against his skin. He did not shake her off.

"He told me. He promised," she whispered. "When he saved me, when he got me on that ship, Nicholas waited on the shores for Takeo and told him everything he'd done. Takeo let him go. When Nicholas got back to the ship, he laughed it off. He said Takeo would never harm him, for Emily's sake. He lied to me. And I believed him."

"He lied to us," Cyrus corrected.

Memories flashed before Cyrus' eyes. Hidden glimpses of Nicholas standing in the cold breeze, taking in the harshness of the world like a savory drink. Little comments on the docks, on the ship, and everywhere else leading up to this moment that seemed to illuminate what should have been obvious all along.

Just then, their solitude was broken. The rocks above thundered as the rest of Takeo's warriors arrived, appearing all along the ridges above. Ropes were flung over the side and soldiers began to descend, slowly but surely, slipping down ice covered surfaces. They gathered around in a wide, half circle about Nicholas, with Takeo at their center. There were dozens of them, a few Cyrus recognized as being a part of Aiguo's crew, but many were new faces. Cyrus searched the crowd for anyone with projectiles: bows, throwing knives, whatever could be flung with deadly precision. He knew Emy was doing the same. There was a fair distance between the two of them and that group, but they were in full view. He saw a few drawing daggers, but none threw. Takeo's men watched their lord out of the corner of their eyes. Emy pulled Cyrus back a few more steps and stood in front of him.

One stepped forward to Takeo's side. Cyrus was certain he'd never seen him before, yet an intense hatred flared over him as he gazed upon this stranger. That's when he knew it was Aiguo.

"If it would please my lord, I'll have this oaf eliminated," Aiguo said, bowing.

"Do not speak again," Takeo replied. "You have failed me."

Aiguo didn't so much as breathe. He bowed low and stepped away from Takeo, whose gaze drifted across the ravine again, but this time to Cyrus. The Dark Lord stared at him curiously.

"Cyrus?" he said.

Cyrus wasn't sure what to do. He hadn't thought about this moment. He'd been so young when Takeo had last seen him that Cyrus had no memory of the man. Yet, the opposite was not true. He should have realized that.

"Cyrus, it is you," Takeo repeated, confidently this time, and then tilted ever so slightly to Aiguo. "It seems you've failed to mention a lot of things. Speak."

"I had no idea these two would be with her, my lord," Aiguo answered, bowing low again. "In truth, I wasn't fully certain she'd be here either. It was simply the next place to search. I told you all of this."

"Yes, but you did not mention whom she might be traveling with, and I want to know why, of all people, she is with Cyrus."

Takeo cut himself off, his eyes going wide.

"The angel," the Dark Lord said, then shook his head. "Of course. Aiguo, when this is over and if I have not killed you, you're going to tell me everything that happened. I don't know why you hid this from me, but I promise we will experience great pain together finding out."

Even from this distance, Cyrus could smell Aiguo's sweat and hear him gulp.

"As for you, Cyrus," Takeo continued, "listen to me. Whatever that creature before you has promised, she lies. Undoubtedly, she's lied to you countless times already. I have no idea what they've told you about me, but I hope they at least warned you that I always speak the truth. So you shall harbor no doubts when I say that if you help her any further, you will die."

"I know," Cyrus replied, and was surprised to hear himself doing so with such confidence. "I've already seen your work, through him."

Cyrus paused and pointed an accusing finger at Aiguo.

"He killed my mother," Cyrus said.

"Oh? He did?" Takeo replied, cocking an eyebrow.

Aiguo remained bowed. Cyrus had expected Aiguo to speak in his own defense, but then he remembered that Takeo had commanded the man to stay silent. However, to not speak in one's own defense. Was Takeo really that terrifying, even to his underlings?

"So, revenge, is it?" Takeo said. "That's what you want? Well, simple enough."

Takeo merely flicked his head, the movement almost imperceptible at this distance, yet the results were immediate. Heavily armed soldiers came forward and grabbed Aiguo, forcing the man to his knees with a swift kick to the back of his legs. The scene nearly erupted into chaos right then as the mercenaries Aiguo had hired tensed and drew back from Takeo's larger group, but when no one came for them, they relaxed. It seemed even they knew who was truly in charge.

Aiguo kneeled alone.

"My lord, wait!" he begged, finally breaking his silence.

Takeo's drawn sword flew up and touched the thickest part of Aiguo's neck, pushing Aiguo's face skyward and his mouth closed.

"Do not speak," Takeo seethed.

He never raised his voice. He did not have to.

"You had one task: to kill her," Takeo said. "That beast was alone when I sent you out. Now, after years of hunting her, she's not only alive but gathering allies. She's trekking through the same mountains as I am, seeking the same angel, plotting who knows what, and I am very disappointed in you. We had a deal, Aiguo. We always had a deal, and you have broken your end of the bargain. It brings me great pleasure to get one final use out of your corpse. Cyrus! Here's your revenge. You kill that wretched creature standing before you, and I will kill this wretched creature kneeling before me."

Cyrus did not answer. He gaped back, completely stunned by what he saw. He thought it was a trick, at first, because how could anyone treat someone who served them this way? Was this a game? If Cyrus attacked Emy, would Takeo simply laugh it off and let Aiguo go? Judging by the hatred in Takeo's dark eyes, Cyrus couldn't help but feel that he spoke the truth. However, none of that mattered. The mere idea of betraying Emy and trying to kill her in cold blood was so foreign that Cyrus couldn't even consider it. Yet the mere proposal was so brutal that it took Cyrus time to respond.

"No," Cyrus said finally. "Never. It's not that simple."

"Of course, it is," Takeo replied. "His life for hers. We'll both be doing the world a favor this way. Did your mother ever tell you that she meant for you to follow me? When you came of age, she wanted me to come and take you away from Angor, to train and develop you. Think of me as your destined mentor and this moment as your first lesson."

Cyrus shook his head. He was dizzy with disbelief. This wasn't a proposal. It was damnation.

"You're, you're a—," he stuttered. "You're a monster. My mother would never want me to follow a man like you. And killing him won't bring her back."

Takeo blinked and glanced down at Aiguo. Then he sighed and drew the sword away from Aiguo's neck. However, the guards did not let him up just yet. Emy glanced back at Cyrus and nodded, gratefully. Nicholas favored Cyrus with a smile.

"Good fellow, ain't he?" the viking said. "Lucky lad that you never came back to fulfill your promise."

"I never made a promise," Takeo replied, eyes still on Cyrus. "I can see you're determined to go down this road, foolish boy. I've already warned you not to help her any further, but perhaps you need a demonstration as to why. I am not one to be defied. Stay, watch, and learn.

"Nicholas, are you ready?"

Nicholas grunted and lowered his head.

"Let's get on with it," the viking said.

Takeo drew back his arms, and his guards moved from their watch over Aiguo. They flanked him and took his heavy jacket, pulling it free and revealing less restrictive clothing below. Across the way, Nicholas set his maul in the snow and began to do the same, stripping away his layers of protection against the cold. They met each other's gaze, paused, and then continued. Nicholas pulled away another layer, revealing his muscle-bound and hair-covered figure. Takeo stripped away until he bore a figure that was lean and chiseled yet littered with scars. As Takeo turned, Cyrus counted four on the man's back, two on his right side, one near his waist, and dozens of tiny marks across his chest. A big, faded blotch stained his stomach, so large that Cyrus couldn't imagine how any normal person could survive whatever blow could make a scar that size. Cyrus swallowed down a dry, aching throat.

"We have to help him," he said.

"How?" Emy replied, her voice pained as much as Cyrus'. "There's nothing we can do."

"I can't look away."

"Then don't."

Nicholas tilted his head until the bones in his neck popped. Then he pushed his hands together until his knuckles cracked.

"What do you say we go out like we went in, eh?" he said. "Barefisted."

Takeo paused. He took his sword, the black one that Cyrus knew was enchanted, and held it out. One of his guards came forward and took it in both hands, bowing deeply. The guard, Cyrus noticed, wore thick gloves while Takeo's hands were exposed.

Takeo held out his palm and another guard came forward, took a knee, and held out his own sword, another katana. Takeo took it in one hand, and Nicholas grimaced.

"Bastard," the viking whispered.

"He gave up his enchanted sword," Cyrus whispered. "Nicholas has a chance now, right?"

Emy didn't reply.

Nicholas grabbed his maul and lifted it up. His muscles bulged from the weight, and his chest hair fluttered in the wind. Nicholas paced off to the left, and Takeo mimicked him. They began a ritualistic circle.

"Your soldiers know that if I kill you," Nicholas said, "I get to be in charge. You haven't ditched your one rule, have you?"

"They know," Takeo replied, emotionless.

Cyrus swallowed again. Something was strange about Takeo. He didn't look at Nicholas. The Dark Lord held his gaze deflected, looking at the ground. It dawned on him a moment later.

"He's sad," Cyrus said. "Why is he so sad?"

"He's already in mourning," Emy whispered breathlessly.

The warriors stopped circling. Takeo raised his eyes and met Nicholas' gaze. He drew in a deep breath as a single tear formed and slid down his cheek. As it dropped into the air, it froze before it hit the ground.

Takeo dashed off the ground in a blur, his feet kicking up snow. He grabbed his sword in both hands and let loose a swing that was almost impossible to follow. Nicholas' maul came about in both hands, blocking the swing just as Nicholas' foot swept off the ground to take Takeo in the ribs. At first, Cyrus could have sworn the kick struck as his foot appeared to connect, yet Takeo came away clean and unharmed. Takeo had dodged so narrowly that Cyrus hadn't seen it.

Cyrus clenched a fist in hope.

"He almost had him," he said.

"No," Emy said, shaking her head. "Not even close."

Takeo came in again, and Nicholas swung early to use his greater reach. Takeo slowed but did not stop, and the maul passed a hair's breadth from his nose before Takeo was inside Nicholas' swing and lunging forward. Nicholas twisted, narrowly avoiding being skewered, yet the sword passed along his right side and drew blood. Bright red splashed into the fading light and splattered across the snow, yet neither warrior paused.

Nicholas' right hand came away from his maul and struck down, connecting with Takeo's shoulder, yet the shorter man rolled with the blow and came away just a touch off balance. Even as he stumbled, Takeo's blade was alive with fury, making several small cuts for Nicholas' heart, falling short thanks to Nicholas' quick backstep. Nicholas swung again, early this time while Takeo was still at a distance and not charging yet. Takeo had to duck to avoid having his head removed. While Takeo was in free fall for that one moment, Nicholas' knee dashed forward to bash Takeo, like a battering ram of blood, bone, and muscle. Takeo dodged again, twisting and falling to the ground where he rolled away. Nicholas' next attack was a heavy stomp to the ground, far too late to make contact. The warriors stepped away for a moment and sized each other up.

"I trained you well," Takeo noted.

"You're getting slow, old man," Nicholas replied.

Cyrus balked. Takeo had been a blur to the eye, even without his enchanted sword. Could Nicholas be serious? Had Takeo Karaoshi been faster than this, once upon a time? He wasn't even that old.

"Is this the part where you reconsider this fight?" Nicholas asked. "Ask me to join you one last time?"

"We both know it's too late for that," Takeo answered. "Please, no more of your humor, Nicholas. Don't make this harder than it needs to be."

"Well now, you didn't think I was going to make this easy, did you?"

They circled again, and Cyrus kept waiting for Nicholas to charge, but he didn't. The big man was cautious and steady, sweating in his intensity. He watched Takeo without blinking, despite the freezing wind, with muscles so taut that Cyrus could see the veins swell. Takeo's eyes were calm and dark as they'd always been, flicking from point to point across Nicholas' form, searching for weakness.

It reminded Cyrus of the way his werewolf clan would circle prey in the night.

Takeo dashed forward again, sword held ready in both hands, thrusting forward for a killing blow. Nicholas swung once more before the other could reach him, trying to put Takeo off balance, but letting go with one hand early this time. As the katana came for his heart, Nicholas' hand swung defensively, sweeping the blade to the side even as it cut along his hand, and then dashed forward with a fist that connected with Takeo's jaw. The Dark Lord jerked from the blow, his head snapping back, and a grin spread across Nicholas' face as he let his maul go altogether and grabbed Takeo's shoulder with his free hand.

And then it was over. It was all over. Nicholas had Takeo in both hands, and Takeo's head was reeling, dazed from the blow, and not a single person breathed as Nicholas went to hammer home another barefisted punch backed by decades of strength.

Yet it never landed. Not before Nicholas' chest exploded in a shower of blood.

While everyone, even Nicholas, had been distracted by the punch, Takeo had fought on. Even dazed and blinded, he had turned his blade and swung upwards, striking where his opponent had last been and still was. Blood sprung from Nicholas' chest as the upwards swing of the sword showered the area in red, staining Takeo's face and everything around him. The two came apart, both hitting the ground with heavy thuds. Takeo collapsed into a pile on his side. Nicholas fell on his back, arms splayed out, eyes looking towards the sky.

Emy let out a breathless gasp. Cyrus felt dread seep into his being.

After a moment, Takeo shook his head and stood to his feet. It was a struggle, but he managed it after spitting blood. His soldiers did not move.

Nicholas stayed on the ground.

Takeo walked over to him, rubbing his jaw and twisting his neck. Nicholas coughed and spit blood, miraculously still breathing. However, the snow around him grew red as the wound across his chest overflowed. He didn't have long.

"You hit me," Takeo said, as he stood over him. "You finally hit me."

He sounded proud, yet equally disappointed. Nicholas didn't reply. He coughed again, and his right hand twitched as it searched the ground for something. Takeo saw the movement, thought for a moment, and then reached out with his sword. He hooked Nicholas' discarded maul and dragged the handle to the flailing hand. Nicholas clutched the weapon tightly.

Takeo raised his sword in both hands over Nicholas' neck and paused.

"Any last words?" Takeo asked. "For your legend?"

Nicholas struggled to reply. He coughed blood with his first deep breath but managed to squeak out words with the second.

"How does it feel?" Nicholas asked.

Takeo blinked, confused.

"How does it feel?" Nicholas repeated, stronger this time. "To know you killed us all?"

Nicholas chuckled, coughed blood again, and then laughed. Teeth bright red, eyes glowing, he laughed into Takeo's face. The Dark Lord snarled and brought the sword down, slicing Nicholas' neck open. Laughter drowned in blood, and the world went silent save for the cold wind that whipped through the ravine.

Takeo stared down at Nicholas' body and once more his form became consumed by sorrow. His eyes glistened as tears began to form. He let one drop onto Nicholas' cold corpse and then reached down to touch Nicholas' cheek. The Dark Lord caressed the fallen warrior for a moment before closing his eyes and standing up. Takeo walked back to his guards and handed back the bloodied sword. He took his enchanted blade and closed his hands tightly around the magic weapon. All traces of sorrow disappeared.

"Come on," Emy whispered softly. "There's nothing more to see here."

"He killed him," Cyrus said. "I can't believe it. Weren't they like brothers?"

"Please, Cyrus, we have to go. We'll need all the distance we can get, especially with your foot. And remember, don't show any weakness."

They turned to go, but both stopped as they heard a chuckle. They looked back to see Aiguo grinning in triumph at the Dark Lord.

"Marvelous, my lord," he said. "Beautiful work. You showed that oaf—"

Takeo's hand flashed out like lightning and struck Aiguo in the stomach. The man who'd stood back up went to his knees again but never got the chance to howl in pain. Just as quickly as he struck, Takeo's fist clenched around Aiguo's throat like a vice and squeezed. Aiguo's eyes bulged as he gasped for air, but he dared not fight back. He stayed on the ground, mouth gaping, and put his hands together in prayer before Takeo. Cyrus could see him mouth words, begging forgiveness, begging for his life, yet Takeo did not relent. He squeezed so tightly that Cyrus thought Aiguo's neck would snap. Aiguo's eyes began to roll back in his head, his hands dropped, and his mouth closed, and only then did Takeo release him.

Aiguo collapsed to the ground, and Cyrus thought him dead until he coughed.

"Thank you, my lord," Aiguo coughed out. "My deepest apologies. You are as merciful as you are wise. I shall not fail you again."

Takeo didn't look at him. The Dark Lord stared out across the ravine at Emy and Cyrus with unyielding focus. Into that gaze, he poured all his malice, his hatred, and his pain. Cyrus couldn't look away, even as his insides turned cold to the touch.

"See that you don't," Takeo said.

Chapter 24

Once they were out of sight, Emy demanded more than requested to carry Cyrus. His pride wanted to deny her, but he could tell she wasn't going to give up. Also, they both knew she was more than strong enough for the task.

Their progress wasn't much faster with her having to carry the extra weight, but it saved Cyrus from having to put any weight on his injury. Besides, as the sun went down and the temperature plummeted, they had to find shelter soon anyway. Cyrus thought about the size of Takeo's warband and realized their enemy would have a hard time finding adequate shelter. Perhaps that was one advantage he and Emy could use.

"How bad is it?" Emy asked once they were set up for the night.

"I don't think it's too bad," Cyrus replied, rubbing his ankle. "I hope."

"If it were me, I'd already be healed by now."

"Well, I'm not you, so. . ."

He trailed off in a way that ended that conversation, but they didn't stay silent long. They had other things on their minds.

"I can't believe he's dead," Cyrus said. "And we just left him."

"We always knew running into Takeo was a possibility," Emy replied, softly. "Almost a guarantee, really. Like you, he'd met Ephron before. However, even still, I just can't believe it either. I can't believe Nicholas lied this whole time. Why didn't he tell me the truth? And how did I not see it?"

Cyrus shook his head.

"You talk like it's his fault, but we're just as guilty."

"He knew, Cyrus. He knew he was going to die if he went with us, but he did it anyway. My life was always in danger, but his was a choice."

"Nicholas tried to talk us out of going, remember? And not once did we listen. Emy, we can't put the blame on him."

Emy turned away and shook her head. She drew her knees up and wrapped her arms around them. For once, she appeared fragile, and Cyrus felt the urge to comfort her.

"But you're right," Cyrus continued. "If he had told us that he couldn't leave home, we wouldn't have let him come."

"Maybe that's why he didn't tell us," Emy replied, speaking as if to herself. "Nicholas hated being trapped, like some sort of caged animal. He wanted to be free, even if it would cost him his life. Perhaps, especially if it cost him his life. He always wanted to die an epic death."

Cyrus shook his head again.

"Emy, what are we up against exactly?" Cyrus said. "I've heard stories about Takeo's cruelty, his sword, and his plans to enslave the world. Yet, somehow, I was completely unprepared for what I saw. I mean, he leapt, literally leapt, off a cliff and dashed across an entire valley to slay us. I can't explain it, but it's like my werewolf side knew, absolutely positively knew, to be afraid. Is he even human?"

Emy didn't answer at first. She rocked against her knees and drew in a deep breath. She stared into the frozen ground as if it stretched on for miles, while just outside their shallow overhang the snow began to fall heavily. This was good news in some regard because this would cover their tracks. For the first time since arriving in these mountains, Cyrus hoped the snow would never stop.

"Most of my kind despise humans," Emy said. "Despise as in look down on them. To us, humans seem like stupid and feeble creatures, probably not unlike the way humans view akki or goblins. To us, your strength is only in numbers, and it is our rightful place to rule over such lesser creatures. It may sound conceited and narcissistic, but how can we think otherwise? A rakshasa lives for hundreds of years while it's rare for a human to last much beyond half a century. And even if one does, they become decrepit and useless, a burden on the rest of their species. To add to this, you are weaker than us, dumber than us, slower than us; some of my kind think it's a miracle that your kind hasn't perished of its own ineptitude.

"But that is only the most arrogant of us, and admittedly, I've only met two rakshasas in my life. If I had to guess, I would say arrogance is the fatal flaw that has kept my kind from dominating yours. Takeo Karaoshi is proof of that.

"You see, he prevents me from believing we are better than humans. Takeo has more than an enchanted sword. He is tenacious, unrelenting, and perhaps the most dangerous thing alive when backed into a corner. Some burning desire to survive ignites within him whenever he is closest to death, and the resulting damage is catastrophic. The logical side of me knows that I am smarter and stronger than him, yet I have witnessed him fight, survive, and win against odds that should be impossible. Takeo Karaoshi is my proof that humans are not to be underestimated and, in some cases, they should be feared.

"You tell me that when you saw him, you were afraid. Well, I'm telling you that is completely justified."

Cyrus swallowed hard and let his gaze fall to the ground.

"Damn," he whispered.

They sat there in silence, the only interruption being the wind blowing across their shelter with a shrill howl. Cyrus felt like he should say something, some words noting the bright side, but he didn't see one. He felt like he'd signed his death warrant already, somehow, and it wouldn't even be Takeo who killed him. They still had the immediate problem of escaping these mountains alive, let alone taking down a being the world over was rightly terrified of.

Emy must have been thinking the same thing because she looked over to him again and spoke up.

"Your ankle, could you walk on it tomorrow?" she asked.

Cyrus shrugged.

"I suppose I don't have much of a choice," he said. "Good news is that it won't swell much, not in this cold. How much of a lead do you think Nicholas gave us by destroying that bridge?"

Emy shrugged, too.

"Depends," she said. "Was there another bridge just down the way? Does the ravine close up further down? The only certainty is that they will find a crossing eventually. After they do, will Takeo join the hunt for us? Or will he leave that to Aiguo?"

"Well, surely Takeo will keep looking for the angel, right?"

Emy sighed, leaned back, and stretched her neck. She turned as if to look for someone but stopped halfway. A silence passed between them as they both recognized she'd been searching for Nicholas. They weren't even shedding tears over him, let alone praising his sacrifice. It seemed heartless, yet Cyrus just couldn't understand it. Why had Nicholas sacrificed himself so willingly? He didn't owe them anything. He hardly knew Cyrus, and he had mentioned before that he couldn't do much to save Emy from herself. Why had he destroyed that bridge?

Had he wanted to die?

"I think he'll leave us to Aiguo," Emy said, interrupting Cyrus' thoughts. "Killing me is really a secondary goal for Takeo. Plus, the more of the world he conquers, the fewer places I have to hide."

"I can't believe Aiguo, let alone anyone, follows that man," Cyrus said. "Takeo's hatred for his underlings is shocking. Does he treat them all like that?"

"Not all," Emy conceded, "but most."

"How?" Cyrus asked. "How can anyone live like that? Those people who served Aiguo didn't even lift a finger to help him. It's like an entire structure of hate and deceit. Do they all sleep with one eye open?"

Emy scoffed.

"Takeo causes it, of course," she said. "It's the natural state of villainy. Takeo trusts no one and he's willing to kill anyone, even those who serve him, if it will further his goals. This attitude, you can imagine, only attracts those of a similar mind, and thus Takeo's closest advisors are all people who do not trust him and would kill him if it would serve their purposes. Takeo sees this in them and hates them for it, and around and around the circle of depravity goes. It's disgusting, and it is Takeo's greatest flaw. His soul is poisoned."

"Well, I guess now that you mention it, I can probably work out why Aiguo serves Takeo at all. If you're wretched scum, the only person you can serve is another wretched scum. Reminds me of my stepfather. He was like that. His closest friends were always some of the worst sorts of people, the type of people who would tolerate beating a defenseless woman and her child for nothing more than existing."

"Imagine, Cyrus," Emy went on. "Imagine for just one moment that Takeo gets his way. After slaying who knows how many people, that's the type of man that now decides the fate of the world. Imagine whom he'll appoint to control each section of the world. Imagine. . ."

Cyrus held up a hand, asking for silence, and then dropped it to his ankle. He rubbed again. He hoped it would heal soon.

"I get it," Cyrus said. "You don't have to convince me anymore. I'm not going back to Angor."

Emy let loose a long sigh of relief.

"Oh good," she said. "Because, honestly, I don't think I can take a dragon by myself."

"According to Nicholas, you couldn't take a dragon even with my help. But we're still going to try, aren't we?"

Her silence was answer enough, as if confirming out loud would lessen their chances of survival. Cyrus was surprised Emy was going along with this, as she was clearly a logical individual. Nicholas had laid out in quite plain terms what a horrible idea fighting a dragon would be, and that if such a thing were possible, it would have been accomplished by the vikings themselves ages ago.

Best not to say anything at all.

"There's just one thing I can't imagine," Cyrus said, switching topics. "The man I saw across the ravine, how is it possible that once upon a time he took me to see an angel? That couldn't have been easy, but he didn't seem to care about it. He remembered me, barely, and then dismissed everything about me a moment later. I don't know why, but somehow I had convinced myself that there would be something more to it when he saw me again."

Emy shrugged.

"What did you expect?" she said. "That he would throw open his arms and say he's been looking for you all this time?"

"I don't know," Cyrus replied, then scoffed. "I guess my views were warped when you had disguised yourself as him and my mother talked and talked about all these plans for me. Even though I know now that wasn't really him, I think I had convinced myself that that was the way we were supposed to meet. I guess my mother made me believe, in a way."

"You felt kinship with him?"

Cyrus shook his head.

"Good," Emy said. "Because this is Takeo Karaoshi we're talking about. All the people he ever cared about are dead, and he's been driven to madness by it. He's on a crusade of suffering and subjugation, to cleanse the world of the power it once had to slay those he lost. It's vengeance, don't you see, Cyrus? And he must be stopped. Get up."

Cyrus snapped out of his trance. It dawned on him that the level of energy in Emy's voice had risen, and she'd moved to her feet. She reached down a hand for Cyrus, and he took it. She pulled him up, and their hands stayed clasped.

"I had hoped against hope that this would be simple," she said. "I thought with the power of a colossus, I could crush Takeo with ease. However, that's not going to happen. So, I'll need other weapons, allies, and I want you to be one of the first. I want you to swear to me—no, swear with me—that we won't stop until this is over. A death oath, if you will."

"Wait, what?" Cyrus balked.

"Cyrus, you've seen what we're up against. You've heard the stories, felt the threat. Takeo is on an endless path of destruction, and it will only end with his death. You and I, we must be a part of that. Together, here and now, we swear an oath to bring him down. Are you with me?"

Cyrus swallowed. He hadn't been prepared for this. Just a moment ago, he'd been talking with remorse about a missed kinship that his mother had planned for years.

"You want me to swear to kill the Dark Lord?" Cyrus said. "Emy, I don't know that I can do that. One of the first things Ven taught me was never to close the door on salvation. It was one of her closest held beliefs. Without it, she may never have given me, a werewolf, a chance."

Emy's energy faded. Her eyes narrowed at Cyrus as if he were a child. He felt like a child, too, to be honest, and he knew what she was going to say long before she said it.

"Cyrus, no more than a few hours ago, we watched the Dark Lord cut down the brother of the woman he loved for the crime of getting in his way. In cold blood, Cyrus, without hesitation. I think we can safely say he's beyond salvation."

Cyrus went to reply but stopped himself. He stuttered over his next words, and Emy pulled him close, their hands still clasped.

"What?" she demanded. "What more excuse do you need? We're talking about the man responsible for killing your mother, your werewolf clan. This goes beyond logic at this point. You should hate this man with a passion. What is wrong with you? What were you going to say next?"

"It's just, Ven had this phrase," Cyrus replied. "She didn't always say it the same way, but it went something like, 'Your enemy is only truly destroyed once you've made them your friend.' I know it can't always work. My stepfather was that way, but I made my childhood bully into my friend, and it was the best thing I could have done."

Emy's gaze bore into Cyrus, and he looked away. Emy released him. She sat down with a heavy plop and shook her head.

"Of all the people I could get stuck with, why did it have to be you?" she said.

Cyrus felt his cheeks grow hot, and he sat back down, as well. He didn't give an answer. He didn't think Emy wanted one.

"So where do we go from here?" she asked.

"I can still help you with that dragon," he said.

"Are you sure? Or are you going to try and make friends with it?"

Cyrus winced. Emy sucked in a breath.

"Sorry," she said.

"No, no, you're right," he replied. "I had that coming. I see what you were trying to do there, to make a bond in an important moment. I just wasn't ready for it, is all. I know you've suffered a lot under Takeo's rule, and you want to fight back. I should, too, you know, for my mother, but it's not that straightforward. Takeo didn't kill my mother. In fact, from what my mother said, she admired him. It's just, it's not as easy for me as it is for you.

"I'll help you stop him. I will. I've seen what he wants, I watched him kill Nicholas. It's just, I don't want to swear an oath of murder. I don't want to be that kind of man. If I did something like that, I'd feel no better than Takeo himself."

Emy froze. Her gaze on Cyrus turned nearly to a glare, then faded to frustration. Cyrus didn't need to read minds to know she disagreed.

"Well, I guess this matter is far from resolved, then," she said.

Emy turned away and lay on her side. Cyrus sighed, staring at her back, and let his shoulders drop. He lay down, too, but didn't turn away.

"Yes," he whispered across to her. "This is far from over."

Epilogue

Sir Mark O'Conner sat in his chair and aimed carefully with his dagger. He held the blade's point in two fingers with the handle tilted ever so slightly back towards his right ear. From this position, he could sight his target best, and although being a vampire had a number of disadvantages, it did come with perks. His two fingers possessed more than enough strength to hold the dagger aloft, his eyes saw through the darkness as if it were a morning fog, and his speed would allow him to propel this dagger with lethal intent even from a seated position.

If his target were not the west-facing stone wall of his office, it would have been in danger.

Mark threw the dagger with a moderate level of strength, and the blade's tip struck the same spot of solid stone it always did. The dagger ricocheted away with violent intent, spinning through the air, bouncing off the floor, another wall, and then skidding across the stone until it bashed into the leg of his chair and spun in place. This was by design, of course. Mark was practiced enough that he could throw the dagger with such precision that it came right back to him, assuming it didn't break.

Mark sighed and picked up the dagger, inspecting it.

"I wonder how long you'll last," he mused aloud.

He'd broken several daggers, all thrown at the same spot on the wall in his office facing the setting sun. Most of Lucifan was a dense forest of buildings, casting more shade than it allowed in sunshine. However, Mark knew that this particular wall had a rare view of the sun's descent. Sunlight poured onto this wall, and Mark could feel it's heat. He imagined the sun scraping at the wall, thirsting for him from the other side.

Mark paused to inspect the dent his dagger-throwing habits had formed in the wall. It wasn't deep, perhaps no more than a finger's tip at the deepest point, so there was still quite a bit of stone left. However, with each throw, with each strike, the daggers whittled away at it. One day, one dagger, one throw, would break through, and Mark would give the sun the kill it so desperately wanted.

He went to throw the dagger again when there was a knock at the door. Mark sighed and stored the dagger in its drawer.

"Come in," he called.

Once upon a time, Mark would never allow anyone entrance who did not shout their name and purpose through the door. He had claimed it was prudent, given the danger of his position, but now Mark knew it was just plain old simple fear of death. It was natural as a mortal to fear death, and it had governed many of his actions, back when he was a human. However, such fear no longer applied to Mark.

"Sir Mathew," came the call through the door. "It's about the leprechauns again, sir."

"By the angels, Mathew, haven't I told you that you can come in when I say so?"

The door creaked open, and Mathew stepped inside.

"Sorry, sir," he said. "Old habits die hard, I guess."

"Yes, quite," Mark muttered his reply. "Were they the only thing?"

Mathew's eyes flicked towards the wall, to the gash in the stone. A sadness passed through his eyes, but he didn't say anything. They'd talked about it once, and Mark had let Mathew voice his concerns. Mathew had droned on about how Lucifan needed a leader, that Mark was the best person for the job, and about other such nonsense that Mark had forgotten the moment he'd heard it. After the speech was done, Mark's only response had been to make Mathew swear to never talk about that again.

So far, Mathew had kept his promise. However, Mark didn't expect it to last.

"Well?" Mark said. "Out with it. The leprechauns?"

"They're insisting on another meeting, sir," Mathew said. "I know you're going to say that we've already settled the terms between them and the Ogre's Guild, but they've gone back on their word. They say they won't sign the contract until they've had another meeting to clarify conditions with the ogres."

"And what does your gut tell you?"

Mathew scoffed.

"I don't need my gut, sir," he said. "My contacts tell me the leprechauns are trying to break up the Ogre's Guild, so they don't have to negotiate anything, especially pay rates and retirement. I can't believe I'm saying this, sir, but I think organizing the ogres into a guild was the most controversial thing you could have done. The underbelly of the city is in an uproar, I swear it. Who would have thought that crime rates could be driven down by something as simple as hired muscle demanding fair pay? Truly, sir, you're a genius."

Mathew's eyes flicked to the gash in the wall again. Mark blinked. An awkward moment of silence crept by before Mathew cleared his throat.

"So, the leprechauns, what should I—"

"You know, I still can't get it out of my head," Mark cut him off.

Mathew groaned and shook his head.

"Sir, we've been over this," he said. "Cyrus is a headstrong youth that dropped in from nowhere. I didn't care for either of my parents at his age, and they raised me."

"Easy for you to say. It wasn't your son."

Mathew shrugged, and Mark struck the desk with his knuckles.

"It's just, when I called him son, he—"

"Listen, you really can't blame the boy. He'd never met you before, and you had never planned on meeting him. Let it go, sir."

"And so what?" Mark responded, bristling. "Am I not allowed to be concerned for his safety, or to crave his respect? Do I have to raise him in order to wish him happiness and wellbeing, or to hope with every fiber of my being that Takeo doesn't find him? Huh?"

"And we've been over this, too, sir. What can we do? Takeo rules an army large enough to invade the world, so Cyrus' best chance at safety is to go unnoticed. It's best to keep one's head down in times like this. Cyrus can do that better with a smaller escort than a larger one."

"It's not just that, Mathew. It's the way he looked at me. You didn't see. The way I sit here, doing nothing. He was . . . disappointed."

"And I've told you, sir, over and over, that it's just a thing that children do at that age. You remember, surely. You grow up thinking adults are infallible, and then you see they are not, and you feel like the whole world lied to you. It turns you bitter. One day, he'll grow old enough to forgive you, and there's nothing you can say or do to hurry that along."

"But he's right, isn't he?" Mark countered. "I do have soldiers at my command and power and privilege. Yet I do nothing! If what you say is true, then why didn't he feel the same about Belen, huh? Cyrus clearly adored her, cherished her, and respected her. That could have been me, Mathew!"

In frustration, Mark slammed a hand down on his desk. He'd meant to make nothing but noise, but he'd forgotten his vampiric strength. The hand struck the table and cracked the wood. The desk groaned and a leg snapped. The whole desk fell to one corner and hit the stone floor, drawers flying open. The heaviest one, the one holding the dagger, flew open the farthest. Mark stared at the exposed blade, and he could have sworn it stared back.

"No, sir," Mathew said calmly. "It couldn't. Let it go."

But Mark wasn't listening. The dagger stared at him. It wanted to kill him, he knew, but it couldn't. It wasn't powerful enough. His curse could withstand all sorts of punishment and torture and keep him breathing. To destroy him, it would take something truly immense, like a basilisk, a kraken, or the sun.

Or an angel.

"Can we move on, sir?" Mathew asked but was silenced by Mark's raised hand. "Sir?"

"I had a thought."

"Hopefully a productive one. About the leprechauns?"

"No, no," Mark said and waved. "Something beyond money. You know, I've always wondered, why didn't Ephron come back for me?"

Mathew blinked.

"Sir?"

"I had a hand in killing Ephron's siblings," he said. "Perhaps that's only a rumor to the public, but you know the truth. Ephron knows the truth. Why hasn't he ever come back to reclaim his throne? His eyes alone could kill me with their sunlight."

"Well, um, sir," Mathew replied. "Well, you know, it's not in an angel's nature to crave revenge."

"But he could still come back and retake the throne and leave me alive. Why not? Huh? Why not?"

Mathew shrugged, growing frustrated.

"Sir, is there a point to all this?"

"Of course, there is," Mark shouted, slamming a fist on the desk again. "Think, man, think. Ephron could come back at any moment but does not. Why?"

Mathew sighed. He could tell this conversation wasn't going to be over quickly. He came further into the room and took a seat on the other side of the desk. His breath turned to mist this close to Mark's aura.

"Because he doesn't want to," Mathew suggested.

"And why not?" Mark replied, stretching out a hand. "Dig deeper. Ephron cares for this city, deeply. Why leave it in the hands of another?"

Mathew thought for a moment but shrugged again.

"I don't know, sir."

"And neither did I," Mark said. "Not until right now."

Mark reached into the drawer at his side, grabbed the dagger, and stabbed the point into the desk. The wood splintered under the force.

"Night after night, day after day," Mark said in a low voice, "I've waited for Ephron's return. I've craved it, that he might come and take his revenge. Prayed for it, even. I got so desperate, I started to help him, throwing knives at the wall. Yet, he's left me alive and in power. Why? To punish me? No. Angels don't understand punishment any more than revenge. Because he trusts me? Pathetic, selfish thought. To protect this city? What faith does he have that I could do that? No, the only thing I can do that the angel can't is exactly what we've gone over: revenge and punishment."

Mathew went still. He swallowed hard and gave his superior an uneasy glance.

"Sir, what are you getting at?"

"I'm saying I finally know," Mark replied, a grin creeping across his lips. "My son asked me. He said I have an army and wealth. I could have done something. I said I couldn't, and I believed it, and yet, couldn't I? If I had commanded you to go to the Forest of Angor and retrieve Cyrus, would you?"

Mathew folded his arms across his chest and said, "Well, I suppose I would. You are my commander, after all."

"Would others, if I commanded them?"

Mathew thought for a moment but frowned and nodded.

"Don't you see, Mathew," Mark pressed. "Lucifan has power, military power. But what's the one thing Ephron could never do? Use it."

"Sir . . . I don't like where this is going."

Mark stood up, leaving the dagger stabbed into the desk. He straightened his coat and cracked his neck.

"Sir?"

"No one will like where this is going," Mark answered, finally. "That's what war is all about."

"Sir?"

"I've got your answer for the leprechauns. After I'm done taxing them, they'll be begging for whatever the ogres would have offered. But there won't be anyone left to hire, because Lucifan isn't going to wait around for the damned Dark Lord to come knocking at our doorstep. Get up, Sir Mathew. We have work to do.

"Lucifan is going to war."

Author's Note

Thank you for reading my books. I hope you found this tale worthy of your time, and know that I enjoyed writing for you. If you received this book for free, please consider showing your support by purchasing a copy, recommending it to a friend, or writing a review online. Your kindness would not go unnoticed, and I would greatly appreciate it.

Sincerely,
Travis Bughi